THE GLAMOUR

THE GLAMOUR

Christopher Priest

Copyright © Christopher Priest 1984, 1985, 1996, 2005

The right of Christopher Priest to be identified as the
author of this work has been asserted by him in accordance
with the Copyright, Designs and Patents Act 1988.

First published in Great Britain in 1984
by Jonathan Cape

This edition published in Great Britain
in 2005 by Gollancz
An imprint of the Orion Publishing Group
Orion House, 5 Upper St Martin's Lane,
London WC2H 9EA

1 3 5 7 9 10 8 6 4 2

A CIP catalogue record for this book
is available from the British Library

ISBN 0 575 07579 1

Typeset at The Spartan Press Ltd,
Lymington, Hants

Printed in Great Britain by
Clays Ltd, St Ives plc

www.orionbooks.co.uk

PART ONE

I have been trying to remember where it began, thinking about my childhood and wondering if anything might have happened that made me become what I am. I had never thought much about it before, because on the whole I was happy. I think this is because my father protected me from discovering what was really going on. My mother died when I was only three, but even this blow was softened: her illness was a long one and by the time she actually died I was used to spending most of my time with the nurse.

What I remember most lucidly from childhood was something I enjoyed. When I was eight I was sent home from school with a letter from the medical office. A viral infection had been attacking children at the school and after we had all been screened it was discovered that I was the carrier. I was placed in home quarantine and was not allowed to mix with other children until I ceased to be a carrier. I was eventually admitted to a private hospital and my two perfectly good tonsils were efficiently removed. I returned to school shortly after my ninth birthday.

The period of quarantine had lasted nearly half a year, coinciding with the warmest months of a long hot summer. I was on my own for most of the time and although at first I felt lonely and isolated I quickly adapted. I discovered the pleasures of solitude. I read a huge number of books, went for long walks in the countryside around the house and noticed wildlife for the first time. My father bought me a simple camera and I began to study birds and flowers and trees, preferring their company to that of my friends. I constructed a secret den in the garden, sitting in it for hours with my books or photographs, fantasising and dreaming. I built a cart with the wheels of an old pram and skittered around the country paths and hills, happier than I had ever been before. It was a contented, uncomplicated time, one in which I built up personal reserves and internal confidence. Inevitably, it changed me.

Returning to school was a wrench. I had become an outsider to the other children because I had been away so long. I was left out of activities and games, groups formed without me, and I was treated as someone who did not know the secret language or signs. I hardly cared, because it allowed me to continue with a reduced version of my solitary life. For the rest of my time at school I drifted on the periphery, barely noticed by the others. I have never regretted that long, lonely summer, and I wish only that it could have lasted for ever. I changed as I grew up and I am not now what I was then, but I still think back to that happy time with a kind of infantile yearning.

So perhaps it began there, and this narrative is the result, the remainder. All that follows is a story, my own, told by different voices, mine amongst them, although at the moment I am only 'I'. Soon I shall have a name.

PART TWO

The house had been built overlooking the sea. Since its conversion to a convalescent hospital it had been enlarged by two new wings built on in the original style, and the gardens had been relandscaped so that patients wishing to move around were never faced with steep inclines. The gravelled paths zigzagged gently between the lawns and flower beds, opening out on to numerous levelled areas where wooden seats had been placed and where wheelchairs could be parked. The gardens were mature, with thick but controlled shrubbery and attractive stands of deciduous trees.

At the lowest point of the garden, down a narrow pathway leading away from the main area, there was a secluded, hedged-in patch, overgrown and neglected, with an uninterrupted view of this part of the south Devon coast. It made it possible to forget, briefly, that Middlecombe was a hospital. Even here, though, there were precautions: a low concrete kerb had been embedded in the grass to stop wheelchairs rolling too close to the cliff's edge, and an emergency signalling system, connected directly to the duty nurse's office in the main block, was prominent among the bushes.

Richard Grey came down here whenever he could. The extra distance exercised his arms as he worked the wheels of the chair, and anyway he liked the solitude. He could get privacy inside his room where there were books, television, telephone, radio, but when actually in the main building there was subtle but constant pressure from the nursing staff to mix with the other patients. There were no more operations to come, but it seemed to him that his recovery was interminable. The physiotherapy was tiring and left him aching afterwards. He was lonely on his own, but mixing with the other patients, many of whom did not speak English well, made him impatient and irritable. His body had been severely injured, his mind too, and he knew that both would have to heal in the same way: plenty of rest, gentle exercise, increasing resolve. It was often all he was capable of, staring at the sea, watching the tides, listening to the waves. The passage of birds excited him and whenever he heard a car he felt the tremor of fear.

His sole aim was to return to the normality he had taken for granted before the blast. He could at last stand on his own using the sticks, and the crutches were permanently in his past, so he knew he was improving. After wheeling himself down the garden he would lever himself out of his chair and take a few steps leaning on the sticks. He was proud of being able to do this alone, of not having a therapist or nurse beside him, of having no rails, no encouraging words. When standing he could see more of the view, could go closer to the edge.

Today it had been raining when he woke, a persistent, drifting drizzle that had continued all morning. It meant he had had to put on a coat, but now it had stopped raining and he was still in the coat. It depressed him because it reminded him of his real disabilities: he could not take it off on his own.

He heard footsteps on the gravel and the sound of someone pushing through the damp leaves and branches that grew across the path. He turned, doing it slowly, a step and a stick at a time, keeping his face immobile.

It was Dave, one of the nurses. 'Can you manage, Mr Grey?'

'I can manage to stay upright.'

'Do you want to get back in the chair?'

'No. I was standing here.'

The nurse had stopped a few paces away from him, one hand resting on the chair as if ready to wheel it forward quickly and slide it behind Grey's legs.

'I came to see if you needed anything.'

'You can help me with my coat. I'm sweating.'

The young man stepped forward and presented his forearm for Grey to lean on while he took the sticks away. With one hand he unbuttoned the front of the coat, then put his big hands under Grey's armpits, holding his weight, letting his patient remove the coat himself. Grey found it a slow, painful process, trying to twist his shoulder blades to get out of the sleeve without compressing

4

his neck or back muscles. It was impossible to do, of course, even with Dave's help, and by the time the coat was off he was unable to conceal the pain.

'All right, let's get you into the chair.' Dave twisted him round, almost carrying him in the air. He lowered Grey into the seat.

'I hate this, Dave. I can't stand being weak.'

'You're getting better every day.'

'How long have I been here?' Grey asked.

'Three or four months. Probably four now.'

There was a silence of memory inside him, a period of his life irretrievably lost. All his memories were of the garden, the paths, this view of the sea, the pain, the endless rain and misted hills. They blended in his mind, each day indistinguishable from the others by its sameness, but there was that lost period behind him too. He knew that there had been the bedridden weeks, the sedatives and painkillers, the operations. Somehow he had lived through all that and somehow he had been signed off, despatched to convalescence, another bed from which he could not get out by himself. But whenever he tried to think back to beyond the pain, something in his memory turned away, slipped from his grasp. There were only the sessions of therapy, the garden, Dave and the other nurses.

He had accepted that those memories would not return, that to try to dwell on them only hindered his recovery.

'Actually, I was looking for you,' Dave said. 'You have visitors this morning.'

'Send them away.'

'You might want to meet the young woman. She's pretty . . .'

'I don't care,' Grey said. 'Are they from the newspaper?'

'I think so. I've seen the man before.'

'Then tell them I'm with the physiotherapist.'

'I think they'll probably wait for you.'

'I've nothing to tell them, nothing to say.'

While they had been speaking, Dave had leaned down on the handgrips and swung the chair around. Now he stood, pushing gently on the grips, rocking the chair up and down.

'Shall I wheel you up to the house?' he said.

'I don't seem to have any choice.'

'Of course you have. But if they've come from London they aren't going to go back until they've seen you.'

'All right, then.'

Dave took the weight of the chair and wheeled it slowly forward. It was a long, slow climb up to the main house because of the uneven path. When propelling himself Grey had already developed an instinct about jolts and their effect on his back and hip, but when someone else pushed him he could never anticipate them.

At last they entered the building by a side door, which opened automatically at their approach. The wheelchair rolled gently down the corridor towards the lift. The parquet flooring had a satin-smooth sheen, with no signs of wear. The whole place was continually being cleaned. It smelled unlike a hospital, with polish and varnish, carpets, international cuisine. The acoustics, too, were muted, as if it were really an expensive hotel where the patients were pampered guests. For Richard Grey it was the only place he knew as home. He sometimes felt he had been here all his life.

They ascended to the next floor and Dave propelled the chair to one of the lounges. Unusually, no other patients were there. At a desk in the alcove to one side James Woodbridge, the senior clinical psychologist, was using the telephone. He nodded to Grey as they came into the room, then spoke quickly and quietly and hung up.

Sitting by the other window was Tony Stuhr, one of the reporters from the newspaper. As soon as he saw him Grey felt the familiar conflict on meeting him: Stuhr was a likeable and frank young man, apparently intelligent, but the paper he worked for seemed to be the worst kind of tabloid rag, with a dubious reputation for chequebook journalism. Stuhr's by-line had appeared in the past few days on a series of stories about an alleged extramarital royal romance. The newspaper was delivered every day to Middlecombe, especially for Richard Grey. He never picked it up from the stall in the reception area and if anyone brought it to his room he rarely glanced at it.

Stuhr stood up as soon as Grey entered the room, smiled briefly at him, then looked at Woodbridge. The psychologist had

6

left the desk and was crossing towards him. Dave stepped on the footbrake of the wheelchair and left the room.

Woodbridge said, 'Richard, I asked you to come back to the house because there's someone I'd like you to meet.'

Stuhr was grinning at him, leaning over the table to stub out his cigarette. Grey noticed that his jacket was falling open and a rolled up copy of the newspaper was stuffed into an inner pocket. Grey was puzzled by the remark because Woodbridge must have known that he and Stuhr had met on several previous occasions. Then he realised there was someone with Stuhr. It was a young woman standing beside him, looking at Grey, her eyes flicking nervously towards Woodbridge, waiting for the introduction. He had not noticed her until this moment. She must have been sitting with the reporter and when she stood up had been behind him.

She came forward.

'Richard, this is Miss Kewley, Miss Susan Kewley.'

'Hello, Richard,' she said to Grey, smiling.

'How do you do?'

She was standing directly in front of him, seeming tall but not really so. Grey was still not used to being the only person sitting. He wondered whether he should shake hands with her.

'Miss Kewley read about your case in the press and has travelled from London to meet you.'

'Is that so?' Grey said.

'You could say we've set it up for you, Richard,' Stuhr said.

'What do you want?' Grey said to her.

'Well, I'd like to talk to you.'

'What about?'

She glanced at Woodbridge.

'Would you like me to stay?' the psychologist said to her over Grey's head.

'I don't know,' she said. 'What's best?'

Grey realised he was at risk of becoming irrelevant to the meeting; the real dialogue would be going on above him. It reminded him of the pain, lying in the intensive care unit in the London hospital after the first two operations, dimly hearing himself being discussed, dimly caring through the shrouds of agony.

'I'll call back in half an hour,' Woodbridge was saying. 'If you need to see me before then, you can use the phone.'

'Thank you,' said Susan Kewley.

When Woodbridge had left Tony Stuhr released the footbrake on the chair and pushed Grey to the table where they had been sitting. The young woman took the chair closest to him, but Stuhr sat by the window.

'Richard, do you remember me?' she said.

'Should I?'

'I was hoping you would.'

'Are we friends?'

'I suppose you could say that. For a while we were.'

'I'm sorry. I can't remember much about the past. How long ago was it?'

'Not long,' she said. 'Just before you were injured.' She looked at him only infrequently when she spoke, glancing down into her lap, or at the table, or across to the reporter. Stuhr was staring through the window, obviously listening yet not participating. When he realised Grey was looking at him he took the newspaper from his pocket and opened it to the football page.

'Would you like some coffee?' Grey said.

'You know I—' She checked herself. 'I prefer tea.'

'I'll get it.' Grey propelled himself away from her and went to the phone, asserting his independence. When he had ordered he returned to the table. Stuhr picked up his newspaper again; words had apparently been exchanged.

Looking at them both, Grey said, 'I might as well say that you're wasting your time. I've nothing to tell you.'

'Do you know what it's costing my paper to keep you in this place?' Stuhr said.

'I didn't ask to be brought here.'

'Our readers are concerned about you, Richard. You're a hero.'

'I'm no such thing. I happened to be in the wrong place. That doesn't make me a hero.'

'Look, I'm not here to argue with you,' Stuhr said.

The tea arrived on a silver tray: teapot and crockery, a tiny bowl of sugar, biscuits. While the steward arranged them on the table Stuhr returned to reading his newspaper. Grey took the opportunity to look properly at Susan Kewley. Dave had described her as pretty, but that was hardly the right word. Neutrally pleasant-looking might be a better way of putting it. She had a regular face, hazel eyes, pale brown hair which grew straight, slender shoulders. She was probably in her middle to late twenties. She sat in a relaxed way, resting her narrow wrists and hands on the arms of the chair, her body erect and comfortable. She would not look at him, but stared at the crockery on the table as if avoiding not only his eyes but his opinion too. Yet he had no opinion, except that she was there, that she had arrived with Stuhr and therefore must be connected, directly or indirectly, with the newspaper.

How had he known her in the past? She said she was a friend, but what kind? A family friend? Someone he had worked with? A lover? Surely he would be able to remember something like that, of all things? What would it have been about her that made him love her? It occurred to him that it might be some kind of setup, cooked up by the newspaper: MYSTERY WOMAN IN LOVE BID.

When the steward had left Grey said to her, 'Well, what is it we have to talk about?'

She said nothing, but reached forward and pulled a cup and saucer towards her. Still she did not look at him and her hair was falling forward, concealing her face from him.

'As far as I can remember I've never seen you before. You'll have to give me more to go on than the fact we were friends.'

She was holding the saucer, pale veins visible beneath her translucent skin. She was shaking her head slightly.

'Or are you here because *he* brought you?' Grey said angrily. He looked at Stuhr, who did not react. 'I don't know what you're after, but—'

Then she turned towards him and for the first time he saw all of her face, quite long, fine boned, wintry in colour. Her eyes were full of tears and the corners of her mouth were twitching downwards. She pushed back her chair quickly, toppling the saucer with its cup on the table, colliding with the wheelchair as she pushed past him. Pain jabbed down his back and he heard a gulping inhalation of breath from her. She ran across the room and went into the corridor.

To stare after her would mean turning his head against the

stiffness of his neck, so Grey did not try. It felt silent and cold in the room.

'What a bloody-minded bastard you can be.' Stuhr threw aside his newspaper. 'I'll call Woodbridge.'

'Wait a minute! What's going on?'

'Couldn't you see what you were doing to her?'

'Who is she?'

'She's your girlfriend, Grey. She thought if you saw her again it might trigger some memory.'

'I don't have a girlfriend.' But he felt again the helpless rage of his lost weeks. Just as he tried to avoid memories of the pain so he shrank away from the time before the car bomb. There was a profound blankness in his mind, one he never entered because he did not know how.

'That's what she told us.'

'Where was she when it happened? Didn't she know about the appeals? If so, why's she taken so long to come forward? And if she is someone I know, what the hell is she doing here with you?'

'Look, it was an experiment.'

'Did Woodbridge cook this up?'

'No. Susan approached *us*. She told us that she had been having an affair with you, not long before the explosion. It was over, and she'd lost contact with you. When she eventually found out you had been one of the victims, she came forward. She thought that if you saw her it might help you regain your memory.'

'Then it is a stunt.'

'I won't deny that if you regained your memory we'd publish the story. But really, I'm only here to mind your girlfriend.'

Grey shook his head and stared angrily through the window at the sea. Since he had been told he was suffering from retroactive amnesia, he had been trying to come to terms with it as best he could. At first he had probed the feeling of blankness, thinking that if he could somehow find a way he would penetrate it, but to do so made him profoundly depressed and introspective. What he was doing instead was trying not to think about it, to accept that the weeks he had lost would stay lost.

'Where does Woodbridge come into this?'

'He didn't set it up. He agreed to it. The idea was Susan's.'

'It was a bad idea.'

Stuhr said, 'That's not her fault. Look at yourself – you're totally unmoved! The only reservation Woodbridge had was that *you* might be traumatised. Yet you're sitting here as if nothing has happened, and Susan's in tears.'

'I can't help that.'

'Don't blame her for it.' Stuhr stood up. He thrust his newspaper back into his pocket. 'There's obviously no point going on with this. I'll call and see you in a month or so. You might be more receptive.'

'What about the – about Susan?'

'I'll come back this afternoon.'

She was there, standing beside his wheelchair and looking down at him, her hand resting on the grip behind his left shoulder. At the sound of her voice Grey started with surprise, jerking the stiffness in his neck, a completion of the movement he had failed to make when she left the room. How long had she been standing there, right beside him, on the periphery of his vision? Stuhr had given no indication she had returned.

Stuhr said to her, 'I'll wait for you in the car.'

He moved past them both and again Grey felt that unpleasant sensation of everyone being taller than him. Susan sat down in the chair she had occupied before.

'I'm sorry about that,' she said.

'No, I'm the one who should apologise. I was rude to you. I was reacting to Tony Stuhr, you were there in the way. Not your fault.'

'I won't stay now. I need time to think. I'll come back later.'

Grey said, 'After lunch I have to go for physiotherapy. Could you come again tomorrow?'

'It might be possible. Tony's driving back to London today, but I could stay.'

'Where are you?'

'We were in Kingsbridge last night. I'll arrange something with the hotel.'

As before, she did not look at him when they spoke, except in short, darting glimpses through the strands of fine hair. Her eyes had dried but she looked paler than before. He wanted to feel something for her, remember her, but she was a stranger.

Trying to offer her something warmer than this cold exchange of arrangements he said, 'Are you sure you still want to talk to me?'

'Yes, of course.'

'Tony said that we, I mean you and I, were once . . .'

'We went out together for a while. It didn't last long, but it mattered at the time. I'd hoped you would remember.'

'I'm sorry,' Grey said.

'Let's not talk about it. I'll come back tomorrow morning. I won't get upset again.'

Wanting to explain, he said, 'It was because you turned up here with Tony Stuhr. I thought you worked for the newspaper.'

'I had to approach them to find out where you were. It was the only way. They apparently own the rights to your story.'

'How did that happen?'

'I've no idea.' She had picked up her bag, a canvas holdall with a long strap. 'I'll come back tomorrow.'

'Come in the morning and stay for lunch, or as long as you like.'

'I should have asked you straight away: are you in much pain? I didn't realise you would still be in a wheelchair.'

'I'm better now. Everything happens slowly.'

'Richard . . . ?' She still had her fingers resting on the back of his hand. 'Are you sure – I mean, you really can't remember?'

He wanted to turn his hand so that she would touch his palm, but that would be an intimacy he knew he hadn't deserved. Looking at her large eyes and her clear complexion, he realised how easy he must once have found it to be with her. What was she like, this quiet-spoken woman who had once been his girl-friend? What did she know about him? What did he know of her? Why had they split up, when their relationship apparently mattered to them both? She was from beyond the coma, beyond the agony of ruptured organs and blistered skin, from the lost part of his life. But until today he had had no idea she even existed. He wanted to answer her question truthfully, but something still stood in the way.

'I'm trying to remember,' he said. 'I feel as if I know you.'

Her fingers briefly tightened. 'All right. I'll come back to see you tomorrow.'

She stood up, went past his chair and out of his sight. He

12

heard her footsteps soft on the carpet, then more distinctly in the corridor outside. Still he could not turn his head, without the pain.

Richard Grey's parents were both dead. He had no brothers or sisters. His only relative was his father's sister, who was married and living in Australia. After leaving school Grey went to Brent Technical College, where he took a diploma in photography. While at Brent he enrolled in a BBC training scheme, and when he had won his diploma he went to work at the BBC TV film studios as a camera trainee. After a few months he became a camera assistant, working with various crews in the studios and on location. Eventually he graduated to full camera operator.

When he was twenty-four he left the BBC and went to work as a cameraman for an independent news agency based in north London. The agency syndicated news film throughout the world, but principally to one of the American networks. Most of the news stories he was assigned to were in Britain and Europe, but he travelled several times to the United States, to the Far East and Australia, and to Africa. During the 1980s he made several trips to Northern Ireland, covering the troubles there.

He established a reputation for courage. News crews are frequently in the thick of dangerous events, and it takes a particular kind of dedication to continue filming in the middle of a riot or while under fire. Richard Grey had risked his life on several occasions.

He was twice nominated for a BAFTA award for documentary or news filming and one year he and his sound recordist were given a special Prix Italia for film reportage of street fighting in Belfast. The commendation read: *Richard Grey, Camera Operator, BBC Television News. Special Award. News filming in circumstances of extreme personal danger.* Among his colleagues Grey was a popular figure and in spite of his reputation he never found people unwilling to work with him. As his professional stature grew it was recognised that he was not foolhardy, endangering himself as well as others, but used skill and experience and knew intuitively when a risk might be calculated.

Grey lived alone in the apartment he had bought with the money his father left him. Most of his friends were people he worked with, and because his job involved so much travelling he had never settled down with a steady girlfriend. He found it easy to drift from one casual encounter to the next, never forming ties. When he was not working he often went to the cinema, sometimes to the theatre. About once a week he would meet some of his friends for an evening in a pub. He generally took solitary holidays, camping or walking; once, he had extended a working trip to the States by renting a car and driving to California.

Apart from the deaths of his parents, there had been only one major disruption to his life and that had happened about six months before the car bomb.

It came about because Richard Grey filmed best on celluloid. He liked the weight of an Arriflex, the balance of it, the quiet vibration of the motor. He saw through the reflex viewfinder as if with an extra eye; he sometimes said he could not see properly without it. And there was something about the texture of the film itself, the quality of the picture, the grain, the subtlety of its effects. The knowledge that film slipped through the gate, halting and advancing, twenty-five times a second, gave an intangible extra feel to his work. He was invariably irritated if people said they could not tell the difference, on a television screen, between a film sequence and one recorded on videotape. It seemed to him that the difference was manifest: video footage had an empty quality, a brightness and sharpness that was unnatural and false.

But while Grey was in the most productive part of his career, a change took place. Celluloid was a slow and unwieldy medium for news gathering. The cans had to be taken to a lab, then to a cutting room. Sound had to be synched in or overdubbed. There were always technical problems during transmission, especially when a local news studio had to be used or if the film had to be sent by satellite to one of the syndicating stations. The difficulties were increased when working abroad or in a war zone. Sometimes the only way to get the story out was by taking the unprocessed film to the nearest airport and putting it on a plane to London, New York or Amsterdam.

News networks around the world were changing over to electronic cameras. Using portable satellite dishes, a crew could transmit pictures direct to the studio as they were being shot.

There they could be edited electronically and transmitted without delay.

One by one the news crews were going over to video and it came, inevitably, to Grey. He went on a retraining course and thereafter had to use an electronic camera, but for reasons he never really understood he found it difficult to transfer his skill. He could not 'see' without the intervention of film, the silent whirring of the shutter. He became selfconscious about the problem, attempting to overcome it by fundamentally rethinking his approach. He tried to adjust his eye so he could see again, a concept to which his colleagues were sympathetic even though most of them were making the same transition painlessly. He kept telling himself that the camera was a mere instrument, that his ability was innate and not a product of the medium. Even so, he knew he had lost his flair.

There were other jobs open to him. BBC News and ITN were also changing over to electronic news gathering, and even though he was offered a film job with ITN he realised that the same problem would arise before long. Another job offered to him was with an industrial documentary unit, but he had cut his teeth on news filming and it was never a real alternative.

The solution came when the agency unexpectedly lost its contract with the American network. Staff had to be made redundant and Richard Grey volunteered. He had no particular idea in mind: he simply took the redundancy money, intending to use it to buy time to rethink his career.

He was not short of money. He had bought his apartment outright with his father's money and the redundancy lump sum would last at least a year. Nor was he idle, because he found occasional freelance work.

But then there was a gap.

His next memories were fitful: he was in intensive care at Charing Cross Hospital in London, surviving on a ventilator, undergoing a series of major operations, in pain and under sedation. Ambulance journeys punctuated the agony, as he was moved from one kind of trauma clinic to the next. Finally there was a day long journey in another ambulance and ever since he had been here at Middlecombe, convalescing on the south Devon coast.

Somewhere in the gap in his life he had been walking innocently in a London street where terrorists had planted a car bomb outside a police station. It exploded while he was passing. He suffered multiple burns and lacerations, back injuries, fractures of pelvis, leg and arm, and ruptured internal organs. He had nearly died. He knew because he had been told, not because he remembered.

This was the extent of his memories on the day Susan Kewley came to see him, and she nowhere fitted into them.

There was a conflict of medical opinion about Grey's amnesia and for Grey himself it was complicated by a conflict of personal opinion.

He was being treated by two doctors at the hospital: the psychologist James Woodbridge and a consultant psychiatrist called Dr Hurdis.

Grey disliked Woodbridge personally, because he found him high-handed and often remote, but he took a clinical line that Grey found comprehensible and acceptable. Woodbridge, while acknowledging the traumatic nature of the injuries, and the effects of concussion, believed that retrograde amnesia could be psychologically based. In other words, that there were additional events in his experience, unconnected with the explosion, which Grey was repressing. Woodbridge believed that those memories should be coaxed out gently by psychotherapy, and that the benefits of using other techniques to open up the memories would not be worth the risks. He thought that Grey should be rehabilitated gradually, and with a return to normality he would be able to come to terms with his past, his memory returning in stages.

On the other hand, Dr Hurdis, whom Grey actually liked, had been pressing him in a direction he tried to resist. Hurdis believed that progress with orthodox analytical psychotherapy would be too slow, especially where organic loss of memory was involved.

Despite his feelings for them as people, Grey had so far responded better to Woodbridge than to Hurdis.

Until Susan Kewley's arrival, Grey had not been too concerned about what might actually have happened in the weeks he had lost. What worried him more was the sense of *absence*, a hole in

16

his life, a dark and quiet period that seemed forever remote from him. His mind instinctively shied away from it, and like the sore places in his body he had been trying not to use it.

But Susan Kewley had come to him from out of the absence, unrecognised and unremembered. She had known him then and he had known her. She was awakening in him the need to remember.

In the morning, when Richard Grey had been bathed and dressed, and was waiting in his room for news of Susan's arrival, Woodbridge came to see him.

'I wanted to have a quiet word with you before you see Miss Kewley,' Woodbridge said. 'She seems a pleasant young woman, don't you agree?'

'Yes,' Grey said, suddenly irritated.

'I wondered if you had any memory of her.'

'None whatsoever.'

'Not even a vague feeling that you might have seen her somewhere?'

'No.'

'Did she tell you anything about what had happened when you knew her?'

'No.'

'Richard, what I'm suggesting is that you might have had some kind of traumatic row with her, and afterwards dealt with it by trying to bury the memory. It would be perfectly normal to do so.'

'All right,' Grey said. 'But I don't see why that matters.'

'Because retroactive amnesia can be caused by an unconscious wish to banish unhappy memories.'

'Is it going to make a difference?'

'Seeing her could deepen your unconscious wish to block her.'

'It didn't yesterday. It deepened my wish to know her better. It seems to me that she might be able to remind me of things I can't remember by myself.'

'Yes, but it's important that you realise she is not going to provide you with the solution on her own.'

'But surely it can't hurt?'

17

'We'll have to see. If you want to talk to me afterwards I will be here for the rest of the day.'

Grey remained stubbornly irritated after Woodbridge left. It seemed to him that there was a subtle but definite distinction between his private life and his presence in the hospital as a patient. He sometimes thought that his amnesia was seen as a professional challenge by the people who were treating him, something unrelated to his real life. If Susan really had been his girlfriend, their knowledge of each other was presumably intimate and their memories would be private. Woodbridge's questions intruded on this.

A few minutes after Woodbridge left, Grey took the book he was reading and went out of his room and along to the lift. He propelled himself out to the terrace and moved to the far end. This was not only some distance away from the other patients, but gave him a vantage point over most of the gardens and the drive leading to the visitors' car park.

The weather was cool and grey, with low clouds moving in darkly from the north-west. The sea was normally visible from the terrace, glimpsed through trees, but today there was a dulling haze over everything.

He settled down to read, but the wind was blustery and after a few minutes he called a steward and asked for a blanket. After an hour, the other patients had retreated inside.

Vehicles arrived at intervals, nosing their way up the turning incline into the steep drive. Two of them were ambulances bringing new patients, and there were several tradesmen's vans and a number of cars. With the arrival of each one Grey's hopes rose and he waited excitedly for her to appear.

It was impossible to concentrate on his book and the morning passed slowly. He felt cold and uncomfortable and, as midday approached, more and more resentful. She had promised, after all, and must have known what the visit would mean to him. He started to invent excuses for her: she had had to hire a car and there had been a delay; the car had broken down; there had been an accident. But surely he would have heard?

With the helpless egoism of the invalid, Grey could think of nothing but this.

The time drew near to one o'clock, when luncheon was served

and he would be taken into the dining room. He knew that even if she arrived in the next few minutes they could only have a short time together. At two he had to go for physiotherapy.

At five minutes before the hour a car turned into the drive. Grey regarded its silver roof and sky-reflecting windows with fatalistic certainty that it was Susan. He waited.

She appeared on the terrace with one of the nurses, Sister Brecon. The two women walked across to him.

'They're serving lunch, Mr Grey. Shall I get them to wheel you in?'

Looking at Susan he said, 'I'll be there in a few minutes.'

'I can't stay long,' she said, to the nurse, not to Grey.

'Would you like me to tell them you're staying for lunch too?'

'No, thank you.'

The nurse glanced from one to the other of them, then walked away.

'Richard, I'm sorry I couldn't get here earlier.'

'Where have you been?'

'I was delayed in Kingsbridge.'

'I've been waiting for you all morning,' he said.

'I know. I'm really sorry.'

She sat down on the tiled parapet of the terrace. Her fawn raincoat fell away on each side, revealing the lower part of her legs. They were thin and clad in ankle socks pulled on over her stockings. She was wearing a flowered skirt, with a white lace trim.

She said, 'I made the mistake of phoning the studio this morning. All sorts of problems have come up.'

'Studio?'

'Where I work. I'm a designer and I do freelance work three days a week for them. It's my only regular work. I thought you might remember that.'

'No.'

She leaned forward to take his hand. Grey stared at the ground, realising dismally that for the second time he was feeling hostile towards her.

'I'm sorry,' he said.

'And there's something else. I have to go back to London

today.' When he looked up quickly, she added, 'I know. I'll try to come back next week.'

'Not before then?'

'I really can't. It's difficult. I need the money and if I let them down they'll find another artist. It's hard getting the work.'

'All right.' Struggling against his disappointment Grey tried to get his thoughts straight. 'Let me tell you what I've been thinking since yesterday. I want to look at you.'

He had already noticed that she rarely turned her face fully towards him, always presenting a quarter profile or keeping her head modestly lowered. Her hair fell about her face, hiding her face. It had seemed an attractive mannerism at first, a shyness, a reticence, but he wanted to see her properly.

She said, 'I don't like being looked at.'

'I want to remember you as I used to know you.'

'You didn't look at me then, either.'

But she tossed her hair back with a light shaking motion of her head and looked straight at him. He regarded her, trying to remember or see her as he might have done before. She held his gaze for a few moments, then cast her eyes downwards once more.

'Don't stare at me,' she said.

'If I can remember you, then I'll remember everything else.'

'That's the reason I'm here.'

'I know, but it's difficult for me. I'm told what to do by the staff, the newspaper wants me to tell my story, I'm stuck in this chair, and all I'm interested in is getting back to normal. The truth is, Susan, I don't remember you. Not at all.'

She said, 'But—'

'Let me finish. I *don't* remember you, but I nevertheless feel I know you. It's the first real feeling I've had since I've been here.'

She nodded mutely, her face hidden from him again.

'I'd like to see you again, as often as you can manage it.'

'It's not easy,' she said. 'I spent most of what I had, renting the car. And there's still the train fare back to London.'

'I'll pay for everything – I've got money. Or the newspaper can pay. Something can be arranged.'

'Maybe.'

He sensed an unstated reason, something more intractable than shortage of cash. She was looking away from him again, staring down the length of the terrace. He wished she would face him.

'I assume there's someone else,' he said.

'There was once, yes.'

'Is he the reason it's taken you so long to get down to see me?'

'No – it's more complicated than that. I came as soon as I felt I could. Niall, the friend, didn't make any difference to that. He knew about you, and knew I was missing you, but he didn't stand in the way. It's all over with him now.'

Grey felt excitement in him, an involuntary contraction of muscles, a feeling he had not known since before he could remember.

'Susan, can you tell me what happened between us? At the end. Why did we part?'

'You really don't know, do you?'

'No.'

She shook her head. 'It seems impossible to me that you could forget. It mattered so much at the time.'

'Couldn't you simply tell me?'

'Surely that part of it doesn't matter any more? It wasn't any one thing. I think the truth is that it had never really worked from the beginning.'

'But it worked enough for you to be here. What happened? Did we have a row? What was said?'

'No, not a row, not that sort of thing. It had been going wrong for some time and we both knew we couldn't carry on as we were. It was complicated. I was with Niall for a time and you were unhappy about that, but there was a misunderstanding. You'd gone away and I thought it was all over between us. You'd actually said you wanted to stop seeing me, but it turned out nothing had been settled. All this was going on, really muddled and upsetting, when the car bomb happened. You must have been told what followed that, the way the terrorists threatened to search for the survivors and finish them off. The police moved you to another hospital and I had no way of knowing where to find you.'

'Until now.'

'Yes.'

'Look, I can sort of guess at that,' Grey said. 'Obviously, the life

I was in before the bomb was not as clear cut as I'd like it to be. I assumed that if I had been involved with someone it couldn't have been all that important.'

'Oh, but it was,' she said, her eyes wide.

'Then tell me more. Where did we meet, where did we go? Give me something to connect to.'

'Do you remember the cloud?' she said.

'Cloud? What sort of cloud? What do you mean?'

'Just, the cloud.'

One of the stewards had appeared on the terrace, a napkin folded over his arm. 'Will you and your visitor be requiring lunch, sir?'

'I don't want lunch today,' Grey said, glancing briefly at him. To his surprise he realised that Susan had taken the interruption as a signal to end their conversation. She was standing. 'What are you doing? You can't leave!'

'I have to turn the car in at Kingsbridge and after that there's a bus to Totnes for the train. I'm already late. I must go.'

'What were you talking about just now? What did you mean about the cloud?'

'It was something I thought you'd remember.'

'I don't,' Grey said. 'Tell me something else.'

'Niall. Do you remember him?'

'No. Am I supposed to?'

'Do you remember how we met?'

He shook his head with exasperation. 'No, I don't!'

'I don't know what you want to hear! Look, I'll come here again and we'll talk properly.'

She was leaving. Already she had turned away from him.

'When will it be? Can you come back at the weekend?'

'It'll be as soon as I can make it,' she said. She crouched down by his chair and squeezed his hand gently. 'I *want* to see you, Richard. I'd stay with you if I could. I should have allowed more time, but the newspaper wouldn't tell me anything about your state of mind, and I thought—'

She brought her face to his and kissed him lightly on the cheek. He raised his hand to touch her hair and turned his head, finding her lips. Her face was cold, from the weather. She held the kiss for a few seconds, then drew away from him.

'Don't go, Susan,' he said quietly. 'Please don't leave me.'

'I really must.' She stood up and moved away from him, but the kiss had changed something already. She was hesitating. Then she said, 'I nearly forgot! I brought you a present.'

She stepped back to him, reaching down into her deep canvas bag. She drew out a small white paper bag, folded over and sealed with a strip of clear tape. She handed it to him, waiting for him to open it. He broke the seal with his thumb and pulled out what was inside. There were about two dozen postcards of assorted sizes and kinds. They were all old and most of the photographs were black-and-white or sepia-tinted. Some of the pictures were views of English seaside resorts, some were expanses of countryside, some were from the Continent: as Grey riffled through them he glimpsed German spas, French cathedrals and palaces, Alpine scenery, fishing ports.

'I saw them in an antiques shop this morning. In Kingsbridge.'

'Thank you. What can I say?'

'I suppose it's possible you already have some of them. In your collection.'

'My *collection*?'

She laughed then, abrupt and loud. 'You don't even remember that, do you?'

'You mean I collect old postcards?' He grinned at her. 'How much more am I going to learn from you?'

'Actually, there is something you can do straight away. You never used to call me Susan. It was always Sue.'

She bent down to kiss him again, this time on the cheek. Then she left, walking quickly along the terrace and disappearing into the building. He waited, and a short time later he heard a car door slam and an engine start. Soon he saw the windows and roof of her car as it drove slowly down towards the lane, the dim sky reflecting off the polished surfaces.

Richard Grey spent part of the following Saturday afternoon with Dr Hurdis, who was making one of his regular visits. Hurdis usually made him feel he was regarded as a participant in a problem shared by them both, rather than as a recipient of therapy or the subject of a theory. Their sessions together were often more like conversations than analysis, and although Grey realised it was probably not the whole case he was nevertheless grateful not to be treated, as almost everyone else at the clinic treated him, as someone halfway between a rich hotel guest and a patient who understood only monosyllabic instructions and sign language.

He was in a communicative mood that day, because not only did he feel at last he had something to talk about, but also he had an interest in himself that had been lacking before.

Not that Sue's short visit had solved anything. His amnesia remained as profound and impenetrable as ever, a fact which Hurdis quickly elicited from him. The principal change she had brought him was something she could not have intended: she had reassured him that he had actually existed in the lost period. Until her visit, he had not truly believed in himself. The sense of blankness and absence behind him had been complete, seeming to exclude him from his own life. But Sue was a witness to the fact of himself. She remembered him when he did not.

He had thought of almost nothing but her since she left. His mind and life were filled with her. He wanted her company, the touch of her hand, her kisses. Most of all he wanted to see her, to look properly at her, but in a strange miniature of his larger problem he found it difficult to remember what she was like. He could visualise peripheral details about her: the canvas bag, the stockinged ankles, the flowered skirt, her masking hair. He knew she had looked him straight in the face, as if allowing him a secret sight of her, but afterwards he found he could not see her face in his mind's eye. He remembered the pleasant plainness of her face, the regularity of her features, but these too acted to mask her appearance.

'I think Sue is my best chance of recovering my memory,' he said. 'She obviously knows me well and she was there during the weeks I've lost. I keep thinking that if only she tells me one thing that jogs my memory, it could be enough.'

'You might be right,' Hurdis said. They were in the office he used during his weekend visits, a comfortable place of big leather chairs, dark wooden panelling and a bookcase stocked with medical texts. 'But a word of caution. You mustn't be too anxious to remember. There's a condition known as paramnesia, hysterical paramnesia.'

'I'm not hysterical, Dr Hurdis.'

'Clearly not, in the usual sense. But occasionally someone who has lost his memory will grasp at any straw, any hint of a memory. If you don't know how reliable it is as a memory, it can sometimes lead to a whole sequence of invented memories.'

'I'm sure that couldn't happen with Sue. She would put me right.'

'As you say. But you might not be able to tell the difference. What does Mr Woodbridge think?'

'I think he's against my talking to her.'

'Yes, I see.'

Grey's preoccupation, since Sue left, had been in trying to pry loose any memories she might have touched on. Fired by his new interest in her, the few things she said became enormously important, and he examined them in his mind from every angle. He talked them out with Dr Hurdis, glad to have an uncritical listener, someone who contributed by encouraging him to talk.

In actual fact she had said remarkably little about their past together. It was symptomatic of paramnesia, according to Hurdis, that he should seize on such fragments and try to find relevance in them.

He had already solved one minor mystery on his own: the question of the postcards. At first he thought he had stumbled on something from his lost weeks, something hitherto forgotten, but then, surfacing from the old past, the memory came to him.

He had been working in Bradford, in the north of England. During an afternoon off he went wandering by himself through the backstreets and discovered a tiny junk shop. He had a collection of antique film equipment and was always on the lookout for more. This particular shop had nothing of the sort, but on the counter he came across a battered shoe box crammed with postcards. He looked through them for a while, mildly interested. The woman who ran the shop told him the prices were marked on the back of each card. On an impulse he asked her how much she would want for the lot. A few seconds later the deal was closed for ten pounds.

When he reached home a few days later, Grey went through the several hundred old postcards he now owned. Many of them had obviously been bought and collected by someone in the past, because they were unused. Others, though, had messages on the back. He read all the ones he could decipher, scrawled in fountain pen or indelible pencil. Almost all of them were prosaic despatches from holidays: a lovely time being had, the weather improving, visited Aunt Sissy yesterday, the scenery is beautiful, raining all week but we're bearing up, Ted doesn't like the food, weather glorious, the gardens are so peaceful, the sun brings out the mosquitoes, we've all been swimming, weather, weather, weather.

Many of the cards went back to the Great War and before, their halfpenny stamps mute tokens of how prices had changed. At least a third had been sent from abroad: grand tours through Europe, rides on cable cars, visits to casinos, insufferable heat. The actual photographs were even more interesting. He saw them as stills from some long-lost travelogue of the past, glimpses of towns and scenes that in one sense no longer existed. Several pictures were of places he knew or had visited: Edwardian gentlemen and ladies strolling on seafront esplanades, which now were littered with high-rise hotels, amusement arcades and parking meters; country vales, where broad motorways had since been driven through; French and Italian shrines, which now were cluttered with souvenir stalls; peaceful market towns, jammed with traffic and chain stores in the modern age. These too were memories of a vanished past, alien but recognisable, unattainable in every real sense.

He sorted the cards into groups by country, then returned them to the box. Whenever friends sent him postcards after that he added them to the stack, thinking that they too would one day come to represent a certain past.

Sue's reminder had surprised him, but the cards did not come from his amnesiac period. He had been in Bradford while still working for the agency, predating by at least a year any possible first meeting with her.

However, the fact that she knew about the postcards meant she must have been in his flat to have seen them, or that he had known her well enough to talk to her about this fairly insignificant feature of his life.

The rest of what she had told him was more vague. They had plainly been lovers, although only, it seemed, for a short period.

They had split up. There was someone else in her life and the name Niall had been mentioned. She was Sue, not Susan. Then odd details: the way they might have met, the cloud.

What had gone wrong with their relationship? The two short times he had seen her at the hospital he had been initially hostile to her. Was it an awakening from the unconscious? If there was someone else, had everything been wrecked by jealousy?

And what was the significance, if any, of the cloud? It was a commonplace. Why did she remember that of all things, and think it would trigger a memory in him?

Taken as a whole, nothing she said stirred the slightest memory in him. From the reference to the postcards he could understand, to the enigmatic cloud he could not, nothing helped.

Dr Hurdis listened with his usual close interest, wrote down a few notes as Grey was speaking, but at the end sat with his notebook closed on his lap.

'There's something else we could try,' he said. 'I think I'd like to try hypnotising you?'

'Would that make a difference?'

'It might. Hypnosis is sometimes helpful in recovering lost memory, but it's an imperfect technique and by no means a sure method. It might make a difference in your case, though.'

'Why haven't you suggested it before?'

Hurdis said, smiling, 'You're motivated now. I'm due to make another call here on Wednesday. We'll give it a try then.'

In the evening, Grey spent an hour in the pool in the basement of the hospital, swimming to and fro slowly, floating on his back, thinking about Sue.

Sue telephoned on the Tuesday evening. One of the nurses wheeled Grey down to the payphone in the corridor. He had a telephone of his own in his room, but she must have been given the other number. As soon as he heard her voice he knew she was going to let him down.

'How are you Richard?' she said.

'I'm a lot better, thanks.'

There was a short silence. Then, 'I'm on a payphone, so I can't talk too long.'

'Hang up and I'll call you back from my room.'

'No, someone's waiting. I've got to tell you something. I won't be able to get to see you this week. Will next week be all right?'

'I suppose so,' he said, against a thudding and inevitable feeling of disappointment. 'You promised you'd come.'

'I know, and I meant it. But it's not possible.'

'What's the problem?'

'I can't afford the train fare and—'

'I've told you, I can pay.'

'Yes, but I can't get the time off. There's a deadline and I have to go into the studio every day.'

Two patients were walking slowly down the corridor, not speaking. Grey held the receiver closer to his ear, trying for privacy. The patients went through the door into the lounge, and he briefly heard music from the television.

When the door closed he said, 'Don't you understand how important it is to me?' but halfway through his sentence he heard the line close and open again, presumably as Sue put in another coin.

'I didn't hear that,' she said.

'I said it's important that I see you.'

'I know. I'm sorry.'

'Will you definitely come next week?'

'I'll try.'

'You'll *try*? You said you wanted to come.'

'I do, I really do.'

Another silence.

Then Grey said, 'Where are you speaking from? Is someone with you?'

'I'm at my flat. The payphone in the hall.'

'*Is* somebody with you?'

'No, and I don't see—'

'You're right,' he said quickly. 'I'm sorry.'

'I'm working in my room, trying to finish a piece of artwork before going to the studio tomorrow morning.'

Grey realised that he had no idea where she lived. A bead of sweat ran down his face beside his eye. Part of him was thinking how ridiculous it was to be so obsessed with this young woman, already checking up on what she was doing when she was away from him. He had rarely felt so isolated, so incapable of free movement or thought, so dependent on another human being. 'Look,' he said. 'The phone will cut off again soon. Do you have any more change?'

'No, I'm going to have to finish.'

'Please, get some more money and call me again so we can talk. Or give me your number and I'll phone you.' Time was slipping away while he pleaded reasonably.

'I'll try to get down to Devon for the weekend.'

'Do you mean that? It would be—'

But the line clicked and went dead. Grey groaned in frustration. He heard the dialling tone, so he put down the receiver. The whole building felt deeply silent, as if his words had sounded about the place for all to hear. It was an illusion, thankfully: he could still hear the television faintly through the door and somewhere below him the central heating boiler was making its customary distant noises. He could hear voices at the far end of the corridor.

He sat in his wheelchair, the telephone in its acoustic perspex hood just above head height. He tried to calm his feelings. He knew he was being unreasonable: he was treating her as if she were answerable to him for all her actions and thoughts, as if vows were being broken.

Ten minutes passed and then the phone rang. He snatched it down.

Sue said, 'I was only able to borrow a couple of coins. We can talk for three or four minutes.'

'All right, about the weekend—'

'Please! Let me say what I want to say. I know you think I'm letting you down, but I went to Devon without really thinking through what I was doing, what I might be letting us both in for again. I didn't realise what seeing you again would do to me. What you want is for me to explain what happened, but that's so close to where we went wrong before that I'm scared of losing you all over again.'

'It means we have to meet soon.'

'Yes, but I can't walk away from my life. I'll come down to see you at the weekend. That's a promise. But you'll have to send me some money.'

'I don't know your address!'

29

'Do you have some paper? Or can you remember it?' Speaking quickly, she dictated an address in north London. 'Have you got that?'

'I'll send a cheque tomorrow.'

'I'll pay you back when I can.'

'You don't—'

'Now, there's something else,' she said, and it was almost as if she was expelling breath held back until this moment. 'Don't interrupt, because there isn't time. I'm all mixed up about you, because you don't seem to recognise me and because of what happened before, but it's my only chance and I've got to say it. I still want you, I still love you.'

'Still?'

'I always did, Richard, right from the start. Almost from before you spoke to me the first time.'

He was smiling. He could hardly believe what he was hearing.

'I won't be here much longer,' he said. 'Maybe a week or two. I'm feeling much better.'

'It's terrible seeing you in that chair. You were always so active, you made me feel lazy.'

'I walked a long way today. Five times across the room, and it's further every day.' He knew he was bragging like a child, but the mood of depression she had cast him into had evaporated. 'I'm sorry about everything. I'm so cut off down here, I get obsessed with my own troubles. It'll be different next time.'

They were still speaking, exchanging half-intimacies, as her money ran out and the line died. He hung up, then propelled himself down the corridor, thrusting down on the push-wheels with all his strength. At the end of the corridor he swung round and sped back to the lift. If one of his arms had been free he would have waved a clenched fist in the air.

Once inside his room he found the cardboard box of personal documents sent down to the hospital by the police, and looked through them for his chequebook. Just to see the pieces of card and paper was like glimpsing his old identity again: a driving licence, credit cards, a cheque guarantee card (date expired), membership of the British Film Institute, a BECTU union card, a BBC Club card, the insurance certificate for his car, a bank statement, membership card for the National Trust . . .

He found the chequebook and wrote Sue a cheque for one hundred pounds. He scribbled a note on the hospital's paper and slipped it into an envelope with the cheque. He wrote the address Sue had dictated to him, then propped up the envelope, ready for posting in the morning.

He sat back in his chair for a while, dwelling pleasurably on the intimate words they had exchanged at the end. He closed his eyes, trying to remember her face.

A little later he returned to the documents he had scattered across the table. They had been in his possession since his transfer to Devon, but he had scarcely looked at them. Nothing could have seemed more irrelevant. His affairs, such as they were, were being looked after by a solicitor retained by the newspaper. As a matter of fact the cheque to Sue was the first he had written on his own behalf since the car bomb.

Suddenly interested in himself he opened the chequebook and looked through the counterfoils. He had used about half of the twenty-five cheques and the dates scrawled on the counterfoils were all in the days leading up to the bomb incident. Hoping for a clue he looked at each one, but he soon realised he would learn little from them. Most of them were cash cheques: two of them for a hundred pounds each, the rest for fifty pounds. There was one cheque made out to British Telecom, one to London Electricity, one to a record shop, two or three of them to filling stations, and one to a Mrs Williams for the sum of twenty-seven pounds. This last item was the only one he couldn't understand, but it was hardly likely to be significant.

His address book was also in the box, a small, plastic bound notebook. He knew most of it was blank because he had never been good at writing down addresses, but nevertheless he turned to the page for the Ks. There was no entry for Sue Kewley, which was unsurprising but vaguely disappointing. It would have been a sort of proof, a link with his forgotten past.

He went through the book, examining everything. Most of the addresses were of people he could remember: colleagues, old girlfriends, his aunt in Australia. Several of the names had only telephone numbers against them. Everything in the book had a familiar feeling of being from his known past, providing him with nothing new. No entry for Mrs Williams. Just as he was about to put the book aside he thought of looking at the back of the last page, remembering that he sometimes used it for scribbled notes. There he found what he was looking for: amid a number of obscure pieces of arithmetic, a reminder of a dental appointment and a couple of doodles, was the word 'Sue'. Next to it was a London 020 8 telephone number.

For a moment he was tempted to pick up his phone and call her immediately, to celebrate the fact that he had found her in his own past, but he held back. He was content with what had passed between them and how their last phone call had ended. Another one might make her change her mind again. There was plenty of time ahead for him to check that it was still her number, to verify this old link with himself.

Grey visited Dr Hurdis's office the following morning, still in the optimistic mood of the evening before. He had slept well and without the need for painkillers. The psychiatrist was waiting for him and introduced him to the young woman who was standing beside him.

'Richard, I'd like you to meet one of my postgraduate researchers, Alexandra Gowers. Mr Richard Grey.'

'How do you do?'

They shook hands formally, Grey slightly taken aback to meet her. She gave him a friendly smile, as perhaps in the circumstances she should, but she did seem pleasant enough. Grey briefly registered that she was wearing a red skirt with a black woollen pullover. Her spectacles and long dark hair gave her a studious look.

Hurdis said, 'With your permission, Richard, I should like Miss Gowers to be present while I hypnotise you. Do you have any objections?'

'I suppose not. Would you mind telling me why?'

'Her research is into spontaneous amnesia as it relates to hypnotic trance, and I thought your case would be of particular interest to her. Of course, if you prefer not—'

'No,' said Grey. 'I don't object.' He had no real will to resist.

'This is anyway only a preliminary session. What I'll do is put you into a light trance and see how you react to that. If it goes well I might try to deepen the trance a little.'

Hurdis and the young woman helped him out of the wheel-chair. Hurdis took his weight as Grey lowered himself into one of the leather chairs and made himself comfortable.

'Do you have any questions, Richard?'

'Tell me what's going to happen. Is it like losing consciousness?'

'No, you'll be awake the whole time. Hypnosis is simply a form of relaxation.'

'I don't like the idea of being unconscious,' he said.

'What I want you to do is try to cooperate with me as far as possible. In a sense, the subject hypnotises himself, so you remain in control. You can speak, move your hands, even open your eyes. Nothing like that will break the trance. The important thing to warn you about is that we might not get results straight away. If we don't you mustn't feel let down.'

'I'm ready for that,' Grey said, remembering numerous other instances in the recent past when he had hoped without result for some breakthrough.

'All right, if you're ready to begin.' Hurdis was standing at his side. He stretched out an adjustable desk lamp so that it was above Grey's head. 'Can you see this?'

'Yes.'

Hurdis moved it back a little. 'What about here?'

'Just about.'

'Keep looking up so the lamp is on the edge of your vision. Relax your body as much as you can and let your breathing get steady and easy. Listen to what I'm saying and if your eyes start to feel tired let them close.' In the room, Grey was aware that Alexandra Gowers had moved away and was sitting on one of the straight backed chairs placed against the wall. 'Keep the lamp in sight and listen to me, and while you do so I would like you to start counting backwards to yourself, count to yourself, count from three hundred downwards, start now, keep counting, and listen to what I'm saying, but keep counting slowly *299* to yourself, and breathing *298* gently and slowly, and think *297* of nothing but looking up at the lamp and *296* counting slowly backwards listening *295* to what I'm saying, and feeling your body relaxed *294* and comfortable, extremely comfortable, your legs *293* feel heavy, your arms feel heavy *292* and now your eyes are

33

beginning to feel *291* tired, so if you wish you can close them, let them close, but keep *290* counting slowly and listening, your body is relaxed *289* and now your eyes have closed but you are *288* still counting slowly, while you feel you are drifting backwards, totally relaxed while you drift slowly backwards, and now *287* you are feeling drowsy, very comfortable as you drift backwards, feeling drowsy, listening to what I'm saying but getting drowsy, drifting deeper and deeper into sleep, but listening to what I'm saying . . .'

Grey felt comfortable and relaxed and drowsy, listening to Hurdis with his eyes closed, but none the less he was still aware of everything around him. It was as if his senses had somehow been made more acute than normal, because he found he could discern movements and noises not only inside the room but from further afield. Outside in the hall two people walked past, talking to each other in quiet tones. The lift motor grumbled. Somewhere in the room Alexandra Gowers made a clicking noise, as if with a ballpoint pen, and started writing on her notepad. The sound of the pen was so delicate, so deliberately contrived by her hand, that Grey suddenly realised that by listening closely he could follow what she was writing: he sensed that she had written his name in capital letters, then underlined the words. She wrote the date next to his name. Why had she put a line through the stem of the '7' . . . ? In the next room a telephone rang, distracting him: someone cleared their throat before picking up the receiver. Grey could hear the words as they were spoken, but decided not to listen in. He was free of pain, completely free, for the first time in weeks. Obedient to Hurdis's suggestions the sensation of the trance . . .

'. . . drifting backwards, feeling drowsy, listening to me, your body is relaxed and you are sleepy. Good, Richard, that's excellent. Now stay breathing steadily, but what I want you to do is concentrate on your right hand. Think about your right hand and how it feels, and concentrate on it, and perhaps you find it is resting on something soft, something light, very light, something that supports your hand, pressing up gently from below, lifting your hand, lifting your hand . . .'

As Hurdis said these words Grey felt his right hand lifting away from his lap. It raised itself quickly and smoothly until his arm was upright, or nearly so.

Alexandra Gowers made another clicking sound and Grey realised that it was being made by a stopwatch. He sensed her writing down with her other hand: *Right arm; 1m. 57s.* The watch clicked a second time.

Hurdis said, 'Good, that's fine. Now feel your hand in the air, feel the air around it, gently supporting it. The air is holding it up, the air is holding it, holding it, and now you cannot pull your hand down again, the air is holding it . . .'

While Grey obediently tried to pull his hand down to his lap once more, Alexandra Gowers again timed him and wrote on her notepad. He realised he was doing well as an hypnotic subject. He was starting to enjoy the sensation of duality: his mind was separate from his body, one could act without the other.

'. . . holding it up, but now I want you to lower your hand as soon as I have counted to five, as soon as I count from one to five, your hand will fall back, but not until I reach five, Richard, one . . . two . . . your hand is still held up . . . three . . . four . . . now you feel the air releasing your hand . . . five . . . your hand is free . . .'

Seemingly of its own will the hand fell slowly back into his lap.

'. . . that's fine, Richard, that's excellent. Now I want you to stay breathing slowly, your whole body relaxed, but when I tell you I want you to open your eyes, not until I tell you, you can open your eyes and look around the room, and when you open your eyes and look around the room I want you to look, but not until I tell you, I want you to look for Miss Gowers, look for Miss Gowers, but although you know she is here you will not be able to see her, she is here but you will not be able to see her, but don't open your eyes until I have counted to five, when I count from one to five I want you to open your eyes . . .'

Hurdis droned on and on. Grey, listening closely, found his quiet voice irresistible and compelling. He concentrated on Alexandra Gowers, a few feet away from him, sitting on the chair so that she leaned forward, one leg crossed over the other, a notepad on her lap, a pen in one hand and the stopwatch in the other. He could hear her breathing, sense the almost inaudible sibilance when her stockinged legs crossed against each other and rubbed minutely as she moved.

'. . . open your eyes when I reach five . . . one . . . two . . . three . . . four . . . I want you to open your eyes . . . five . . .'

Grey opened his eyes and saw Dr Hurdis standing slightly to one side, looking at him, half smiling in a friendly way.

'You can't see Miss Gowers, Richard, but I want you to look for her, look around the room but you cannot see her, look now . . .'

Grey immediately turned towards where he knew she was, expecting to see her, already familiar with how she appeared, but she was not there. Thinking she must have moved, Grey looked quickly around the room but there was nowhere she could be. He looked back at her chair, *knowing* she was there, but he was unable to see her. Weak sunlight came through the window and struck the wall, but there was not even a shadow of her.

'You can speak if you wish, Richard.'

'Where is she? Has she left?'

'No, she is still here, but for the moment she is invisible. Now, please sit back and make yourself comfortable once more. Close your eyes again, steady your breathing and allow your limbs to relax, you're feeling drowsy.' (Grey closed his eyes, heard the stopwatch click, heard the silky friction of one leg against another, heard the ballpen move across the paper.) 'Fine, that's fine. You can feel yourself drifting again, starting to move slowly backwards, and you feel sleepy, very sleepy indeed, and you are drifting deeper and deeper, that's fine, deeper and deeper, and now I'm going to count from one to ten, you will drift deeper and deeper, and with every number you hear you will drift deeper, and feel sleepier and sleepier, one . . . very deep . . . two . . . you are drifting further and further . . . three . . .'

But then there was a gap.

Grey next heard, '. . . seven . . . you will feel refreshed, happy, calm . . . eight . . . you are beginning to awaken, you will be fully awake, fully alert, calm . . . nine . . . your sleep is now light, you can see daylight against your eyelids, and in a moment you will open your eyes and be fully awake, and you will be calm and happy . . . ten . . . you can open your eyes now, Richard.'

Grey waited a few more seconds, comfortable in the chair, his arms folded in his lap, sorry that it was over. He was reluctant to break the spell. The trance had freed him from pain and stiffness and that was worth anything to him. But his eyelids fluttered against the sunlight and a moment later he opened his eyes fully.

Something had happened.

This was his first thought as he looked at the other two. Both stood beside the chair, looking down at him. The casual air they had worn at the start was gone and they seemed strained, concerned.

'How do you feel, Richard?'

'Fine,' he said, but already the pain was returning, the familiar stiffness was creeping over his hip, his scarred back, his shoulders. 'Is something wrong?'

'No, of course not.'

Hurdis's manner was abrupt and awkward. He moved to the other chair and sat down. Alexandra went to the window and stood where Grey could not easily see her. The sun had gone in.

'Do you recall what happened?' Hurdis said.

'I think so.'

'What is the first thing you remember from what we have just done?'

Grey half closed his eyes again, wondering. In spite of the returning sensations of pain, he felt buoyant, light-hearted, refreshed, the way people are supposed to feel after a good night's sleep or a long holiday. He remembered, in fact, little of what had transpired, only the monotonous counting, Hurdis's voice, the sharp sense of Alexandra Gowers sitting beside him. That was distinct, a clear memory. But somehow, he discerned, that wasn't part of what he was supposed to know.

He said, 'I remember you counting, then something with my hand. You made Miss Gowers disappear. I think after that . . . You wanted to go further, but I'm not sure what happened then. I started waking up.'

'Is that all?'

'Yes.'

'Are you absolutely sure? There was nothing between?'

Trying to cooperate, Grey said, 'All the way through, I felt I could sense both of you. It was extremely clear—'

'No, after that. Before the end. Do you remember writing anything down?'

'Not at all.'

Behind him, still at the window, Alexandra Gowers said, 'Then it is spontaneous.'

'I agree.' To Grey Hurdis said, 'You're an excellent hypnotic subject. I was able to take you into deep trance without any difficulty. I regressed you to the period obscured by the amnesia. Do you have any memory of that?'

It was all a complete surprise to Grey, who shook his head, still trying to cope with the confusions of what he was learning. It seemed he was forgetting a part of the hypnosis, but it had been the part where he remembered what he had forgotten. It seemed too convenient, double-speak from the unconscious.

'I asked you to try to recall the events of last year. We can roughly date the amnesiac period to the summer weeks, the car bomb incident being at the beginning of September. That's right, isn't it?'

'Yes.'

'You accepted the regression smoothly, but your voice was emotional and it was difficult for us to follow what you said. I asked you to describe where you were, but you didn't answer. I asked if there was anyone with you and you said there was a young woman.'

'Susan Kewley!'

'You called her Sue. But none of this is conclusive of anything, Richard.'

'If Sue was with me, that must prove something!'

'Indeed, but we will have to hypnotise you again. This session was too short and what you were saying was unclear. For instance, some of it was in French.'

'*French!* But I don't speak French! Hardly any. Why should I speak French under hypnosis?'

'It can happen.'

'What did I say?'

Alexandra Gowers glanced at her notepad. She said, 'You were ordering a meal. You asked for red wine with it. Does that ring any bells?'

'Not from last year.'

In fact, Grey remembered exactly when he had last been in France. Three years earlier he had travelled to Paris with a crew to cover the French presidential elections. They had taken a French-speaking researcher with them from the news agency and she had done most of the interpreting for everyone. During the entire trip he had uttered hardly a word of French. His sole remaining memory of the trip was that one night he had slept with the researcher. Her name was Mathilda; she was still at the agency, and, having risen rapidly through the firm, was now deputy managing director.

'The next time we hypnotise you I'll tape record the session,' Dr Hurdis said. 'I didn't do that today because I wasn't expecting to take you any further than into a light trance. But I think you ought to see this.' He passed Grey a sheet of notepaper, apparently torn from a pad. 'Do you recognise the handwriting?'

Grey glanced at it, then in surprise looked more closely. 'It's mine.'

'Do you remember it?'

'Where did you get this?' He read the words quickly: they described a passenger departure lounge in an airport, with crowds of people, children charging around, loudspeaker announcements, airline desks. 'It looks like part of a letter. When did I write this?'

'About twenty minutes ago, while you were being regressed.'

'Oh no, that can't be true!'

'You asked for some paper and Miss Gowers gave you her notepad. You said nothing while you were writing and you only stopped when I took the pen away.'

Grey read the page again, but nothing about it struck any chord of familiarity. The passage had a familiar ring to it, but only in the sense that it described the bustle, boredom and nervous anticipation of an airport lounge, somewhere he had been through numerous times. That last half-hour before boarding a plane was usually an edgy period for him. Hanging around in a departure lounge might then be something he would conceivably describe, but nothing could have been further from his mind that morning.

'I can't help you,' he said. 'I've no idea what it means. What do you think?'

'It could be part of a letter, as you say. It could be an extract from a book you read a long time ago, or a film, a trick of memory. Or it could be something that happened to you that was released under hypnosis.'

'It must be that. Surely?'

'Yes, but of all the possibilities, I believe it's the one we should be most cautious of.' Hurdis glanced briefly at the clock on the wall.

'But that's exactly what I'm looking for.'

'And that's why you have to be careful. There's a long way to go. Next week, when we meet again . . . ?'

Grey felt a stirring of discontent. 'I hope to be out of here soon.'

'But not by next week?'

'No, but soon, I hope.'

'Very good.' Hurdis was clearly on the point of leaving. Alexandra Gowers had moved towards the door, holding her notepad cradled in both arms against her chest.

Still in the armchair, unable to move without assistance, Grey said, 'But where does it take me? Have we made any progress at all?'

'Next time I'll implant the suggestion that you retain what happens in deep trance. Then we might have a better chance of interpreting what you experience.'

'What about this?' Grey said, meaning the page of handwriting. 'Should I keep it?'

'If you wish. No, on second thoughts I'll file it with my case notes. Next week we might use it as the basis for another regression.'

He took the page from Grey's unresisting fingers. Grey was curious about it, but in itself it did not seem important.

Before she left, Alexandra came across to him.

'I'm grateful to you for letting me stay,' she said. She extended her hand and they shook as formally as they had at the beginning.

'When I was trying to see you,' Grey said, 'were you here, in the room?'

'Yes.'

'On that chair?'

'I didn't move an inch.'

'Then how could I not see you?'

'It's called an induced negative hallucination, a standard test of hypnotic trance. You knew I was there, you knew how to see me. At one point you looked straight into my eyes, but if you couldn't see me it was because your mind wouldn't register me. Stage hypnotists work a similar effect, but they usually make their subjects see people without their clothes on.' She said it seriously, clasping her notepad to her breasts. She pushed her glasses up to the bridge of her nose, staring deliberately at him. 'Apparently it works best on members of the opposite sex.'

'Yes,' said Grey. 'Well, it was a pleasure to look for you, anyway.'

'I do hope you regain your memory,' she said. 'I shall be fascinated to know what happens.'

'So will I,' Grey said, and they both smiled politely. She turned away and walked into the corridor. Grey waited for one of the nurses or orderlies to come to help him back to his wheelchair.

That evening, alone in his room, Richard Grey levered himself painfully out of his wheelchair and walked to and fro across the room, using his sticks. Later, feeling like a non-swimmer casting off from the side, he walked the length of the corridor and returned. After a short rest he did it a second time, taking much longer, pausing for rests whenever he had to. At the end of it his hip felt as if it had been hammered and bruised, and when he went to bed he could not sleep for the pain. He lay awake, determined that his long convalescence must end as soon as possible, sensing that his mind and body would heal in unison, that he would remember only as soon as he could walk, and vice versa. Before, he had been passively content for time to take its course, but now his life was different.

The following day he had a session with James Woodbridge, but said nothing of what had apparently happened under hypnosis. He wanted to hear no more interpretations, no more technical terms, no more warnings about reading too much into anything. He was convinced that his forgotten past had to be remembered, and remembered in detail. It was in some way symbolic of his overall recovery and would open the way to the rest of his life. Those weeks leading up to the car bomb had been significant. Perhaps what had happened was no more than a love affair with Sue, but because of the timing it was important to remember even that.

There too the silent gap in his memory, the invisible past, gave promise of the future.

Thursday passed slowly, but at last it was Friday. He tidied his room, obtained clean clothes from the hospital laundry, exercised his body, and concentrated again, and again, on trying to remember. The staff knew he was expecting a visit from Sue and he took their teasing with good grace. Nothing could deflate his mood. Everything was heightened by his expectation of her. The day went slowly by, the evening came, and as her lateness became apparent he found hope turning to apprehension. Late in the evening, far later than he had expected, she called him from a payphone. The train had been delayed but she was at Totnes station and was about to hire a taxi. She was with him half an hour later.

PART THREE

The board was showing that my flight was delayed, but I had already gone through security and passport control and there was no escape from the departure lounge. Although it was a large area, lined along one side with plate-glass windows overlooking the apron, it was noisy, warm and oppressive. It was the busiest week of the holiday season. The lounge was packed with package tour groups heading for Alicante, Faro, Athens and Palma. Babies cried, children ran in energetic games, a group of shaven-headed youths sprawled in a corner surrounded by empty lager cans, there was a line of people waiting to use the telephones. Boarding announcements came through at intervals, but they were invariably for other flights.

Already I was regretting that I had not taken the train, but air travel had the attraction of speed, even for a short journey like mine. Since leaving home that morning, though, I had been subjected to one delay after another: crossing London on the Underground, with two changes of train, a slow journey to Gatwick Airport with the railway carriage crowded to the doors, and now the wait for the plane.

Restlessly, because in spite of having flown more times than I could remember I always felt apprehensive before a flight, I walked around the lounge, trying to distract myself. There was nowhere left to sit, nothing much to do except stand or walk about and look at the other passengers. As I crossed the lounge for the third or fourth time I noticed a middle-aged man with two immense pieces of hand baggage, a pleasant-faced young woman dressed demurely in a light jacket, a businessman with a financial newspaper held close to his face, apparently trying to isolate himself within it from the casually dressed crowds around him. I speculated idly about each of them in turn: how do some people get bulky hand baggage on to planes?; she's attractive and how would I ever get to speak to her?; and why should a businessman be flying during a holiday weekend? As usual, idle speculation led nowhere and I lost interest.

Whatever had caused the delay was finally sorted out and three flights were called in quick succession. The crowd started to disperse. The next flight announced was mine and I went through with the other people to the boarding gate. It was only a short flight to Le Touquet, adding to my frustration that I had bothered to fly at all, and less than an hour after the flight had been called I was on a French train heading for Lille. Knowing that the journey was to take several hours I bought a supply of food at Le Touquet: fresh bread, cheese, some fruit and a large bottle of Coca-Cola.

The train to Lille stopped at every station on the way and it was mid-afternoon before we arrived. The Basle express was waiting, which at first came as a relief as the lateness of the other train had made me nervous about the connection, but once it moved off it travelled even more slowly than the first. We meandered in an unhurried way across the plains of north-east France, frequently stopping in open countryside. The train was almost empty and during each halt a great silence descended. The sun beat down on us. Alone in my compartment, I started to read one of the paperbacks I had brought with me, but I was sleepy.

During one of the long halts in a station the door to the corridor opened, bringing me out of my doze, and I looked up. It was a young woman of medium height and build, standing in the doorway. I recognised her, but for the moment could not think how.

She said, 'You're English, aren't you?'

'Yes.' I raised my paperback for her to see, as if proof were needed.

'I thought so. You flew from Gatwick, I think, and I saw you on the other train to Lille.'

I remembered briefly noticing her in the departure lounge.

'Are you looking for a seat?' I said, because I was already bored with my own company.

'No, I booked one in London. I thought the train would be full. The trouble is, I'm in a compartment crowded with seven other people and the rest of the train is almost empty. It seems crazy to stay cooped up in there, in such heat.'

The train lurched as if more carriages were being coupled, then halted again. Somewhere under the carriage a generator started churning. Two men in SNCF uniforms walked slowly along the platform, past the window.

She slid the door to, then sat in the window seat opposite mine. She was carrying a canvas holdall with a long strap, bulging with her possessions, and she placed it on the seat beside her.

'How far are you going?' she asked.

'To Nancy.'

'That's a coincidence. So am I.'

'I'm planning to stay only one night. What about you? Do you know people in Nancy?'

'No, I'm passing through,' she said.

'To Switzerland?'

'To the Riviera, actually. I'm visiting a friend who's staying near Saint-Raphaël.'

'Isn't this a rather long way round?'

'I'm not in a hurry. It doesn't cost me anything and so I thought I would see a bit of France on the way.'

'You didn't choose the scenic route, did you?' I said, glancing out at a dull town of factories and small houses, shimmering in the heat.

She had straight brown hair, a pale face, thin hands. I guessed her to be in her middle twenties. I found her company agreeable, partly for the relief she had brought me from my own boredom but mostly because I had liked her almost at once. She seemed interested in me, making me talk. We sat across from each other, leaning forward, talking about our separate lives in London, comparing experiences, getting to know one another. She said she hadn't eaten anything since breakfast, so I shared some of my food with her and bought several bottles of beer from a trolley passing down the train corridor.

The long journey across France continued, the sun shining straight in through our window. When she first came into the compartment she had been wearing the jacket I had seen her in at the airport, but a few minutes later she removed it and placed it on the rack overhead. While she turned away from me I could not help appraising her. She was slim, slightly bony around the shoulders, but she had a lovely body. I noticed the white lines of her bra, visible beneath her blouse. I was thinking speculatively carnal thoughts, wondering where she was planning to stay that night, and with whom, and whether she would like a travelling companion for more than the first train journey. I wondered how unhurried her trip to see her friend in the south could be. It was almost too good to be true, to meet an appealing young woman on my first day. I had planned and expected to spend the holiday on my own, but not because I wanted to.

We continued to talk while we finished off the food together, and exchanged names at last: hers was Sue. She lived in Hornsey, a part of London close enough to West Hampstead, where I had my flat, for us to know many of the same places. There was a pub in Highgate we both knew well and must frequently have visited at the same times in the past. She said she was a freelance illustrator, had been to art school in London but originally came from Cheshire, where her parents still lived. Naturally, I too talked about myself, telling her about some of the news stories I had covered and the places I had been to, why I had given up work and what I was planning to do next. We were interested in each other; there was no doubt about that, and I could certainly not remember the last time I had met someone I had got to know so quickly. She listened to me intently, leaning forward across the space between our seats, her head slightly to one side so that her hair fell forward, partly hiding her face. I tried to change the subject several times and get her to talk about herself. She answered direct questions but volunteered nothing. She did not seem closed or secretive about herself, merely quiet.

I kept wondering: why is she alone? Because I found her so fascinating I could not imagine that other men would not feel the same. It was difficult to believe she did not have a boyfriend – most likely the undescribed friend in Saint-Raphaël she was travelling to see – but she spoke about herself in the singular, never gave any hint that she was one of a couple. I did not ask her about it because I was already willing her to be available to me. I had my own background: there was a friend called Annette, the closest to a regular girlfriend I had, although nothing between us had been settled and we both saw other people. My job often took me away from home for weeks on end and I sometimes had flings while abroad. Annette had her own life. She was partly the reason

I was travelling alone in France, because she had flown to Canada a month earlier to visit her brother's family, leaving me at a loose end in a hot summer in London.

But Sue and I stayed away from the subject of others. To mention them would have been to admit, too soon perhaps, what we were both feeling. Always there is an undercurrent of reserve, a way out of a potential relationship if it starts to look as if it isn't going to work. Otherwise we were at ease with each other, exchanging minor confidences, passing opinions, talking about people we knew. I kept wanting to touch her, wishing that she would come over and sit beside me, or that I had the nerve to move across to her side. I was shy of her but excited by her.

It was late evening when the train arrived in Nancy. We were both tired after the long day of travelling and much of the nervous curiosity between us had worn down to an easy familiarity. We were still opposite each other, but Sue was resting her legs on the seat next to me, and I could feel the light touch of her ankle against my thigh. She had been dozing as the train crawled on and I had returned to my paperback, trying to take my mind off the closeness of her slim legs. It was almost by chance that I looked up and realised we had arrived. A flurry of minor activity ensued. I became preoccupied with Sue's luggage, presumably still in the other compartment, but she simply said she had no other bags. She was already waiting for me on the platform as I dragged my suitcase out.

When we left the platform an official took and checked my ticket, but Sue neither offered hers nor was asked to show it.

We enquired at the tourist office for an inexpensive hotel reasonably close to the station, then set off down the road in search of it. Outside the door, Sue turned to face me.

'Richard, there's something we haven't discussed,' she said.

'What's that?' I said, although I could guess what she meant.

'No misunderstandings about tonight, OK?'

'I wasn't assuming anything,' I said, not entirely truthfully. 'Would you like to find another hotel for yourself?'

'No, but we should have separate rooms. I told you I'm going to see a friend, in Saint-Raphaël. That's the way it is.'

'Of course,' I said, regretting that I had left it to her to bring up the subject and moreover for leaving it until the last moment. I was disappointed, though, and found it difficult to disguise the fact. The hotel was able to let us have a room each, and outside the lift we prepared to separate.

Sue said, 'I need a shower, but I'm hungry. Are you planning to go out somewhere for supper?'

'Yes, but I can wait. Will you join me?'

'I'd love to,' she said. 'I'll knock on your door in half an hour.'

In the centre of Nancy was a magnificent broad square, surrounded by eighteenth-century palaces, known as the Place Stanislas. We entered it from the south side, coming into great emptiness and peace. It was as if the bustle of the main part of town had not penetrated to this place. No more than a few people strolled or stood in its vastness. The sun beat down, striking sharp shadows on the sandstone pavings. An autobus was parked outside the Hôtel de Ville, formerly the Duke of Lorraine's palace, and some distance behind this four black painted saloon cars were parked in a neat row. No other traffic entered the square. A man wearing a cloth cap wheeled his bicycle slowly across the plaza, passing the statue of the Duke, at the centre.

In one corner of the square was the Fountain of Neptune, a glorious rococo construction, with nymphs and naiads and cherubs, water trickling across scalloped levels into the pools below. The wrought-iron archways of Jean Lamour surrounded the fountain. We walked over the cobbled road, gazed up at the Arc de Triomphe, then passed through into the Place Carrière. This was lined on both sides with terraces of beautiful old houses. Two rows of mature trees ran down the centre, with a narrow park between them. We walked through, utterly alone. Over the roofs to our left we could see the spire of the cathedral.

An ancient car drove through, trailing smoke and a clattering noise. At the far end there was a colonnade in front of the former Palais du Gouvernement, and here another couple walked slowly past. We looked back the way we had come, to the vista of Place Stanislas glimpsed through the Arc: the bright sunlight made the clean lines of the buildings, the stately sculpted view, seem static and monochrome. The car with the smoke had passed through into the square and now nothing moved anywhere we could see.

We left Carrière and walked through a narrow shaded lane to

one of the main shopping streets. Sounds grew around us and we saw the press of people. In the Cours Léopold there were a number of pavement cafés, so we went to one of them and ordered *demis-pressions*. The evening before, when we went out for our late supper, we had been to one of the restaurants on the other side of the same street, and after the meal had stayed drinking wine together until after one o'clock. We had spoken about the other people in our lives. I told Sue then about Annette, perhaps as a counterbalance to Sue's boyfriend, waiting for her in Saint-Raphaël, because I was already jealous of him.

Now, after our short sightseeing walk, Sue seemed more ready to talk about the present.

'I like living in London,' she said, 'but it costs so much money simply to stay alive. I've never really had any money, not since leaving home. I'm always broke, always scraping along. I wanted to be a real artist, but I was never able to get started. It's all commercial work.'

'Do you live alone?' I said, seeing a chance to lob in one of the leading questions.

'I have a room in a house. One of those large terraces in Hornsey. It was divided up into flats and bedsitters years ago. My room is on the ground floor, quite large, but it's difficult to work in natural light. The house is on a hill and at the back the garden is higher than my window.'

'Is your friend an artist?'

'My friend?'

'The one you're on your way to see.'

'No, he's a sort-of writer.'

'What sort of writer is a sort-of writer?'

She smiled. 'That's what he says he does. He seems to spend most of his spare time writing, but he never shows it to me and I don't think he's had anything published. I don't ask about it.' She shook her head, thinking about him, and stared at the little plate of salted *bretzels* the waiter had brought with the drinks. 'He wanted to move in with me, but I wouldn't let him. I'd never get any work done.'

'Then where does he live?'

'He moves around from one place to another. I'm never really sure where he is until he turns up. He sponges off other people.'

'Then why . . . ? Look, what's his name?'

'Niall.' She spelt it for me. 'Niall's a hanger-on, a born parasite. It's the only reason he's in France. The people he was staying with were going on holiday. I imagine, faced with the choice of leaving him alone in their house or taking him with them, that they decided to take him. So Niall gets a free holiday in the south of France and that's why I'm going down there to see him.'

'You don't sound keen on the idea.'

She looked frankly at me. 'If you want the truth, I was enjoying not having Niall constantly around me when he started calling me from France.' She swallowed the rest of her beer. 'I shouldn't say it, but I'm sick of Niall. I've known him too long, he's a blood-sucker and a pest, and I wish he'd leave me alone.'

'Ditch him.'

'I wish it was as easy as that. Niall hangs on. He knows how to get his way. I've kicked him out a dozen times and yet every time he manages to worm his way back in. I've given up trying.'

'But what sort of relationship is that? Does he have some kind of hold over you?'

'Let's have another drink.' She signalled to the waiter as he was passing. The waiter didn't acknowledge her, so we waited until he was on his return journey, and this time I ordered two more beers.

'You didn't answer my question,' I said to Sue.

'I didn't want to. What about your girlfriend, the one in Canada? How long have you known her?'

'You're changing the subject,' I said.

'No, I'm not. How long have you known her? Six years? That's how long I've known Niall. When you've been with someone as long as that, he *knows* you. He knows how to hurt you, how to manipulate you, how to twist things round against you. Niall's good at that.'

'Why don't you . . . ?' I paused, trying to imagine such a relationship, trying to think of myself in something similar. It was completely outside my experience.

'Why don't I what?'

'I can't understand why you let it go on.'

The waiter arrived with our order and removed the old glasses.

'I can't understand it either,' Sue said. 'Except that it's often easier just to keep going. It's my own fault, really. I should take a stand against him.'

I said nothing for a while, leaning back in the seat and pretending to watch the passers-by. I had only just met her, yet she didn't seem to me anything like the compliant victim she was describing. I wanted to switch into male competitiveness mode and say to her: I am different, I do not cling, I will not bully you, you've found someone else, you don't have to put up with this man Niall, leave him, stay with me.

Eventually I said, 'Do you know why he wants to see you?'

'It won't be anything in particular. He's probably bored, wants someone to talk to, wants someone to go to bed with.'

'I don't understand why you put up with it. You say you're broke, yet you're travelling across France to see him. He's a – what did you call him? – a bloodsucker and a clinger, yet you're going out of your way so he can spend some time with you.'

'You don't know him.'

'It seems irrational to me.'

'Yes. I know it does.'

We stayed one more night in Nancy, then took a train to Dijon. The weather had changed, and as the train moved slowly through the extensive suburbs of the city heavy rain began to fall. We discussed whether or not to stay, but I was no longer in any hurry to reach the south, and we agreed to stick to the plan we had worked out the previous evening.

Dijon was a busy industrial city, with some kind of business convention in progress, and the first two hotels we called at were full. The third, Hôtel Central, had only double rooms available.

'We can share,' Sue said, as we retreated from the reception desk to consult. 'Ask for a twin-bedded room.'

'Are you sure you don't mind? We could try somewhere else.'

She said quietly, 'I don't mind sharing.'

Our room was on the top floor, at the end of a long corridor. It was small, but it had a large window with a balcony and a pleasant view across the trees of the square below. The rain poured down relentlessly, making a rushing noise on the broad leaves. The two beds were placed close together, separated by a small table with a telephone. As soon as the porter had left, Sue threw her canvas bag on the bed by the window and came across to me. She embraced me tightly and I put my arms round her shoulders. Her hair, the back of her jacket, the vee of her blouse at the front, were wet from the rain.

'We don't have long together,' she said. 'Don't let's wait any more.'

We started kissing, she with great passion. It was the first time we had held each other, the first time we had kissed. I had not known what she would feel like, how her skin and lips would taste. I knew her only to talk to, only to look at. Now I could hold her, press her against me, feel her body eagerly moulding itself to mine. Soon we were impatiently undressing each other and then we lay on the nearest bed.

We did not leave the hotel until after dark, driven out by hunger and thirst. We had become physically obsessed with each other and could hardly stop touching. I held her close to me as we walked along the rain swept street, thinking only of her and what she meant to me. So often in the past sex had merely satisfied physical curiosity or need, but with Sue it had released deeper feelings, greater intimacy and affection, a new appetite for each other.

We found a restaurant, Le Grand Zinc, although we nearly passed it by, thinking it must be closed. When we went in we discovered we were the only customers. Five waiters, dressed in black waistcoats and trousers, with stiff white aprons that reached to their ankles, stood in a patient row beside the serving door. When the *maître d'hôtel* had shown us to a window table they moved into action, attentive but discreet. Each had short dark hair, plastered to his scalp with unguent, and each had a pencil thin moustache. Sue and I exchanged glances, suppressing giggles. It did not take much to make us laugh; I had never felt like this before.

Outside, a storm had started: brilliant pink-hued flashes of lightning, far away, thunderless. The rain continued to sheet down, but traffic was scarce in the street. An old Citroën was parked by the kerb, glistening in the rain, the double inverted vee on its radiator grille reflecting back the red-lamped lights in the restaurant.

At the end of the meal, sipping brandy, we held hands across the tabletop. The waiters stared away.

'We could go to Saint-Tropez,' I said. 'Have you ever been?'

'Isn't it crowded at this time of year?'

'I suppose so, but that might be more reason to go there.'

'It would be expensive.'

'We can live cheaply.'

'Not if we keep eating out in places like this. Did you notice the prices?'

Because of the rain we had not checked the prices before hurrying in, but they were clearly shown on the *carte*. The prices were in old francs, or seemed to be. I had made a half-hearted attempt to convert them to a sterling equivalent, but had come to the conclusion they were either ridiculously low or outrageously high. The quality of the cooking and service indicated the latter.

'I'm not going to run out of cash,' I said.

'I know what you mean and it's not going to work. I can't sponge off you.'

'Then what's going to happen? You say you've no cash with you, but if we're together for a while either I've got to pay or we can't do it.'

She said, 'We've got to talk about that, Richard. I still have to see Niall.'

'After everything that's happened today?'

'Yes.'

'If it's just money, let's go home to England tomorrow.'

'It's not simply the money. I promised I would go and see him.'

'Break the promise.'

'I can't do that.'

I took my hand away from hers and stared at her in exasperation. 'I don't want you to go. I can't think of anything I'd like you to do less.'

'Neither can I,' she said in a low voice. 'Niall's a bloody nuisance, I realise that. But I can't just fail to turn up.'

'I'll come with you,' I said. 'We'll see him together.'

'No, that would be impossible. I couldn't stand it.'

'All right. I'll go to Saint-Raphaël with you and wait for you while you tell him. After that we'll get the first train home.'

'He's expecting me to stay with him. A week, maybe two.'

'Can't you do *something* about him?'

'I wish I could. I've been wishing that for the last five years.'

'Well don't leave it too long.' I snapped my fingers at the *maître d'* and in seconds a folded bill on a plate was put in front of me. The total, *service compris*, came to three thousand francs, written the old way. Tentatively, I put thirty francs on the plate, and it was accepted without demur. 'Merci, Monsieur.' As we left the restaurant the *maître d'* and the waiters stood in an impeccable row, smiling and nodding to us, 'Bonne nuit, à bientôt.'

We hurried along the street, the storm effectively postponing any more wrangling over the problem. I was angry, but as much with myself as anything: only hours before I had been congratulating myself on being open-minded about women, and now I was feeling completely the opposite. The way out was clear: to give in, to let Sue go on to see her boyfriend, and hope perhaps to run into her in London one day. But she had already become acutely special to me. I liked her and she made me happy, and our lovemaking had confirmed all that and promised more.

Upstairs in the bedroom we towelled our hair and stripped off our damp outer clothes. It was oppressively warm in the room and we threw open the window. Thunder rumbled in the distance and traffic swished by below. I stood for a while on the balcony, getting wet again, wondering what to do. I wanted to put off the decision until morning.

From the room Sue said, 'Will you help me?'

I went in. She had pulled back the covers from one of the beds. 'What are you doing?' I said.

'Let's put the beds together. We'll have to move the table.'

She looked hot, dishevelled and sexy, standing in her bra and pants, her hair tousled and still damp. Her body was slim, slightly curved, her skin was glowing in the sweltering air of the room and the light underwear barely concealed her. I helped her move the beds and table and threw the sheets across to make a large double bed, but before the job was half finished we were all over each other. We never finished making up the beds that night and slept uncovered and wrapped around each other, lying across the divide.

In the morning I made no decision, suspecting that no matter what I said I was going to lose her. After breakfast at a table on the pavement outside the hotel we set off to explore the town. We said nothing about continuing our journey south.

In the centre of Dijon was the Place de la Libération, the ducal palace confronted across a cobbled plaza with a semi-circle of seventeenth-century houses. It was on a smaller, more human scale than Nancy's, but we noticed that here too the crowds and traffic stayed away. The weather had changed again and the sun was hot and brilliant. Several wide puddles lay in parts of the plaza. An area of the palace had been made into a museum, and we wandered around, admiring the grand halls and rooms as much as the exhibits. We lingered for a time before the eerie tombs of the Dukes of Burgundy, stone mannikins set amongst gothic arches, each mounted in a grotesquely lifelike pose.

'Where is everybody else?' Sue said to me, and although she spoke softly her voice set up sibilant echoes.

'I thought France would be crowded at this time of year,' I said.

She took my arm and pressed herself against me. 'I don't like this place. Let's go somewhere else.'

We wandered for most of the morning through the busy shopping streets, rested once or twice in cafés, then came to the river and sat down on the bank under the trees. It was a relief to escape temporarily from the crowds, the endless noise of traffic.

Pointing up through the trees, Sue said, 'The sun's going to go in.'

A single cloud, black and dense, was drifting across the sky in the direction of the sun. It was an inexplicable cloud: it was dark and bulbous in an otherwise clear sky, large enough to blot out the sun for many minutes to come. I squinted up at it as the shadow crossed us, thinking about Niall.

'Let's go back to the hotel,' Sue said.

'Suits me.'

We returned to the city centre. In the room we discovered that the chambermaid had made up the beds for us. They were where we had left them, standing together and when we undressed and pulled back the covers we found that a single large sheet had been placed across the mattresses, making a double for us.

We travelled further south, changing trains at Lyon to reach Grenoble, a large and modern city in the mountains. We found a suitable hotel, asked for a room with a double bed, and after we had dumped my suitcase went out to look at the town. It was still mid-afternoon.

'Shall we go up the mountain?' I said. We had come to Quai Stephane Jay, where the terminal of the funicular system was situated. From the broad concourse at the front of the building it was possible to see the cables stretching up out of the town, rising steeply towards a high rocky ridge.

'I can't stand cable cars,' Sue said, gripping my arm. 'They're not safe.'

'Of course they are.' I wanted to see the view from the top. 'Would you rather walk the streets for the rest of the day?'

We had yet to discover the old part of the town, and much of modern Grenoble was concrete high-rise. The city guide urged visitors to tour the university, but that was out on the eastern edge.

In the end I talked Sue into the cable car ride, but she feigned nervousness and held on to my arm. Soon we were lifting away from the city, gaining height quickly. For a while I stared back at the city, seeing its huge spread through the valley, but then we moved to the other side of the car to watch the escarpment of the mountain rising beneath us. It was a modern cable system, four glassy globes moving together in convoy through the sky.

As the cars slowed down at the top we had to scramble to get out, and then we walked through the noisy engine house into the freezing cold wind of the ridge. Sue slipped her arm under my jacket, holding me close. To be with a woman I really liked, whom I wanted to go on liking, was a unique feeling for me. To myself I was renouncing my past, never again seeking easy sexual conquests.

'We can get a drink here,' I said. A café had been built on the furthest extremity of the crag, with a viewing platform that overlooked the valley. We went inside, glad to be out of the wind. A waiter brought us two glasses of cognac. Later, we went out into the wind, hugging each other again, and walked to the edge of the platform. Three coin-operated telescopes tipped down towards the valley. We stood between two of them, leaning against the concrete wall and staring. The air was limpid under a naked sky. On the horizon were the mountains adjoining the southern edge of the city. To our left, the snow-capped peaks of the French Alps were sharp against the blue.

Sue said, 'Look, I suppose that's the university.' She was pointing towards a group of beautiful old buildings, turreted and spired, along by the river. 'It's closer to town than we thought.'

There was a plan built into the top of the parapet, indicating what could be seen from here. We traced the various landmarks.

'The town is much smaller than I thought,' I said. 'When we came in on the train it seemed to spread all the way up the valley.'

'Where are those office blocks?' Sue said. 'You'd think you could see them from up here.'

'They were by the hotel.' I looked on the plan, but it was not marked. 'There was a whole area of tower blocks, near where the cable car started.' I traced the cables down the mountainside, but the terminal was hidden from us. 'It must be a trick of the light.'

'Perhaps they were designed that way, to blend in with the older buildings.'

'They didn't blend too well when we were in the middle of them.'

It said on the plan that Mont Blanc could be seen to the north-east, so we turned in that direction. There were clouds behind us, though, and the view of the mountains was indistinct. Beyond the café were the ruins of an old fort, and we walked across to them. There was an additional charge for entering, so we changed our minds.

'Another brandy?' I said. 'Or back to the hotel?'

'Let's do both.'

Half an hour later we returned to the platform for another look at the city. Lights were coming on down there and tiny points of warm orange and yellow glinted from the buildings. We watched the evening for a while, the deep mountain shadows creeping quickly along the valley floor, then took the cable car down the mountain. After we had breasted one of the rises, the city again came into view. A mist was forming, but we could see the newer section with great clarity: blue-white fluorescent strip lights shone from the glass towers.

It seemed impossible that we should not have been able to see these modern towers from the top of the mountain. I took out the postcards I had bought: one of them was a photograph of the view, and in this the modern buildings were clearly visible. It did not seem a sufficient mystery to make a return trip to the viewing platform worthwhile.

'I'm getting hungry,' Sue said.

'For food?'

'That too.'

We arrived in Nice in the busiest tourist week of the year. The only affordable hotel we could find was in the north of the town, lost in a maze of narrow streets, a long walk from the sea. With our arrival my feeling of dread became dominant. We had at best another day or two together, because Saint-Raphaël was only a few kilometres along the coast.

What Niall represented had become a forbidden subject, ever present in our minds but never discussed. Even the silence about him became intrusive. By this time each of us knew exactly what the other would say and neither of us wished to hear it. If I had a strategy for dealing with the problem it was to give my best to Sue, to hope to convey to her what we were about to lose.

I was in love with her. The feeling had started in Dijon, and every waking minute with her confirmed and enlarged it. She delighted me and I was obsessed with her. Yet I drew back from saying the words, not through any doubts but because they would raise the stakes against her. I still hoped without any basis that she would change her mind, not leave me to return to this other man.

I still did not know what to do. During our first night in Nice, after making love, Sue fell asleep beside me while I sat up with the light on, ostensibly reading but in fact brooding about her and Niall.

Nothing would work. An ultimatum, a choice between me and him, would fail. There was a stubbornness in Sue about Niall and I knew I could not shift her that way. Discarded too was the idea of portraying myself as the wounded lover, hoping to arouse her sympathy. That was close to how I felt, but nothing would make me use it as a ploy. Reason, too, was out. She freely acknowledged that her relationship with him was irrational.

She had rejected my other ideas: my hanging around in the background while she saw him, a premature return to England. I was left with only the impossibility of extreme measures: a violent confrontation with Niall, or one with her, or some kind of self-inflicted one with myself. It was pointless even to think of them.

We stayed in our hotel room for most of the next day, leaving it every two or three hours for a change of scene: a walk, or a drink or a meal. We saw little of Nice, but because of my preoccupations I began to hate the place. I identified the town with my own sense of loss and blamed it for that. I disliked the ostentatious wealth on display: the yachts in the harbour, the Alfas and BMWs and Ferraris that choked the narrow streets, the women with their face lifts and the men with their business paunches. I equally disliked the flashy inverse: the English debs in rusty Minis, the worn out Nike trainers, the chopped off jeans, the faded clothes, the showy tattoos on half exposed buttocks. I resented the topless sunbathers, the palm trees and aloe vera plants, the long curving beach, dark green mountains, exquisite blue sea, the casino and the hotels, the gated villas, the skyscraper apartment blocks, the windsurfers and para-skiers, the speedboats and pedalos. I begrudged everyone their pleasure because I was soon to lose mine.

My pleasure was Sue, but she was also the source of my misery. Provided I pushed Niall to the back of my mind, provided I did not think beyond the next few hours, provided I held on to my lame hope of a last minute change of mind, I was as happy as any fool in love can be.

We decided to stay for a second night in Nice, even though it would only prolong the wretchedness. We somehow agreed that we would set out for Saint-Raphaël in the morning and there we would part. This was to be our last night together. We made love as if nothing was to change, then, restlessly, we sat together on the bed, the window and shutters wide open to the night and the clamour of the unceasing traffic. Insects hummed around the lightbulb. At last she broke the silence between us.

'Where will you go tomorrow?' she said.

'I haven't decided yet. I might get the first train out.'

'But what were your plans before we met? Couldn't you go back to those?'

'I was travelling around to see what happened. You happened. There's no point going back to before that.'

'Someone else might happen.'

'You want that?' I said in amazement.

'Of course not. Why don't you go somewhere with distractions, like Saint-Tropez?'

'On my own? I can't think of anything I'd enjoy less. I want to be with you.'

She was silent, staring down at the rumpled sheets on which we sprawled. Her body was so white. Suddenly I had a jealous image of meeting her again in London in a few weeks' time and finding that she had acquired a suntan.

'It's the end for us, isn't it?' I said.

'I think that's up to you.'

'You're acting as if we can't see each other again. Why does it have to be final?'

'All right. I'll see you in London. You've got my address.'

She shifted position, pulling at the creased sheet, laying part of it over her bare legs as she kneeled beside me. Her hands fretted with it as she spoke.

'I've got to see Niall. I'm not going to break a promise. But I'll get it over with as quickly as possible. You go on with your holiday, tell me where you're going to be, and if I can I'll join up with you.'

'What will you say to him? Are you going to tell him about us?'

'I suppose I have to.'

'Then why don't I wait for you here?'

'Because . . . I can't simply *tell* him. I can't walk in, say, oh by the way I've met someone else, and goodbye.'

'I don't see why not.'

'You don't know Niall. He's expecting me to stay for two weeks. I'll break it to him gently. I will tell him about you, but I know he'll take it badly. There's never been anyone in six years.'

'So how long will it take?'

'Two days, maybe three.'

I left the bed and poured us both some wine. It was a ridiculous situation and whenever we tried to address it I ended up angry and frustrated. I couldn't imagine what kind of hold Niall could possibly have over her, and in trying to get her free of it I was in danger of losing everything. All I wanted . . .

My head reeled with irritation. I drank down the glass of wine I had poured myself, then refilled it. I sat beside Sue and passed her the other glass, but she put it aside untouched.

'When you see Niall tomorrow, will you sleep with him?'

'I've been sleeping with him for six years.'

'That's not what I asked you.'

'It's none of your business.'

It hurt to hear it, but there was truth in what she said. I looked frankly at her naked body, trying to imagine this other man Niall with her, touching and arousing her. I found the idea abhorrent. She had become so precious to me. She was face down, her hair concealing her face. I went to touch her, laying my hand on her arm. She responded at once and clasped my hand.

'I didn't know it would be as difficult as this,' she said.

'Let's do what you suggest,' I said. 'I'll leave you in Saint-Raphaël tomorrow and go on down the coast. If you haven't caught up with me within a week, I'll head back to England on my own.'

'It won't take a week,' she said. 'Two days. Maybe less.'

'What about money?'

'What about it?'

'You're skint. How are you going to get around without it?'

'I don't need money.'

'You mean you'll borrow some from Niall.'

'If I have to.'

'You'll borrow his money, but you won't have mine. Don't you realise it gives him one more thing over you?' She shook her head. 'Anyway, I thought you said he didn't have any money.'

'I said he didn't have a job. He's never short of cash.'

'Where does he get it? Does he steal?'

'Please, Richard, drop it. Money means nothing to Niall. I can get what I need.'

I dressed in trousers and T-shirt and left her there on the bed, closing the door noisily behind me. I went down the four flights of stairs to street level. Outside, in the warm night, I walked along the street to the bar on the corner. It was closed. I turned the corner and started down the next street. This was a neglected, ill-lit part of Nice, the houses crowding one on the next, the plaster peeling and broken in many places. Lights showed from a few windows and ahead of me, at the next intersection, I could see the constant traffic moving quickly across. I went as far as this road, then came to a halt. I knew I was being unfair, that after three or four days I had no legitimate claim on her, that in my own way I was being as manipulative as Niall. Just then I did not care. I wanted her more than I had ever wanted any other woman. I was in love.

My quick anger subsided. I blamed myself. She had blundered into this as I had, and found me insisting that she immediately change everything in her life. By demanding what I did I was forcing a choice on her, Niall or me, and there was no easy way out for her. She knew Niall better than she knew me and I knew nothing of him. I was on the brink of losing her altogether.

I hurried back to the hotel, convinced that I had ruined everything. I rushed up the stairs and went quickly into the room, half expecting to find her gone. But she was there, lying in the bed with her back to the door, a single sheet covering her slim body. She made no move as I entered.

'Are you asleep?' I said.

She turned over to look at me. Her face was damp and her eyes were red.

'Where have you been?'

I pulled off my clothes and climbed on the bed beside her. We put our arms around one another, kissing and holding tenderly. She cried again, sobbing against me. I stroked her hair, touched her eyelids, and then at last, far too late but wholly meant, I said the words I had been holding back.

All she said, indistinctly, was, 'Yes. And I love you. I thought you realised.'

The morning brought another deep silence between us, but I was reasonably content. We had made plans, we had an arrangement. She knew my itinerary for the next few days, and where and when we could meet.

We boarded a bus in the centre of Nice and soon set off westwards. Sue held my hand and pressed herself to me. The bus drove first to Antibes and Juan-les-Pins, then to Cannes. Passengers climbed on or off at every stop. After Cannes we passed through some of the most beautiful scenery I had seen in France: wooded mountains, steep valleys leading down to the sea, and of course one vista of the Mediterranean after another. Cypresses and olive trees grew beside the road and wild flowers flourished in every untended patch of ground. The roof panels of the bus were open and rich scents blustered in: sometimes, because of the road, the smell was of gasoline or diesel oil. The coastline was scattered with houses and apartment blocks, high on the mountainsides or standing among the trees; occasionally they ruined the views, but so too, in a different way, did the road.

We saw a sign saying that Saint-Raphaël was another four kilometres and immediately Sue and I drew closer, holding each other tightly and kissing. I wanted both to prolong the farewell and to be done with it, but at least there was nothing more to say.

Except, it turned out, one thing. As the bus halted in the centre of Saint-Raphaël, a square opening out on the tiny harbour, Sue put her mouth to the side of my face and said quietly, 'I've some good news for you.'

'What's that?'

'I started my period this morning.'

She squeezed my hand, kissed me lightly, then went down the centre aisle with the other passengers. The little square was crowded with holidaymakers. I looked down at them from my window seat, wondering if Niall was somewhere among them. Sue stood by my window, smiling up at me, and I wished the bus would leave. At last it did.

Once I was on my own my spirits began to rally. I found somewhere to stay in Saint-Tropez and went for a walk around the village. I discovered I liked the place. Perversely, what I enjoyed were more or less the same things I had disliked in Nice. The same kinds of people were there, the same candid displays of wealth, the same glamour and hedonism. The place smelled of money. Unlike Nice, though, Saint-Tropez was small and the architecture mostly vernacular. It was also noticeably more classless than Nice: large numbers of young people were apparently staying in campsites around the edge of the village, numerous backpackers thronged the streets during the days, and many slept rough on the beaches. It was possible to believe, just, that at the end of the season the place would have its own identity, return to something of the peace and obscurity it had enjoyed before its discovery in the 1950s by film stars and playboys.

Now that Sue was not with me, the dilemma she presented no longer held the same constant fascination and urgency. I continued to feel love and tenderness for her, but without her at my side I quickly resumed some of my old self-confidence, reminding myself that before I met her I had planned the holiday on my own. I had been looking forward to a break from everyone and everything, no work, no girlfriends, no London, no phone calls.

As for the jealousy I felt about Niall, that too faded much sooner than I would have thought the evening before. I closed my mind to as much of the affair with Sue as I could and began to plan and enjoy the next few days on my own.

The first thing I did in Saint-Tropez was to call in at the local Hertz office to book a rental car in three days' time, when I was planning to move on. It turned out that I had made a wise decision to book early, as there was only one car still available. I signed the form and paid the deposit. The Hertz clerk had a name badge pinned to her blouse: Danièle. She spoke American English with a French accent and told me she had worked for two years in the Hertz New Orleans office.

My arrangement with Sue was that I would wait for her every evening at six at Sénéquier, the large pavement café overlooking the inner harbour. I did walk past on my first evening, but there was no sign of her, nor did I really expect there to be.

I spent most of the following day on the beach, dozing, reading and from time to time walking down for a swim. I barely thought of Sue, but in the evening I went to Sénéquier. She did not appear.

I was on the beach again the next day, although as a result of my incaution the day before somewhat better prepared. Liberally smeared with sun-blocker, and sitting under a rented parasol while not moving my head, legs or arms too suddenly, I passed much of the day regarding the other holidaymakers around me. Sue had aroused in me a physical need and she was no longer on hand to satisfy it.

I was surrounded by naked female flesh: bare breasts and buttocks lay exposed in the sun on every side of me. The day before I had hardly given it a second thought, but now I was missing Sue again, thinking of her with Niall. I could not pretend away these nubile French, Germans, British, Swiss, with their *cache-sexe* bikini briefs, their glistening suntanned bodies. Not one of them could replace Sue for me, but each one reminded me of what I was missing.

That evening I waited again in Sénéquier for Sue, hungering for her to appear. I wanted her more than ever, but in the end had to walk away without her.

I had one more day and one more night in Saint-Tropez, and in the morning I decided to kill time a different way. The beach was too distracting. I spent the morning in the village itself, walking slowly around the boutiques and souvenir shops, the leather goods stores, the craft workshops. I strolled around the harbour, looking with frank envy at the yachts, their scrupulously neat crews, their affluent owners and guests. After lunch I walked along the shore away from the centre of the village, clambering over rocks and walking along a concrete sea wall.

At the end of the wall I leapt down to the sand and continued. The crowds were more sparse here, probably because the beach did not present a favourable aspect to the sun: trees shaded much of the sand. I passed a sign: *Plage Privée*. Beyond, everything changed.

It was the least crowded beach I had seen in Saint-Tropez and by far the most decorous. Many people were enjoying the sun and some were swimming, but no women exposed their breasts, and not one of the men was wearing G-string briefs. Children played in the sand, a sight I had not noticed elsewhere, and on this beach there was no open-air restaurant or bar, there were no parasols or beach mats, no magazine vendors or photographers. I walked slowly across the beach, feeling conspicuous in my sawn off denim shorts, my Southern Comfort T-shirt, my sandals, but no one took any notice of me. I passed several groups of people, most of them middle-aged. They had brought picnic meals to the beach, vacuum flasks and little paraffin-fired Primus stoves for heating their kettles. Many of the men were wearing shirts with rolled-up sleeves and grey flannel trousers or baggy khaki shorts. They sat in striped deckchairs, clenching pipes between their teeth. Some of them were reading English newspapers. Most of the women were wearing light summer dresses, and those who were sunbathing sat rather than lay and were clad in modest one-piece suits.

I went down to the water's edge and stood near a group of children who were splashing and chasing each other in the shallows. Beyond, heads protected by rubber bathing-caps bobbed in the waves. A man stood up and waded out of the sea. He was wearing shorts and a singlet and rubber-and-glass goggles over his eyes. As he passed me he took off his goggles and shook out the water, making a spray across the white sand. He grinned at me, wished me good afternoon, then moved on up the beach. A cruise liner was at anchor some two or three hundred metres off shore.

Ahead, a para-skier rose up on his cable, soaring behind the speedboat that was towing him. I walked on, out of the private section and to another beach where rows of straw-roofed shelters had been erected in straight lines across the sand. In their shade, or spread out in the full glare of the sun, crowds of nearly naked sunbathers lay all about. This time I went up the beach to one of the open-air bars and bought myself a glass of expensive iced orange juice. Sipping it thankfully after my long walk, I sat down on the sand.

Not long after I noticed a young woman walking along the beach. Unlike every other woman in sight she was wearing clothes, and doing so with considerable panache. She had on skin-tight designer jeans, a long sleeved white blouse and a wide sunhat. As she passed near me I realised I knew who she was: it was Danièle, from the Hertz office. She came to within a few metres of me. I watched her while she stripped off her jeans and blouse, to reveal that underneath she was wearing the bottom part of a bikini. She walked calmly into the sea. When she came out she put on the blouse over her wet body, but not the jeans, and sat back elegantly on the sand to dry out.

I went to speak to her and in a while we agreed to meet for supper that evening.

I was at Sénéquier at six, looking for Sue. If she turned up I would drop my date with Danièle without a qualm, but if she did not this evening would not be another lonely one. I was not yet feeling guilty about Danièle, but defiant: my emotions had turned again and whenever I thought of Sue I thought instead of Niall, the sort-of writer, the bullying manipulator.

I went from Sénéquier to a boutique I had been to earlier, where I had noticed they sold a good selection of picture postcards. Feeling vindictive about Sue, I chose a card. The picture was a reproduction of a pre-war view of Saint-Tropez, long before it became fashionable. Fishermen mended nets on the crumbling harbour wall and the only boats in sight were fishing smacks in various states of disrepair. Beyond the harbour, where now the holidaymakers milled past in an endless flow, and where the fashionable Sénéquier was situated, was a narrow yard fronting a wooden warehouse.

I took the postcard back to my room and before changing my clothes I sat on the bed and addressed the card to Sue's address in London.

'Wish you were here,' I wrote sardonically, and instead of signing it I printed an X.

A few minutes later, on my way to meet Danièle, I posted it.

Danièle knew a backstreet restaurant called La Grotto Fraîche, the only one, she said, that stayed open all year round, the restaurant used by the locals. Afterwards, we went to the apartment she shared with three other young women. Her bedroom was next to the main room and as we made love I could hear the raucous noise of a television game-show coming through the wall. When we were finished I could think only of Sue, and regretted everything. Danièle made us some coffee laced with brandy, and we sat side by side on her bed sipping the warm drink, but not long afterwards I was walking back to my room.

I saw Danièle again in the morning, when I collected the Renault. She was wearing the Hertz uniform and was friendly, unremorseful, professional. Before I drove away we exchanged a double-cheek kiss.

I drove inland from Saint-Tropez to avoid the heavy traffic along the coast roads. I found the Renault difficult to drive at first, because the gear lever was stiff to move and positioned on my right. Driving on strange roads on the right-hand side demanded my constant attention, especially as the road wound sharply through mountain country. At Le Luc I joined the main *autoroute* and headed west on the broad divided highway, and the driving became less of a strain.

At Aix-en-Provence I left the *autoroute* and turned south towards Marseille. By lunchtime I had checked into a small *pension* in the dock area, and I spent the afternoon exploring some of the city. Long before six o'clock I went to the rendezvous I had agreed with Sue, the Gare Saint-Charles, and waited for her in as prominent a place as I could find. At eight, I went to find a meal.

I had another day to kill in Marseille. I visited the Quai du Port, with its trams and wharves, the three- and four-masted barques lined up against the docks, the whole area filled with the deafening noise of the steam cranes. I spent the early part of the evening wandering on the concourse of the station, standing at the gate whenever a train arrived from the Riviera. The crowds pushed past me and I scanned all their faces, looking for Sue. As time went by and she failed to appear I started to wonder if I had somehow missed her. I thought I knew her so well that I would never have any problem recognising her, but doubts were assailing me.

I waited until the last train from the coast had drawn in, then returned to my room.

I drove on westwards, into the Camargue. First to Martigues, my last agreed meeting place with Sue, only a short drive from Marseille. Martigues was no place in which to be lonely, for there were few distractions.

The place we had agreed on was the Quai Brescon, where the canal was situated. It was a placid backwater of the town, the houses built directly against the water, with numerous small rowing boats and skiffs tied up along the narrow towpaths. Few outsiders found the quai and there were no restaurants, shops or even a bar. Here the old people of the village gathered in the evenings and when I arrived for my vigil they had already assembled, sitting outside their peeling houses on an assortment of old boxes and wicker chairs. The women all wore black, the men wore weathered *serge de Nîmes*. They stared at me as I sauntered along the quai, their conversation dying around me as I passed. At the mouth of the canal, looking out at the smooth black lake water of Etang de Berre, I could smell sewage.

The warm evening darkened, night fell, lights came on in the tiny houses. Sue had not appeared and I was on my own.

The next day I was unsure what to do next, and while I tried to distract myself I drove further into the Camargue. Then I changed my mind. I decided to head north to Paris, leave the car there and catch the first flight back to London. Soon after I had turned the car around I came to a small town called Aigues-Mortes.

When looking at the map with Sue I had noticed the name and wondered what it meant. We had looked it up and found it was a corruption of the Roman name, Aquae Mortuae, the 'dead waters'. The town itself turned out to be a walled city, massively fortified in the Middle Ages, and surrounded by a number of shallow lagoons. I parked the car outside the wall. In the humid heat I walked around the fortifications, following the course of the former moat. I soon tired of this and climbed a low hill close by, staring back. The town had a monochrome quality, like an old sepia-tinted photograph: light fell flatly, bleaching colours. I could see the roofs within the walls and in the near distance, beyond the old town, there was an industrial site with a number of high but unsmoking chimneys. The lagoons reflected the sky.

It struck me that without Sue to enliven me I was seeing France as a static, silent and unreal place, drifting past almost unnoticed as I travelled, locking into immobility whenever I stopped and stared. Sue distracted me, first by her presence then by her absence. The empty plazas of Nancy, the old-fashioned restaurant in Dijon, that mountain sight of Grenoble, the modest bathers of Saint-Tropez, the docks of Marseille – they were static in my mind, moments I had passed through with my thoughts else-where. Now Aigues-Mortes, frozen in the shimmering sun like some vestige of memory. It had an arbitrary quality, its stillness reflecting some forgotten thought or image, something distinct from Sue. France was haunting me, a place made up of images I descried beyond my preoccupations.

My presence on the hill was attracting flying insects, which were whining unpleasantly around my face, so I hurried back to where I had left the car, walking briskly through the streets of the old town to get to the other side. I found the Renault and opened the door to let out some of the heat before I climbed in.

'Richard! *Richard!*'

She was running between the cars, dodging round them, her

hair flying about her face. I felt the sense of unreality lifting from me, the shadowy town receding, and all I thought was how much she looked the same, how like herself she was. Holding her again, feeling her willowy body against mine, I loved the familiarity of her and rejoiced to know she was once again in my arms.

Driving south-west again, the windows open against the heat, the blast of tyres and engine and slipstream:

'How did you find me?' I said over the noise.

'Just luck. I was about to give up.'

'But why that place?'

'We talked about it in Nice and I thought you might go there. I arrived this morning and I've been hanging around since.'

We were looking for somewhere to stay, somewhere to be alone together. She had been on buses for three and a half days, travelling from one place to another, trying to catch up with my itinerary, then trying to anticipate where I would be after that.

We stopped in Narbonne and checked into the first hotel we found. Sue plunged into the bath and I went in and sat on the side, looking down at her. I noticed she had a bruise on her leg, one that had not been there before.

'Don't stare.' She slumped low in the water, raising a knee to conceal her sex from me, but bringing the bruise fully into view.

'I thought you'd like me to,' I said and rested a hand on her knee, intending an affectionate touch. She moved her leg away.

'You know I don't like you to look at me.'

I left the tiny bathroom, pulled off my clothes and lay on the bed. I listened to Sue splashing around, then draining the water. A long silence, followed by the rustle of a tissue as she blew her nose. When she appeared at the door she had put on panties and a T-shirt. She glanced at me, then prowled around the room, stared out through the window at the yard below, fidgeted with her little pile of clothes. Finally she came to sit on the end of the bed, where I could not reach her without sitting up and stretching towards her.

'How did you get that bruise?' I said.

She turned her leg to look. 'A sort of accident. I fell against something. There's another.' She twisted around and pulled up her T-shirt to reveal a second dark bruise on her ribs, under her arm. 'They don't hurt,' she said.

'Niall did that, didn't he?'

'Not really. It was an accident. He didn't mean it.'

I wanted to hold her again, but there was a distance between us, a familiar feeling. So soon. After half an hour we dressed and walked into the town for a meal. I hardly registered the surroundings. I was travel fatigued, had been in too many different places. And Sue preoccupied me, distracting me from noticing the town. Over dinner, served on the pavement in the dusty street, she at last gave me an account of what had happened.

Niall's friends were staying outside Saint-Raphaël itself, in a holiday-let converted farmhouse. Niall was not there when she arrived and she had had to wait around until the evening. When he finally turned up he was in a group of five people: another man and three young women. No one explained what they had been doing or where they had been, and Niall did not appear pleased to see her. There were now nine people, including Sue, crammed into the house, and regardless of any other considerations she had been forced to share a bed with him. He was in an argumentative, violent mood, and in the morning he left again, taking Joy, one of the other women, with him. Sue decided to leave to join up with me. She got as far as walking away down the lane towards the village when Niall returned. She told him about me, and he started attacking her with his hands. The others pulled him off her, and as she again began to leave Niall's mood changed: first he became melancholy and clinging, but when she insisted that this time it was all over, he immediately put on an air of indifference.

'I should have taken him at face value,' she said. 'He was telling me he didn't care any more and suddenly it seemed to me I couldn't simply walk out on him. In the end I had to.'

'OK, so is it over?' I said, calming down.

'Yes, but I don't trust him. He's never acted like this before.'

'Are you saying he might have followed you?'

She was looking tense, fidgeting with the cutlery on the table. 'I think it's more likely he was sleeping with Joy and he couldn't make up his mind whether he preferred her or me.'

'Can we forget him?'

'All right.'

We went for a walk around the town after the meal, but our real interest was in each other and we soon returned to the hotel. In the room we opened the windows wide to the warm night and closed the curtains. I took a bath and lay in the water staring blankly at the ceiling, wondering what to do. Nothing seemed to be the right thing, not even getting into bed with her. The bathroom door was open and although the tub was behind it, preventing me from seeing out, I could hear her moving about in the main room. I thought I heard her speak, but when I asked what she wanted there was no reply. I heard her bolt the door to the room. She did not come in to see me, and it meant nothing that she did or did not. We appeared to have reached a sort of sexless familiarity, one in which we shared a room, undressed in front of each other, slept in the same bed, yet still were kept apart by Niall's unseen presence.

When I had dried myself I went into the bedroom. Sue was sitting up in bed, leafing through a copy of *Paris Match*. She was naked. She put the magazine aside as I climbed in beside her.

We should have finished our holiday then, but we wanted to see the Pyrenees and we planned to fly back to England, so we headed for Biarritz. It took two days to drive through the mountains and they passed pleasantly and without incident. In the Biarritz hotel the reception clerk booked our plane tickets to London, but there were no flights until the day after next. With no further need of the car, I turned it in at the local Hertz office the morning after we arrived.

Sue was waiting for me at the hotel, and I realised as soon as I saw her that something was amiss. She had the evasive, indirect look I had grown to recognise from the bad times, and I felt a sudden familiar dread. I guessed at once it must be something to do with Niall.

But how could that be? Niall was hundreds of kilometres away and could have no idea of where we were.

I suggested a walk to the beach and she agreed, but we walked apart, not holding hands. When we reached the path that zigzagged down to the Grande Plage Sue came to a halt.

'I don't feel like the beach today,' she said. 'You go if you want.'

'Not without you. We can do something else.'

'I'd like to go shopping on my own.'

'What's the matter, Sue? Something's happened.'

She shook her head. 'I want to be on my own for a while. An hour or two. I can't explain.'

'You could but you won't.'

'Don't start accusing me of things again. Please, Richard.'

'If this is what you want.' I gestured irritably at the beach. 'I'll go and lie around until you feel like being with me again.'

She had already moved away from me. 'I need some space to think, that's all.' She came back, pecked me on the cheek. 'It's nothing you've done, I promise.'

'That's a relief!'

She had already started walking away and showed no sign of having heard. I walked off in a huff, going quickly down the cliff path.

The beach was uncrowded. I chose a place for myself and there I spread out my towel, took off my jeans and shirt, and sat back to brood. She had distracted me yet again, but now I was alone I at last took in my surroundings. The beach was . . . still.

I sat up straight, looking around, aware that something had ceased around me. This beach was different from the ones I had seen on the Med. There was no topless sunbathing, and the heat of the sun was pleasantly tempered by a sea breeze. The sea itself had muscle: long steady breakers came rolling in, making the satisfactory roaring noise familiar to me from British beaches. So there was movement and sound, denying the impression of stillness, but still I felt locked in a place that had come to a halt, become inert.

Looking around at the other people on the beach I noticed that many of them were using changing huts, like tiny *yurts*, erected in three parallel rows, one behind the other. The occupants emerged with almost bashful movements, hastening down the beach and running into the surf with a peculiar crouching motion, reaching forward with their arms. As the first breaker hit them they would jump up against it, turning their backs and yelling in the cold Atlantic water. Most of the swimmers were men, but there were a few women and they all wore shapeless one-piece bathing-suits, and rubber caps.

I lay back in the sunshine, still uneasy, listening to the cries of the holidaymakers and thinking about Sue's behaviour. How had Niall contacted her? How on earth did he know where she was?

Could she have contacted him?

I felt irritated and hurt. I wished Sue would take me more into her confidence about Niall, to give us a chance of solving the apparently unsolvable problem.

I sat up again, in agitation. Overhead, the sky was a deep, pure blue, and the sun was striking down from above the casino. I glanced up at it, narrowing my eyes.

There was a cloud, the only one in sight, the sort of cloud you see on a summer's afternoon in England, when the sun raises thermals from the fields and woodlands. This one stood close to the sun, apparently unaffected by the ocean breeze. It made me think of Niall, as once before another cloud seen from a river-bank in Dijon had made me think of Niall. Then, as now, I was preoccupied with him.

Niall was invisible to me. He existed only through Sue, her descriptions, her reactions.

I wondered what he was really like, whether he was as unpleasant as Sue made out. The odd thing was that we had much in common, not least because we were attracted to the same woman. Niall would see and know Sue much as I did, her sweet nature when happy, her evasiveness when she felt threatened, her maddening loyalties. Above all he would know her body.

And Niall, of course, would also know me. Again, the intermediary was Sue. How would she have portrayed me to him? It could only be as she had seen me: impulsive, jealous, petulant, unreasonable, gullible? All of these were reactions to him, through her. I would have preferred to think that Sue saw me the way I saw myself, but I had a feeling this would not survive the closed loop of our triple relationship. She had a way of conveying only the unpleasant qualities of someone's character, and therefore she kept alive the rivalry and mistrust between us.

The beach was beginning to bore and repel me. I felt as if I were an intruder there, entering a living diorama and interfering with its natural balance. There was still no sign that Sue was coming to join me, so I dressed and walked up the cliff path, heading for the hotel. At the top I glanced back. The beach looked more crowded now, the rows of changing huts had vanished and out beyond the breakers a number of people were windsurfing and bucking along on water scooters.

I left a note in the hotel room, telling Sue that I was going out for a meal, then walked down into the busy streets to find a café. I deliberately passed a few, hoping I would find her somewhere around, but there were so many people that I knew I could easily miss her.

I was tired of travelling. I had been in too many different places, slept in too many different beds. I began to wonder what might be waiting for me in the accumulation of mail at home, if any of the long-awaited payments had arrived, or if I had been offered any freelance work. I had almost forgotten what it was like to feel the weight of a camera on my shoulder.

I found a pavement café and ordered a dish of scallops in wine sauce, with a carafe of white wine. I was irritated with Sue for leaving me like that, for not being at the hotel, for not telling me what was going on. But it was none the less pleasant there in the sun. After the meal I ordered another carafe and decided to sit out the rest of the afternoon in the café. I sat there drowsily, watching the crowds go by.

Unexpectedly, I saw Sue walking down the street on the other side. I had been staring inattentively in that direction, and my first impression was that she was walking with another man. I sat forward at once, craning to see better. I must have been mistaken: she was on her own, but even so she was walking in the way people do when they are with someone else. She walked slowly, kept turning her head to the side, appeared to nod agreement from time to time and was not looking where she was going. By all appearances she was deep in conversation with someone, but I could see nobody with her. She reached an intersection and paused, but not for a gap in the traffic. She was frowning, then she shook her head angrily. She turned away with an irritable gesture and set off quickly down the side road, staring moodily at the ground.

She looked as if she had taken leave of her senses, gesticulating to herself, talking to herself, so wrapped up in her monologue that she was forcing passers-by to step out of her way. Irritation with her gave way to concern.

As she passed out of sight I threw some coins on the table to pay for the meal, and hurried to follow her. I briefly lost sight of her, but by the time I had turned the corner I could see her again, for all the world in the middle of a furious argument with her unseen companion. She appeared to be about to come to a halt again, so I turned and walked away from her. I went back to the main intersection and walked quickly along the main road until I found another side street. I hurried along this and at the next crossing I doubled back in her direction. When I walked around the corner she was standing still, facing towards me. I went up to her, hoping for a sign that her mood had changed, perhaps because of the antics she had been going through. She gazed blankly at me, and for a moment the clean lines of her face and the plainness of her expression conspired to give her an unhinged, bewildered look. The shock of this flash of insight again diverted me from what I had intended to say.

'There you are,' I said. 'I've been looking for you.'

'Hello.'

She was not carrying any shopping bags, and clearly had no recollection of having said what she wanted to do on her own. We walked together in the direction she had been heading, but it was already plain that it did not matter whether I was with her or not. She glanced from side to side, and would not meet my eyes.

'What would you like to do this evening?' I said. 'It's the last night of our holiday.'

'I don't care. Anything you like.'

Irritation surged in me again, in spite of the disconcerting effect she was having on me. 'All right. I'll leave you alone.'

'What do you mean?'

'It's obviously what you want.'

I stalked off from her, angry with her sullen passivity. I heard her say, 'Richard, don't be difficult,' but I walked on. When I reached the corner I looked back. She was still where I had left her, making no attempt to follow or pacify me. I made an exasperated gesture at her and stormed off.

I returned to the hotel room. I took a shower, put on fresh clothes then lay on the bed and tried to read. I was profoundly fed up with the whole thing. I wished for nothing more than the means to go immediately to the airport and step on a plane to London. At that moment I frankly did not care if I ever saw her again.

She returned, though, and I was still there, still awake. It was after ten o'clock. As she entered the room I pretended to ignore her, but I could not help but be acutely aware of her as she moved around, putting down her holdall, slipping off her sandals, brushing out her hair. I scowled and looked away. Apparently to provoke a response in me she took off her clothes in front of me, tossing them in a little pile on the floor. She was in the shower cubicle for a long time, and I lay on the top covers of the bed, mind and emotions in neutral. Everything was at last over between us. Even if she made one of her about faces, and became loving and affectionate and sexy once more, I would reject her. It had all happened again once too often. There was something insurmountable between us, whether it was Niall himself or simply something he embodied. I could not stand the sudden withdrawals, her obstinacy, her irrationality. I wanted an end to it all.

At last she emerged from the shower and stood at the end of the bed towelling her hair. I stared frankly at her naked body, finding it for the first time unappealing. She was too thin, too angular, and with her hair wet and swept back from her face she had a plain, vague expression. She knew I was watching her and she bent forward, towelling her hair from the back of her head. I could see the bony ridges of her spine.

With her hair still damp she pulled on a T-shirt, then turned back the sheet and slid into the bed. I had to shift my weight to let her in. Sitting up, the pillow propped behind her, she regarded me with wide eyes.

'If I tell you the truth, will you forgive me?'

'I doubt it.'

'Won't you listen?'

'Why wouldn't you tell me the truth this morning?'

'Because you'd have tried to stop me doing what I had to do. And you could have, you know, if you'd tried. Richard, listen. It's Niall. He's here, in Biarritz. I've spent the day with him. But you knew that, didn't you?' I nodded, shocked in spite of everything by the news, confirming the inevitable. 'He came to the room this morning, while you were taking the car back. He said he wanted to talk to me alone. I had to let him have that. I'll never see him again after this. That's the truth.'

'What did he want?' I said.

'He's miserable and he wanted me to change my mind.'

'What did you say?'

'I told him I'd made a final decision and that I was with you now.'

'And it took all day to say that?'

'Yes.'

I still felt cold towards her, unforgiving of the truth. Why wouldn't she *act* on her decision?

I said, 'How the hell did he follow us here?'

'I don't know.'

'All right.' I subsided, realising how futile it all was. Sue's face was drained of colour: her skin, her lips, even her eyes looked paler than normal. As her hair dried her face looked less gaunt, but she was as angry as I was. I was thinking: what we should do is hold each other, kiss, make love, put the clock back, all the other clichés and formulas for making up after a tiff, but this time it was not possible.

We sat up late into the night, both of us entrenched in our needs, angry with each other because it all mattered so much. In the end I took off my clothes and got under the sheet with her, but we lay awake without making love. Neither of us would make the first move.

At one moment in the night, knowing she was awake, I said, 'When I met you in the street this afternoon, what were you doing?'

'Trying to work things out. Why?'

'Where was Niall?'

'Waiting for me somewhere. I had gone for a walk, then you appeared.'

'You looked to me as if you were talking.'

'So what? Don't you ever talk to yourself in the street?'

'You were waving your arms at someone, ranting at them.'

'I couldn't have been.'

We lay on in the warm darkness, the sheet thrown down from our bodies. When I opened my eyes I could make out her shape next to me. She usually lay still in bed, without tossing, and in the dark I was never sure if she was asleep or not.

I said, 'Where is Niall now?'

'Somewhere around.'

'I still don't understand how he followed us here.'

'Never underestimate him, Richard. He's clever, and when he wants something he's persistent.'

'He has power over you, whatever you say. I wish I understood what it was.'

'Yes, he has the power.' She breathed in deeply, and as she exhaled it sounded to me as if she sobbed a little. A long silence followed and her breathing steadied, and I thought she must have fallen asleep at last. But as I was starting to drift, she said, quietly, 'Niall's glamorous.'

We were travelling for most of the next day: a taxi to the airport, then two flights with a long wait in Bordeaux for a connection. From Gatwick we caught the train to Victoria and took a taxi to Sue's house. I asked the driver to wait while we went inside.

There was a small pile of mail waiting for her on a table in the hall. She picked it up before unlocking her door. Her room came as a surprise: I think I had expected the usual cramped chaos of bedsitter existence, but the room was large and tidy, and what furniture there was had been chosen discerningly. In one corner was a single bed and next to it were bookshelves packed with expensive artbooks. Under the only window was a desk, with a drawing board, several glasses filled with brushes, pens and knives, a container for paper and a large extensible desk lamp. An Apple Mac stood on a table of its own next to the desk. There was stereo equipment but no television. Against one wall were a hand basin, a small cooker and a massive, antiquated wardrobe. As she closed the door I noticed she had fitted two heavy bolts, one at the top, one at the bottom. The window too was secured with locks.

'I'd better not keep the taxi waiting,' I said.

'I know.'

We were facing each other, but avoiding eye contact. I felt tired from the journey. She came up to me and suddenly we embraced, more warmly than I would have expected.

'Is this the end?' I said.

'Only if you want it to be.'

'You know I don't. But I can't put up with the stuff about Niall any more.'

'Then there's nothing to worry about. Niall won't bother me again.'

'All right. Let's not discuss it now.'

'I'll ring you later this evening,' she said. We had exchanged addresses and numbers soon after meeting, but we went through the routine of making sure we still had them. Sue's address was easy to remember, so I had never written it down, but I had scribbled her telephone number in the back of my address book.

We kissed again and this time we let it linger. It reminded me of how she tasted, how she felt against me. I was regretting my behaviour of the day before, and felt a mad urge to apologise to her, but when we pulled back from each other she was smiling.

'I'll call you this evening,' she said.

Fifteen minutes later the taxi dropped me outside my flat. I let myself in and put down my bag, glancing at the pile of mail on the mat. I left it there and went upstairs.

After being so long away, and with so many different places seen, the rooms had for me a disorientating air of familiarity and strangeness. There was a background smell of damp or mould, so I opened some windows for fresh air and switched on the water heater and fridge. My apartment had four main rooms, apart from kitchen and bathroom: there was a lounge, bedroom, a spare room, and a fourth room which I thought of as my study. It was here that I kept the various pieces of elderly film equipment I had collected over the years, as well as copy prints of some of the stories I had worked on. I had a 16mm projector and screen, and an editing bench. All were tokens of a half-hearted intent to set up one day as an independent film producer, even though I knew that most of the stuff would have to be replaced with modern equipment of professional standard. I should also have to rent a proper studio.

The flat felt cool after the summer weather in France and outside it had started to rain. I wandered around, feeling anti-climactic, and already lonely for Sue. It had been a bad note on which to end the holiday. I still didn't know her well enough to judge the changes in her moods, and I had left her just as we were on another upswing. I thought for a moment I should phone her, but she had said she would call me. Anyway there was much to do around the flat. I had a suitcase full of dirty clothes which needed to be washed soon, and there was no fresh food. But I felt unmotivated and lazy, missing France.

I made a cup of black instant coffee and sat down with it while I opened the mail. Heaps of accumulated envelopes always look more interesting before they are opened. What had piled up for me was a number of bills and circulars, subscription copies of magazines, half-hearted replies to half-hearted letters I had written before I went away.

A postcard had arrived from Canada: *Richard – I may have to stay a few weeks longer. Would you mind phoning Megan at work and asking her to forward my mail? She's got the address. Missing you. Love – Annette.* (There was an X after her signature.)

The three most interesting pieces of mail I found were two cheques, and a note from a producer asking me to phone him urgently. His letter was a week old.

My life was putting itself together again. How Sue had the ability to distract me! When I was with her she put everything else out of my mind. Maybe in London she would seem different, the relationship would continue at lower pressure in the context of familiar, everyday existence. I knew for sure that we could not possibly conduct a long term affair at the intensity with which we had started.

I telephoned the producer who had written to me. He had left his office but there was a message on his answering machine to contact him at home. I called him there, without luck. I walked down to the lock-up garage where I kept my car, and much to my surprise the engine started at the first attempt. I drove back to the flat and parked outside. I collected my dirty clothes and a shopping bag, dumped the clothes in a machine at the local laundromat, and went to buy some groceries. When I had finished I went home.

I read a copy of the morning's newspaper while I was eating, wondering what had been going on in the world while I was away. My job had given me a peculiar attitude to news reporting: either I saturated myself in stories as they developed, or I cut myself off from them entirely. While away I had been content to let a vacuum of non-interest build up around me. From the paper I discovered that most of the news was the same as ever: renewed tension in the Middle East, a cabinet minister denying reports of an adulterous affair, an air crash in South America, rumours of an upcoming general election.

I called the producer again and got through to him. He was pleased to hear from me: one of the US networks wanted documentary footage of US military involvement in Central America, and because of political sensitivity an American crew could not be used. He had been trying to find a camera operator all week, but no one wanted the job. I thought about it while we talked, then said I'd do it.

The evening passed and I felt increasingly restless. It was for a reason I had grown accustomed to: I was waiting for Sue. I had been out of my flat for an hour and a half, and she might have tried then, but surely she would have called again later? I could as easily have telephoned her, but she had said twice she would ring me, and there was a sort of emotional protocol involved. We were not yet on an even footing. Precedence and omission and timing still assumed significance.

I waited for her, growing sleepy, and after about ten o'clock increasingly irritated. I had a feeling in my bones about the silence, the familiar dread of Niall's intrusion. If he could mysteriously follow us to Biarritz, it would be as nothing to follow us home.

When I went to bed I was still irritated with her, but soon fell asleep. I was restless in bed and woke up several times. At one dark low-point of the night I resolved never again to have anything to do with her. If the resolve survived to the morning it was broken by her telephoning me before I was fully awake. I reached over for the receiver.

'Richard? It's me, Sue.'

'Hello.'

'Did I wake you?'

'It doesn't matter. I thought you were going to call me last night. I waited up.'

'I rang an hour or two after you left here, but there was no answer. I was going to try again later but I fell asleep.'

'I thought something might have happened.'

She was silent for a moment. 'I've got to go into the studio today, and see about some work. I'm more broke than I thought.'

'Shall we meet this evening? I'd like to see you.'

We made the practical arrangements as if we were setting up a business meeting. Sue sounded preoccupied and distant, and I was making an effort to keep a querulous tone out of my voice. I was deeply suspicious of why she had not phoned.

'By the way,' she said. 'Did you send me a card? There was one here when I got home?'

'Card?'

'You sent me a postcard from France. I think it was you. It wasn't signed. I suppose it could have been—'

'No, I sent it,' I said. 'It was from me.'

Old Saint-Tropez – fishermen, nets and a warehouse. It was an unwelcome reminder of being alone while she was with Niall, and it also reminded me of how things had become since. All caused by Niall.

'I didn't recognise your handwriting,' she said. 'Well, I'll see you later.'

'All right.'

I went through the day trying not to think about her, but she had become so entangled with me that I could not disregard her. She still informed everything I did or thought. I disliked the effect she had on me, but I could not escape the truth that I was still hopelessly in love with her. Even so, everything was based on two brief periods: a day or two before she went to see Niall, and a day or two that had followed. I loved her, but it was all based on a glimpse of her. I had never really seen her for what she was.

Full of forebodings I walked down to Finchley Road Underground station. Sue was already there when I arrived and as soon as she saw me she ran forward, kissing me and holding me tightly. Forebodings dispersed.

She said, 'Let's go to your flat.'

'I've booked a table.'

'Then we can phone the restaurant and tell them we're going to be late.'

Bemused, I let her lead me off, hurrying along. As soon as we reached my flat she began kissing me again, with more ardour and affection than I could ever remember from her. I felt emotionally detached, so hard had my defences built up during the day. But there was no question of what she wanted and soon we were in bed together. Afterwards, she left the room and walked around the flat, looking at everything, before returning to me. I had never known her so spirited, so active. She brought two cans of beer from the fridge in the kitchen, and passed one to me. She sat on the bed, cross legged and naked. I lay back against the headboard, looking lazily at her.

'I've got to make a speech,' she said, wrenching off the ring-pull and tossing it across the room. 'I want you to listen.'

'I don't like speeches. Come back here.'

'You'll like this one. Anyway, I've been working on it all day.'

'Is it written down?'

'Listen. The first thing I want to say is I'm sorry I saw Niall without telling you. It's never going to happen again and I'm sorry if I hurt you. The second is that Niall's going to be back in London any day now and I can't stop him contacting me. He knows where I live and he knows where I work. What I'm saying is, if I see Niall it's not going to be my fault. The third—'

'But the same thing will happen all over again if you do see him.'

'No it won't. The third thing is that I'm in love with you, you're the only person I want to be with and we must never let Niall interfere again.'

I felt calm after our lovemaking, felt fond of her, felt the warmth radiating from her, but damage had been done. Only that morning it had seemed to me that we had been forced apart irreparably by events, but here was yet another reversal. Sue was saying the very words I wanted her to say. What she did not know, and what I was myself only beginning to sense, was that it was the reversals themselves that did all the harm. Each time I accommodated the new change, something of the past became lost. There was so much disruption I could barely remember the good times.

'Why don't we meet Niall together?' I said. 'I don't like the idea of you being alone with him. How do I know he wouldn't beat you up again?'

Sue shook her head. 'You can never see him, Richard.'

'But if we're together he would have to accept that everything's changed.'

'No. You don't understand.'

'Then make me.'

'I'm *scared* of him.'

I suddenly remembered the job I had been offered, and that I was due to leave London in two days' time. I now regretted accepting, thinking of Niall's imminent return, the certainty he would see Sue while I was away. I imagined the worst, yet to do so was to disbelieve her sincerity, her own freedom to act for herself. I had to trust her.

We eventually dressed and went to the restaurant, and while we were there I told Sue about the trip to Costa Rica. I said nothing of my fears, but she knew at once what I had been thinking.

She said, 'The worst thing about it is not seeing you until you get back. Nothing else will happen.'

She stayed with me in my flat for the next two days, and we were happy. Then I left her to go to earn my living.

It was fifteen days before I returned, red-eyed and exhausted from the thirteen hour flight. I was worn out from the pressures of filming: the delays while getting permission from officials, the extreme heat and humid conditions of the tropical terrain, the problems we had had in setting up certain interviews. At every new place we went to film we had to be approved by the local bureaucrats, or army officers, and all of them were suspicious of us or hostile to us. In the end the job had been done, the money paid to me, and I was safely home. I was glad it was over.

I went back to my flat and although I was tired I was restless and discontented. London felt cool and damp, but after the shanty towns and slums of Central America it looked tidy, prosperous, modern. I stayed in the flat long enough to look through my mail, then collected my car and drove over to see Sue.

One of her bedsit neighbours opened the door to me, and I went straight to her room and knocked. There was a delay, but I could hear her moving inside. In a moment the door opened and Sue was there. She was holding her dressing gown around her, and it was obvious that beneath it she was naked. We stared at each other for several seconds.

Then she said, 'You'd better come in.'

As she said this she gave a half-look over her shoulder, as if someone was there in the room behind her, and when I walked in I was braced for a confrontation. Dread filled me.

The air smelt stale and the room was in semi-darkness. The curtains were closed, but daylight filtered through the thin material. Sue pulled them open. Her room was below ground level at the back of the house. Outside was a brick wall forming a small drainage well, and bushes and uncut grass stood in the garden above the wall, shading the room. The air had a faint blue haze to it, as if someone had been smoking there recently, but I could not smell tobacco.

She had been in bed when I arrived because the sheets were thrown back and her clothes were draped over a chair. On the bedside table was a small, shallow dish, and lying in it were three cigarette ends, used matches and a lot of ash.

I glared around suspiciously, looking for Niall.

Sue closed the door behind me. She stood by the door, leaning back against it and holding the gown wrapped over her body. She would not look at me, and her hair, untidy and tangled, concealed most of her face. I could see, though, that her mouth and chin were reddened.

I said, 'Where is he?'

'Where is who?'

'Niall, of course!'

'Can you see him here?'

'You know I can't. Where did he go? Out of the window?'

'Don't be ridiculous!'

'What else were you doing in bed in the middle of the day?' I shouted.

But suddenly unsure of myself I glanced at my wristwatch. It was still set on Central American time. The plane had landed at Heathrow soon after dawn, so I guessed that by now it must be past midday.

'I didn't have to work today. I was having a lie in.' She pushed past me and sat down on the bed. 'Why didn't you phone before you came round?'

'Why? I just arrived back and I came straight over to see you!'

'I thought you'd telephone first.'

'Sue, you promised me this wouldn't happen.'

'It's not what you think.'

'It's everything I think!' I gesticulated wildly at the ashtray. 'Do you think I'm stupid? Don't lie to me, not any more!'

Her eyes were full of tears, but she held my gaze.

She said quietly, 'Richard, I'm sorry. Niall found me. He followed me home from work one evening and I couldn't argue with him.'

'How long ago was this?'

'A couple of weeks. Look, I know what it means. Don't let's make it worse than it already is. Niall isn't going to leave me alone, so it's never going to work for you and me, whatever we do, whatever you make me promise.'

'I never extracted a promise from you,' I said.

'All right, but it's finished now.'

'You're damned right it's finished!'

'Let's leave it at that.'

I could barely hear what she said. She was huddled on the bed, her arms folded in her lap, leaning forward so that all I could see of her was the top of her head and her shoulders. She had turned slightly, facing the bedside table. I noticed that the ashtray was no longer there, that somehow she had quickly hidden it. The guilty concealment confirmed everything I had assumed from the moment I knocked on her door. Niall had been here with her until a short time before I arrived.

'I'll go now,' I said. 'But what *is* the hold Niall has over you? Why do you let him do this to you?'

She said, 'He's glamorous, Richard.'

'You said that before. What's glamour got to do with anything?'

'Not glamour . . . *the* glamour. Niall has the glamour.'

'You can't be serious!'

'It's the most important thing in my life. Yours too.'

She looked up at me then, a thin, sad figure, sitting in the mess of crumpled sheets that were heaped across the mattress. She was crying, silently, hopelessly.

'I'm going,' I said. 'Don't contact me ever again.'

She stood up, uncoiling stiffly as if in pain.

'I love you for your glamour, Richard,' she said. 'It's what attracted me to you.'

'Not another bloody word!'

'You can't change. The glamour will never leave you. This is why Niall won't let me go. It's the same for him, as for me. You too, wrapped up in glamour, you can't let go—'

Then, somewhere in the room, somewhere behind me, I heard the unmistakable sound of a male laugh. It was a contemptuous snort, as if from a bully who could hold back his mirth no more. I whirled around in horror at the realisation Niall had been standing there all along, but there was no one in sight. Then I noticed that the full-length door of the wardrobe had been open all the time I was in the room, and that there was a space behind it where someone could be hiding. It was the only place he could be. Niall was standing there!

Heady with a renewed surge of anger and despair, I wanted only to escape from this place. I lunged at the door to the room, wrenched it open, saw the bright glint of the stainless steel bolts. I went outside, and slammed the door behind me. I was far too angry to drive my car so I hurried down the road, moving away from her as quickly as I could. I walked and walked, heading home, wanting only in the blackness of rage to be free of her.

I went up the long hill towards Archway, crossed the viaduct into Highgate, then started down towards Hampstead Heath. My anger was narcotic, spinning through my brain in a relentless swirl of vicious resentments. I knew I was tired from the long flight, that jetlag was no condition in which to be rational about anything, least of all this. London seemed like a hallucination around me: the glimpse from the heath of the tall buildings to the south, the old red-brick terraces on the far side, the people in the streets and the endless noise of traffic. I cut through side streets lined with Victorian villas; plane trees and ornamental cherries and crab apples now exhausted at the end of summer; cars parked on both sides, their wheels up on the pavements. I pushed past people, hardly seeing them, ran across Finchley Road, dodging traffic. It was downhill to West Hampstead, long straight roads with cars and trucks, people waiting for buses or moving slowly from one shop to another. I shoved past them all, thinking only of getting home, going to bed, trying to sleep off my anger and my jetlag. I turned into West End Lane, almost home. I passed West Hampstead station, passed the twenty-four-hour supermarket, passed the police station; all familiar landmarks, all part of my life in London before Sue. I was making plans, thinking of another job the producer had mentioned on the long flight home; not news, but a documentary for Channel Four, a major project, much travel. When I had recovered I would call him, leave the country for a while, sleep with foreign women, work at what I did best.

The walking had clarified my mind. No more Sue, no more Niall, no more raised hopes or broken promises or evasions or lies. No more sex in the afternoon, regrets at night. I hated Sue and everything she had done to me. I regretted every word I had confided in her and every act of love we had performed. From the time I had seen her ranting to herself I had worried she was half-mad, and now I was convinced of it. And Niall! There was only one reason why I never saw him. He was a figment of her deranged mind! *Niall did not exist!* Something hit me low in the back and I was hurled forward. I heard nothing, but crashed into the brick surround of a shop window; the thick glass shattered and fell on me. Some part of me was rolling along the ground, twisting my back, while unthinkable heat scorched my neck and legs and arms, and burned my hair. As I came to a halt the only sound I could hear was glass breaking and falling, slabs of it slicing down on top of me, an endless tormenting rain, and somewhere an immense and total silence out and around me, beyond my unseeing eyes.

Part Four

For the first few miles after they left the hospital the road followed the narrow routes of ancient ways between the high Devon hedges. Because of the number of tractors which used these lanes the road surface was muddy. Sue drove nervously and hesitantly, braking sharply as they approached blind corners and steering round them with elaborate caution, craning her neck to see ahead. It was always dangerous for her to drive, demanding constant concentration, but narrow country roads presented an extra hazard to her. Fortunately, the few oncoming vehicles they met were being driven slowly, so there was never any real danger of a crash, but the car felt large and unfamiliar and she wished they would reach the main road.

Richard was beside her in the passenger seat, staring ahead, hardly speaking at all. He held the cross-over seat belt with one hand, keeping it from pressing against his body, but whenever she braked for a corner he jerked forward. Several times he drew in breath sharply. She knew that the lurching of the car was probably painful, but trying to compensate for it only made her more nervous and selfconscious.

A few miles beyond Totnes they came at last to the A38, a modern two lane highway with no sharp corners and only gentle gradients. Almost at once she felt more confident. She accelerated to a comfortable cruising speed of around sixty. A fine drizzle was falling, and whenever they overtook a truck or some other large vehicle the windscreen was blurred with a muddy spray. Once they were past Exeter the road joined the M5 motorway, leading directly to London via the M4.

At her suggestion Richard leaned forward and switched on the radio, tuning it to a number of stations before finding one they agreed on.

'Let me know if you'd like to stop somewhere,' she said.

'I'm all right now, but I'll need to get out and walk around in about an hour.'

'How do you feel?'

'Fine.'

Sue felt fine too, glad to be returning permanently to London. She was exhausted by the journeys she had made to Devon in recent weeks. Richard had been walking unaided for almost a month, and they had both grown impatient for his discharge. It was Dr Hurdis who had delayed matters, saying he was not convinced that the traumas had been dealt with adequately. They had several more sessions of hypnotherapy, but these, like the first, were inconclusive. Richard himself appeared to be untroubled by the outcome, but was anxious to finish the treatment.

Sue's own dilemma was that privately she agreed with Hurdis. She knew that Richard had not yet come to terms with his past, but she was convinced there was nothing more to be gained from conventional therapy. She was undecided about it for her own reasons. Richard had lost his glamour and knew nothing of hers, so the potential of what had once ruined their lives together was still there, like a time bomb. Still, he had been discharged at last.

During Sue's several visits to Middlecombe they had found it almost impossible to spend time together alone. There was always someone around, so their conversations had necessarily lacked intimacy and they still knew as little about each other as they did when Sue first went to the hospital. They had managed to be alone in his room only once. Then, tentatively, they had tried to make love. It was a failure: they were both too aware of the lack of real privacy, the bed was functional hospital apparatus, and anyway his body was still too sore and stiff. In the end they had settled for lying naked in each other's arms for a few minutes, but even that had given her an unpleasant shock. Until then she had had no notion of the extent of his injuries, and she was horrified to see the disfiguring scars from burns, lacerations and surgery. It had marked a fresh phase in her feelings about him: the sheer scale of hurt he had suffered awakened a new tenderness.

But now the problems of being in Middlecombe were behind them, and her own personal dilemma about Richard was the priority. What she most wanted was a clean start, a second chance.

Richard, though, was intent on rediscovering his past and she could not in conscience deny him that.

They had been silent for most of the journey, listening to Radio 3. She wondered what music he liked best, whether it was just classical or if his taste was broader. Richard's amnesia aside there were so many small things they did not know about each other, the finding out swept away first by the urgencies of the start of an affair, and later by its sudden end. She had her own discoveries still to make.

They were approaching Bristol. A mile before the Avon Bridge she turned off the motorway and drove into the service area. She slowed down on the slip road and turned into the parking area, looking for somewhere to leave the car. Beside her, Richard suddenly stiffened.

'Sue!' he shouted. 'For God's sake!'

A man had stepped out in front of their car. Sue slammed her foot on the brake pedal and wrenched the wheel to one side. The car lurched and skidded forwards, dipping down at the side. The tyres made a scraping sound on the wet ground as the wheels locked. The man, who had frozen in terror when he realised what was going on, took a half step back. As the car halted, Sue wound down the window on her side.

'Are you all right?' she said in genuine distress. 'I didn't see you! I'm terribly sorry.'

The man stared back at her, but said nothing.

Leaning uncomfortably across Sue, Richard called to the man, 'Are you hurt?'

'No, I'm all right.'

He turned and walked quickly away. Sue let the tension burst from her in a loud exhalation of breath. She rested her forehead on the knuckles of her hands, closing her eyes.

'I hate driving!' she said.

'I thought you'd seen him. You were looking straight at him!'

'No, I wasn't thinking.' She looked at Richard. 'What about you? Did that do any damage?'

'No more than before.'

She restarted the engine, her hands trembling. After parking the car she went around to the passenger door and stood by it while Richard climbed out. He could do this on his own, insisted on it, but she wanted to be close by him. She reached into the back seat for his walking stick, then locked up. It had stopped raining, but the tarmac of the parking area was wet and puddled. A cool wind blew in from Wales, across the Severn estuary.

She bought two cups of tea and some pieces of cake, and took them to the table where Richard was waiting. The cafeteria was as usual crowded with other motorists. She had never seen one of these places empty. Through the wide opening to the entrance hall they could hear the electronic groans and whines, and bursts of insane musical jingles, from the games machines.

'What are you thinking about?' she asked.

'Getting home. I keep remembering what the flat was like when I bought it. The builders had only recently finished the conversion and it was empty. I find it difficult to imagine it with furniture. Even mine.'

'I thought you said you *could* remember it.'

'It's all mixed up in my mind. I keep thinking of the day I moved in. I'd stupidly put the carpets at the back of the van, so I had to unload them last and move all the furniture around to put them down. And I can remember later, when you were there, but the flat I remember then doesn't feel like the same place. They're one on top of each other. Do you know what I mean?'

'Not really,' she said.

'You haven't been back there, by any chance?'

'No.'

It had occurred to her that she ought to call in to see if everything was all right, but she had never done so.

Since she had started visiting Richard at the hospital she had been afflicted by two mundane problems: lack of time and lack of money. She tried to say as little as possible about them, because at first he had been so suspicious of her excuses. Since then, in the greater cause, she tried to minimise her problems when talking to him. Richard paid for everything he knew about: her travel expenses, the lodgings when she was in Devon, car rental, meals when they were together, but they had little to do with the central predicament. She still had to produce the rent money every month, she had to eat, pay for heating, had to move around London, clothe herself. Her working life had been thrown into chaos by her frequent absences from London. The studio seemed less and less inclined to commission her because she had become unreliable, and she never had enough time to go out and look for other work.

That she had supported herself for some years was a matter of great importance to her. It had been difficult, as a freelance existence always is, but she had survived somehow. Independence and an honestly earned income were equated in her mind with her growth away from Niall's influence, two or three years ago, when she first started to stand up to him.

The temptations were constant, though, because there was always a solution to lack of cash. Niall had taught her how to shoplift and she knew she could get away with it if she had to. Her glamour was much weaker, but it was still there if she needed it. So far she had resisted temptation and Richard knew nothing of the internal struggle.

They left the cafeteria and returned to the car. Richard carried his stick without putting his weight on it, but he was limping. She watched over him protectively as he lowered himself backwards into the passenger seat, then swung his legs one at a time into place. His efforts to move normally touched her, and after she had closed the door on him she stood for a few seconds, staring vacantly across the car's roof and remembering, briefly, a moment from their first affair when she had seen him running.

Soon they were back on the motorway, heading for London. Thinking about the man she had nearly knocked down, and the real dangers implied by the incident, she drove more cautiously than ever.

She found Richard's apartment with some difficulty, in spite of his directions. She had always been scared of driving in London. After a wrong turning into a one way system, and several near misses with oncoming cars in the narrow back streets, she found the road and parked the car not too far from the front of the house.

Richard leaned forward and peered up through the windscreen at the houses.

'It doesn't seem to have changed much,' he said.

'Were you expecting it to?'

'It's been so long, I somehow imagined it would look different.'

They left the car and went to the house. The main door led to a tiny hall with two more doors, one for the ground floor flat and one for his own upstairs. As he fumbled with the key ring Sue watched his face, trying to judge his feelings. He revealed no expression and slipped the Yale key into the lock and pushed the door open. There was a rustling, scuffing sound, and the door jammed briefly. He pushed again and this time it opened fully. On the floor at the bottom of the stairs was a huge pile of letters and magazines.

He said, 'You go first. I can't step over those.'

He pressed back to make room for her and she went in first, pushing the papers to one side against the wall. She scooped up as many of them as she could and cradled them in her arms.

Richard led the way up the stairs, taking the steps slowly and carefully. She followed, thinking how strange yet familiar it was to be here again, when for a time she had thought she would never even see Richard again. The place had memories for her.

At the top of the stairs he halted unexpectedly, and because she was immediately behind him she was forced to take a step down.

'What's the matter?'

'Something's wrong. I can't tell what it is.'

There was frosted-glass window built into the wall beside the stairs, but because all the room doors were closed the landing at the top was in semi-darkness. The flat felt chilly.

'Would you like me to go first?' she said.

'No, it's all right.'

He moved on and she followed him on to the landing. He opened one door after another, peering inside, then going on to the next. Apart from the kitchen and bathroom, directly to the right at the top of the stairs, there were three main rooms. She went into the living room and dumped her armload of magazines and mail on one of the chairs. The air in the room had that indefinable smell of someone else's home, but there was also an impression of neglect, that the air had not circulated in a long time. The curtains were half drawn, so she pulled them back and opened one of the windows. Street noises came in. On the sill in front of the windows was a row of houseplants, all dead. One of them was one she had given him as a present, *Fatsia japonica*, the castor oil plant, but most of the leaves had long ago fallen off and the single remaining one was brown and brittle. She stared at it, wondering whether to touch it and make it fall.

Richard hobbled in from the landing, looked around at the furniture, the bookshelves, the dusty television.

'Something's different,' he said. 'It's been moved around.' He ran his hand through his hair, sweeping it away from his eyes, a gesture of frustration she remembered well. 'I know it sounds crazy, but that's what has happened.'

'Everything's the same.'

'No. I knew it was different as soon as we walked in.'

He swivelled around, balancing his weight on his good leg, and went out again. Sue heard his irregular step as he went down the thinly carpeted landing. She was thinking about the first time she had been here, soon after they met. Because it was summer the room was full of light and the newly painted walls had seemed bright and refreshing. The same walls now showed the effects of a few months of neglect, needing pictures or wall hangings to cheer them up. The whole flat should be cleaned and revived. It brought out tidy instincts in her but the thought of doing house-work for someone else was daunting. She was tired after the long drive from Devon, and felt like going out for a drink.

She heard Richard moving around in the next room, where he kept his pieces of antique film equipment, and she went in to talk to him.

'There's a room missing, Sue!' he said at once. 'Down at the end, next to the bathroom. There was a spare room!'

'I don't remember that,' Sue said.

'I had four rooms! This one, the living room, the bedroom and a spare. Am I going mad?'

He went down the hall and gestured at the blank wall at the end.

'That's an outside wall,' she said.

'You were here before. Don't you remember it?'

'Yes, but it was exactly like this.' She squeezed his arm gently. 'Your memory's playing you tricks. Don't you remember this morning, on the motorway? You said you could remember the flat in two ways.'

'But now I'm *here*.'

He stumped away from her and limped down the landing. Sue wondered what she could say. Unknown to Richard she had been to a private meeting with Dr Hurdis the day before. The psychiatrist had warned her that the return of Richard's memory might be only partial. Hurdis was convinced there were still important gaps in his memory and that some of what he thought of as actual memories might be misremembered details.

'But how can I tell the difference?' Sue had said. 'And what can I do about it?'

'Use your judgement. Memory loss often concerns small, irrelevant matters, but they can be perplexing.'

As perplexing as a room he thought had gone missing from the flat in which he used to live?

Sue went into the bedroom, another room that smelled musty. She pulled open the curtains but the windows here had swollen in their frames, or were seized with paint, and she could not shift them. A fanlight opened for her. The bed stood against the wall inside the door. Someone had made it up, far more neatly than either she or Richard would have done it. Who could it have been? She knew the police had visited the flat after the car bomb, and suddenly she had a grotesque mental image of two uniformed constables in helmets, painstakingly smoothing the sheets and pulling up the covers, plumping the pillows.

She lifted back the bedclothes. While Richard continued to move around in the other rooms she stripped the bed and struggled to turn over the mattress. This too smelled stale, but there was nothing she could do about that. She remembered there was an airing cupboard in the bathroom, over the hot-water tank. She found a complete set of sheets and pillowcases, none of which smelled damp. While she was there she switched on the electric immersion heater, thinking how, piece by piece, a home was brought back to life. With the same thought she went into the kitchen and plugged in the fridge, but the compressor did not start and the interior light would not work. She went out to the landing, found the fuse box and turned on the mains supply. The overhead light came on. Back in the kitchen the fridge was whirring, but when she looked inside she discovered the white insulated walls had grown large areas of spotty black mould. A carton of milk smelled foul, so she poured it away. A yellow liquid glugged horribly into the sink. She washed it down with water. She was kneeling on the floor, wiping the fridge clean, when Richard came in. He stood behind her, resting his weight with one hand on the table. One look at his face told her that his dilemma about the number of rooms was unresolved.

She closed the fridge door, stood up, and went to him.

'Do you want to talk about it?' she said.

'Not now.'

'I'm organising your life for you,' she said. 'We'll go to a restaurant tonight, but after that I'll cook for you.'

'Does that mean you're going to stay?'

'For a day or two.' She kissed him lightly. 'I'll start bringing your stuff in from the car. I've got to return it this evening.'

'While it's still ours, why don't we drive over to collect mine?'

'Where is it?'

'If no one's pinched it, I assume it's where I parked it, in the road outside your place.'

'I don't remember seeing it.' She frowned, knowing she would have remembered the car which for a while had figured so much in her life. 'It's a red Nissan, isn't it?'

'It was. It's probably covered in leaves and dirt.'

'Yes, probably.'

She was certain she hadn't seen it anywhere near her house. He normally kept it in a rented lock-up, and she had assumed it was there.

'If we find it, are you able to drive?' she said.

'I won't know until I try, but I think so.'

The next hour was occupied with chores, and after they had returned to his flat and put away the groceries they set out on what she was convinced would be a wasted journey to find his car. The evening rush hour had begun and driving across north London was a nightmare for her. At last they escaped the crush of traffic in Highgate, and crossed the Archway into Hornsey. She motored slowly down her street, bringing the car to a halt outside the house.

'It's further down,' Richard said. 'On the other side.'

'I can't see it.' But she drove the length of the street and at the end executed an awkward turn.

As she drove back Richard said, 'I distinctly remember leaving it here. Under that tree, where the Mini is. When I left I walked home, so it must still be here.'

'Could you have come back for it later?'

'No, that was the day of the car bomb.'

They reached her house again, and because there was a space opposite she parked and turned off the engine. Richard was obviously confused by the absence of his car, because he turned in his seat and looked along the row of parked cars.

'Let's at least look in your garage,' Sue said. 'The car might have been moved there by the police. They had your papers, didn't they?'

'Yes,' he said, and sounded relieved. 'Maybe you're right.'

She opened the driver's door. 'I want to see if there are any messages for me. Would you like to come in too?'

'I think I'll stay here.'

A sudden tightness in his voice made her glance at him, but his expression revealed nothing. She wondered if his memory of leaving the car here meant that he could also remember what happened the last time he went to her bedsit. Neither of them had yet said anything about that. She left the car and went to the house.

Inside, she found two scribbled messages pinned to the communal noticeboard beside the phone. One was from the studio, and her immediate instinct was to call back at once. She looked at her wristwatch but knew the office was closed now. The message was undated, so it could be up to four days old. When she went into her room she found everything as she had left it. Her old habit, looking around for signs of a visit from Niall, had not left her yet. She took a change of clothes and underclothes from the wardrobe and thrust them into her holdall. She had everything else she needed in the bag she had left at Richard's flat.

Alone for a few moments she stared around the familiar room, recalling how it had felt three years earlier when she moved in. That had been her first real attempt to reject Niall and his way of life. Without fully realising it at the time, she had already made the decision about herself which was only implemented when she met Richard. In the meantime, Niall had continued to hang around on the fringes, unwilling to let her go, while she lacked the drive to free herself of him. By the time she moved into this room she knew there was more going on in the world than Niall could show her. The art-school education her parents had paid for was being squandered, but she was growing up and she wanted more than a life of petty crime and useless drifting. The bedsitter, legally rented and paid for with money she earned herself, had marked a new turning. But with time it had simply become the place she lived in, symbolic of nothing.

She returned to the car and they drove back to West Hampstead. The traffic was lighter now, and she was beginning to remember the way, but Richard had to direct her to the exact location of his garage. When he unlocked the door they found the car inside. Two of its tyres were flat, and so was its battery, but otherwise it was exactly as he must have left it, all those months ago.

They ate dinner in an Indian restaurant in Fortune Green Road, then returned to his flat. Earlier, using jump-leads from the rental car, they had managed to start the Nissan and Richard tried driving it. He took it as far as the nearest filling station where they pumped up the tyres, but after that he had been too tired for more driving.

He seemed relaxed during the meal, though, and for the first time since leaving Middlecombe he became talkative. He said he wanted to get back to work as soon as possible, perhaps overseas; he enjoyed foreign travel. When they were back in the flat they watched the television news. He talked about the style of television reporting and how there were subtle differences between British and American conventions. He had had to learn the American way while working for the agency.

Then they went to bed, and of course she could not help thinking about the past. The physical act of love was a reminder for them both: how long ago it had been, how good it could be, how much it mattered. Afterwards, she lay close against him, resting her head on his chest. She could see none of his scars from this position; an illusion of the past because his injuries affected everything in the present.

Neither of them was sleepy, and after a while Sue left the bed and made some tea for herself and took a can of beer from the fridge for Richard. Because the room was chilly in spite of the electric heater, she put on her pullover and sat facing him while he propped himself against the pillows.

'You never did redecorate this place,' she said, looking around the room in the low light from the bedside lamp. 'You said you were going to.'

'Did I? I don't remember that.'

'You said you'd put up some wallpaper. Or paint the walls with a colour.'

'Why? They look all right to me. I like white paint.'

She was amused by his mock-aggressive reply, recumbent in the bed, the beer can held in his fingers. There was a pink lattice of graft tissue around his neck and shoulder.

'Don't you remember?' she said.

'Have we talked about this before? The colour of my walls?'

'You said you had regained your memory.'

'I have, but I can't remember every tiny detail.'

'This isn't a detail.'

'But it can't *matter*, Sue!'

'How many more tiny details have you forgotten?' She said the words, not thinking until too late of the warning from Dr Hurdis.

'I don't know and frankly I don't care too much. I know I'm having trouble with my memory, but some bits of it aren't going to matter as much as other bits. I want to concentrate on the things that count. You and me, for instance.'

'Richard, I'm sorry. I'll shut up about it.'

'It's difficult for both of us. So why don't we get to the point? What *did* happen to us before?'

'Nothing important.'

'I know that's untrue and so do you.'

'It went wrong. We're having a second chance, and I don't want to risk it again. Let's make the most of it.'

But she was feeling the familiar perverse excitement of their earlier affair. She knew how dangerous it would be to go back, yet she was still fatally drawn to it.

'Sue, it seems to me this is completely bound up in what happened to me. I'm certain you are the key to it.'

'I need a drink,' she said. Before he could answer she swung her legs from the bed and left the room. She walked into the kitchen and took two more beer cans from the fridge. She had had to get away from him because she felt the rapture in her, the risky thrill of wanting to try again.

She stared blankly into the interior of the fridge, holding on to the open door, feeling the refrigerated air circulating down and around her naked legs.

She was fooling herself to think they could be together again without the glamour to link them. It had always been their natural state, intrinsically fascinating, binding them together. Their affair had failed before, but that had been because of Niall. Now he was out of the equation. Wouldn't it be different?

She closed the fridge, went back to the bedroom. She placed the two cans on the table next to him, and sat again on the top of the bed, crossing her legs and tugging down the front of the pullover into her lap.

She said, 'I don't think you remember everything about me yet.'

'I thought I did. You're making me wonder.'

She moved closer to him and took his hand. 'You haven't really got your memory back at all, have you?'

'Yes I have. Most of it, the important stuff. I remember that you and I fell in love, but you already had a boyfriend called Niall who wouldn't let you go, and in the end he split us up. That's right, isn't it?'

'Can you remember why Niall did that?'

'I imagine he was jealous. After we met in France.'

That startled her. She said, 'But I've never been to France. I've never even been out of Britain. I don't have a passport.'

'That's where we were when we met. In France, on a train. I was going to Nancy and you were on your way to somewhere on the south coast.'

'Richard, I've never been to France.'

He shook his head, and his face had the same shaken look she had seen earlier, when he was confused about the number of rooms.

'Help me,' he said softly. 'Tell me the truth.'

'I've never lied to you, Richard. We met here in London. A pub in Highgate.'

'That can't be true!'

He turned his face away from hers, his eyes closed. Sue felt a sudden helpless fright, thinking how unqualified she was to cope with this. The doctor had been right: Richard had been discharged too soon, his memory was permanently damaged. She looked at his scarred body, his trunk and arms not only stouter than before but flabbier too through lack of exercise. Was she wrong to challenge his memories? Were they in their own way as valid as hers? Why should he think they had met in France? It was a shock to discover this, something so unexpected that she could not even begin to understand.

All she knew was her own truth, the one principal matter in their affair.

She said, 'Richard, do you remember the glamour?'

'Not that again!'

'So it means something to you. Can you remember what it is?'

'No, and I don't want you to tell me!'

'Then I'll show you.'

The decision was made. She scrambled away again from the bed, charged with purpose. The rapture of their past together had fixed itself around her, and she knew everything else would have to wait until this was settled. The glamour was their condition.

'What are you doing?' Richard said.

'I want something bright-coloured. Where do you keep your clothes?'

'In the chest of drawers.'

But she already had one of the drawers open and was rummaging through it. Almost at once she found a woollen sweatshirt, a rich royal blue in colour. She took it out. He must have used it for jobs around the house, because one of the elbows had frayed away and there was a smudge of cream paint across the front.

It gave her a stimulating, dangerous feeling to hold it, knowing that it was a bold colour, something she would never choose for herself. To her it had an inherent sexual quality, like a dress with a front that was cut too low, or a skirt that was too short.

'Look at me, Richard. Watch everything I do.'

She stripped off the beige pullover she was wearing and tossed it on the bed. For a few seconds she stood naked, turning out one of the sleeves of the blue sweatshirt so she could put it on. She dragged it over her head, wrestling her arms against its weight. As it passed over her face she briefly smelled him in it, his body, overlaid with the faint mustiness of months undisturbed inside the chest of drawers. She brought her head through and pulled the sweatshirt down over her breasts. It was too large for her and reached to her thighs.

'I preferred you naked,' Richard said, but it was a weak attempt at humour.

'Do you realise what I'm doing?' she said. 'Do you remember?'

'No.'

But she could see in his eyes that he could.

'That man, today, at the motorway service station! The one I nearly ran over? You thought I hadn't seen him and I pretended I wasn't paying attention. But you were right. I hadn't seen him, I *couldn't* see him. He was invisible. I had no idea he was there until you yelled, and made me look properly. He was someone with the glamour, someone who is naturally invisible. Do you understand?'

'Come back to bed, Sue.'

'No, we have to face up to this. I know why you say you've lost your memory, because you're denying what happened last time, you're trying to block it out. But you mustn't any more!'

As she spoke Sue felt the peril of what she was doing coursing through her, exhilarating her.

'Look at the sweatshirt, Richard.' Her voice had thickened with her excitement, as if with desire. 'See how dark and strong it is. Can you see?'

He was staring mutely at her, and he nodded almost imperceptibly. She knew she had him at last.

'Watch the colour. Don't lose sight of it.'

She concentrated, thinking of the cloud, recalling the glamour to her. Once it had always been there somewhere in her, but now she had to force it. She felt the cloud gathering around her.

She became invisible.

Richard continued to stare at the place she had been, so she moved away, unseen by him, and walked to the other side of the bed.

It was invariably like this when the glamour was consented to. It was like stripping in front of strangers, like those dreams of nakedness in public places, like sexual fantasies of total vulnerability and helplessness. Yet invisibility was secure, a concealment and a hiding, a power and a curse. The half-guilty surge of sexual arousal, the sweet desire of unprotected surrender, the sacrifice of privacy, the exposure of hidden desire, the realisation that it had started and could not be stopped. Once before there had been a first time with Richard, but because he had forgotten, because his mind had been changed, she had been granted the chance of a second first time.

Her body trembled with the release of the desire and her breath rasped in her throat. She pulled up the front of the sweatshirt and pressed her fingers into her sex, held them tightly against the moist delivery of her passion. Richard continued to stare silently across the room, completely unaware of where she was or what she was doing.

She said, and she heard her voice still speaking with the thickness of desire, 'Do you remember how we met?'

Richard turned his head sharply towards her, a shocked expression on his face, and he looked at the place where now she stood, an invisible woman, protected by her glamour, naked to his own, irresistibly drawn to the glamour and bound to her by it.

PART FIVE

I thought I had seen you first, but Niall had quicker reactions. He said nothing, and waited for me to notice you.

Then he said, just as your presence was registering on me, 'Come on, let's find another pub.'

'I want to stay here.'

It was Saturday evening and the pub was crowded. All the tables were occupied and several people stood in the spaces between, with many more clustering around the bar itself. The room had a low ceiling and cigarette smoke was thick in the air, blending with your cloud. If I had seen you earlier I had not actually noticed you. In your seeming normality you had been, by paradox, unnoticed by me.

I watched you from our table, with all the fascination like has for like. The woman you were with must have been a girlfriend, but one you had probably not known long. You were trying to please her by making her laugh, paying attention to her, but you never touched her except by chance. She appeared to like you. She smiled a lot, nodding whenever you spoke. She was a normal and therefore did not know as much about you as I did. In a sense I already possessed a part of you, even though you were unaware of me. I felt excited and predatory, lying in wait, knowing that in the end you would sense me, see me, and recognise me.

Niall and I were both invisible that night, sitting at a small table behind the main door, sharing it with two normals. They of course had not noticed us. Earlier, before I realised you were there, Niall and I had been arguing in an all too familiar way about his behaviour. There was an adolescent streak in him and one of his ways of amusing himself was to steal other people's cigarettes. He had already pinched three cigarettes from the man's packet, and used his lighter. It was a petty trick to play, one he should have grown bored with years ago, but he did it out of

106

habit. I knew he wouldn't be caught, but it invariably irritated me. He also insisted on getting all the drinks at the bar, going behind the counter and helping himself. He knew that if I went for the drinks I would make myself temporarily visible, wait to be served with everyone else, and pay for them. Niall interpreted it as one of my ways of standing up to him, a reminder that for me the glamour was only one aspect of my life.

Watching you, I started to wonder if you would ever notice me. You were completely wrapped up in your girlfriend. When you glanced around the bar you did so with unfocused eyes, glancing without seeing.

Niall said, 'He's only halfway glamorous, Susan. Don't waste your time.'

'Are you jealous?'

'Not of him. I know what you're up to and it isn't going to work.'

I could not stop watching you because it was exactly that incipient, halfway quality that interested me. Like me, you straddled the two worlds, partly normal, partly invisible. It seemed impossible that you could not know you were able to cross over, that you managed to get by in the normal world without realising. Your confidence in yourself was certainly unlike any I had ever known in an invisible, with the possible exception of Niall.

He was drinking heavily and pressing me to keep up with him. He relished drunkenness, lapsing into it like so many of the other invisibles. Sometimes, at the end of an evening, when Niall was so plastered he could hardly stand, even I could only just see him. His cloud became dense, impenetrable, a frightening absence around him. That night, while Niall receded, I continued to stare at you. You were drinking moderately, wanting to keep your wits about you, or because you had to drive, or because you were saving yourself for later in the evening when you would be alone with her. How I envied her!

I said to Niall, 'I'll get the next round.'

Before he could argue I walked across to you and stood deliberately between you and your girlfriend, pretending to wait to be served by the barman. You shifted your position to see round me, knowing subconsciously that I was there but nevertheless failing to notice me. I was invisible to you, standing so close I could feel the tendrils of my cloud combining with yours, a deeply sensual imagining.

I moved away, satisfied for the moment, then went behind the counter to help myself to drinks. When I had poured them I put money in the till, and carried the glasses back to our table. I did not sit down.

'What were you up to, Susan?'

'Just looking. I had to be sure.'

'You took too long. I don't want you sniffing around other men.'

'You *are* jealous,' I said. 'Wait here. I'm going to the Ladies'.'

I left him again, wanting to escape for a few moments from the beery dullness in his eyes. As I crossed the room I let the cloud disperse so that I became visible. When I came out of the lavatory I walked across to you and stood beside you. Now I was visible I could barely see or feel the effect of your cloud, but I was almost as close as before. Then you noticed me at last and eased back slightly.

You said, 'Sorry, are you trying to get past?'

'No. I wondered if you might have change for the cigarette machine?'

'Couldn't one of the barmen change it for you?'

'Yes, but they're busy.'

You reached into your pocket and brought out a handful of coins, but there were not enough to exchange for my fiver. I simply thanked you and walked away, knowing that you had seen me properly. Still visible, I sat down next to Niall.

'Will you quit this, Susan?'

'I'm not doing anything you never do.'

I felt defiant. I was staring across the bar at you, feeling like a teenager again, hoping that now you knew I was there you would look in my direction. For the first time I did not feel intimidated by Niall. He took me for granted, knowing that I disliked most of the other invisibles, and that meeting a normal person was virtually impossible. But I had never made a secret of my wish for something better, and seeing you made me reckless.

Because of Niall's proximity I was slipping back into invisibility, and as the process completed itself Niall said, 'Finish your drink. We're leaving.'

'You go if you want. I'm going to stay a bit longer.'

'You're wasting your time. He's not one of us. You can see that as easily as I can.'

He had already finished his last glass of beer, and he belched. He was anxious to leave and take me with him. He knew I often noticed other men I found attractive, but because they were normals he felt safe from them, as in fact he was. Niall called you 'halfway', but I suspected you simply weren't *aware* that you had the glamour. You appeared to be integrated into the real world. It was this that excited me.

I was only partially an invisible woman, barely under the surface of normality, able to rise to visibility if I made the effort. Niall had no such choice. He was deeply invisible, profoundly lost from the world of normal people, and so he realised immediately what you represented to me. You were the next transitional stage, more visible than not, just as I was more invisible than not.

Concentrating, I forced myself to become visible again, deliberately provoking him.

'Come on, Susan. We're leaving.'

'You go,' I said. 'I'm staying here.'

'I'm not leaving without you.'

'Then do whatever you like.' To say such words to Niall, flaunting my independence, was a risky thrill to me.

'Don't fuck around with me. There's nothing you can do about him.'

'You're scared of me getting involved with someone else.'

'You can't keep it up without me,' he said. 'You know you'll revert.'

This was true, but stubbornly I refused to accept it. It was only after I met Niall that I had perfected the technique of forming or unforming the cloud, and it was only when he was present that I could achieve it effortlessly. Visibility was a strain and it exhausted me. I knew that this was because my cloud was linked with his. We had become interdependent, each of us holding on to the other long after we should have parted.

Niall did not know what I had felt the first time I stood behind you. Those tendrils of the cloud reaching out, teasing me . . . You were a true threat to his domination of me, a normal with a cloud, whose closeness could let me become visible too.

'I'm going to try anyway,' I said. 'If you don't like it you can leave.'

'Fuck you!'

Niall lurched up, clouting the edge of the table and slopping the drinks. The people opposite looked at me in surprise, thinking I had done it. I muttered an apology and slid a beer mat across to soak up the splashes. Niall had already left, shoving through the crowd. The people made way for him, stepping back automatically as he elbowed brusquely past them. None of them reacted, none of them noticed him.

I stayed visible when he had left, proving to myself that I could do it. I had never before stood up to Niall so determinedly, and I knew there would be a price to pay. At that moment, though, I hardly gave him a thought because you were more important.

I considered carefully what to do, then left the table and moved across to stand in the crowd close to you. You had turned so that you were leaning with both elbows on the bar, inclining your head to speak to your girlfriend. Hovering an arm's length away from you I felt predatory again. Your lack of awareness of me made you seem defenceless, and it gave an extra edge of guilty excitement. I waited, still visible, but unnoticed in the press of people. You carried on talking to your friend, completely absorbed by her. She was drinking bitter, and so I knew I had only to bide my time. Sure enough, after I had been waiting for about ten minutes she moved away from you. She pressed past me and headed towards the Ladies'.

I went forward at once and laid my hand on your arm.

I said loudly, over the noise of the crowd and the music, 'I know you, don't I?'

You looked at me in surprise. 'Are you still trying to change a fiver?'

'No. I've been staring at you all evening. I'm sure I know you from somewhere.'

You shook your head slowly, obviously wondering what was going on. I saw in your face an expression I had sometimes noticed in men when they met a woman for the first time. It was curiosity mixed with a wish to be found interesting, a fairly crude and blatant signal of sexual availability. I guessed that you knew many women, found it easy to meet more, and that you did not always stay with the same one. This simple male reaction, in which you treated me as one more chance encounter, gave me an extra thrill, one I had never felt before. You were behaving as if I were non-invisible, a normal.

'I don't think we've met,' you said. 'Unless it was at a party?'

'You're here with your girlfriend, aren't you?'

'Well, she's . . . Yes.'

'Do you ever come to this pub on your own?'

'I could do.'

'I'll be here again later in the week. On Wednesday evening.'

'All right,' you said. 'But what do you want?'

'I'm curious about you. Have you any idea why?'

'No. Would you mind telling me what's going on?'

'Take no notice. I'm a bit nervous, chatting up a stranger.'

'Is that what you're doing?'

You were obviously nonplussed by this unexplained intrusion from a complete stranger, and spoke to me in an amused way, but you weren't mocking me. I was quite able to embarrass myself on my own, and after our few words I was wishing I had never started. I knew I was blushing and was hardly aware of what I was saying. I backed away from you, ashamed of my brazenness. I hurried as best I could through the crowd, wanting to hide, yet also hoping fervently that whatever had been said was indeed enough, and that you would come to meet me on the night, if only out of curiosity.

I went outside and stood in the street, as hot and bothered by my ineptitude as ever I had been. I expected to find Niall waiting for me, but there was no sign of him so I breathed deeply, making myself calm down, letting my natural state of invisibility seep over me. Invisibility has its own kind of reassurance. I could hear the noises from inside the pub: conversation, sound system, the tills, the glasses. It was warm in the open air because it was summer, but also, because it was a London summer, a light drizzle was falling. I was tormented by the discovery of you, thrilled that you had reacted to me as if I were normal, and yet wincing inside at the clumsy way I had chatted you up. I wondered if this was what normal people went through when they tried to meet someone from the opposite sex. Being glamorous had saved me from that before.

111

The customers were leaving the pub, sometimes in groups, sometimes in couples. I watched for you, hoping you wouldn't use the rear exit from the building. I wanted to see you once more before you went away, in case we never met again. At last you appeared, walking with your friend and holding her hand. I followed you closely, hoping I would hear her say your name or that I would be able to pick up some other clue about you.

You walked to a sidestreet and I followed you to your car. The red Nissan. You held the passenger door open for her and closed it gently when she was seated. When you were inside you kissed her before starting the engine. As you drove away I memorised the registration number, thinking that if all else failed it might help me trace you again.

Niall's voice beside me said, 'Susan.'

I had guessed he would be there. I turned towards him, but he was invisible. Of course, invisible. But this time I could not see him at all.

'Where are you?' I said.

'Give it up now, Susan.'

'No. Let me see you!'

'You know how to do it. Get down to my level and you'll see me.'

'I can't do that, Niall.'

'Then you know the score. I'll be around when you change your mind.'

He said no more. I tried to find him in that darkened street, used every technique I knew to detect his cloud, bring it to me, but Niall was an adept. He had done this to me once before when he was angry about something, and had sunk so deep into the abyss of invisibility that I had thought I should never find him again. That time he had returned after a few hours. This time, I didn't know. And, because of you, I really no longer cared.

I spent the next day alone, thinking of you, wondering about you, remembering our brief conversation. Everything depended on your being sufficiently intrigued by me to visit the same pub on the Wednesday evening, but I was immature and inexperienced. I felt as unsure of myself as a teenager. Niall knew that, naturally.

At that time I was working on some draft layouts and illustrations for a children's book, and it was an absorbing, detailed job. Late on the Sunday evening I settled down to look at what I had already done and quickly found myself immersed in it again. I continued to work steadily for the next three days. The only distraction was Niall, who had not contacted me since that brief, angry exchange in the street outside the pub. In one sense I had no excuse, because I had known that I was provoking him, but he and I had gone through several bad patches in the past, and after those it was Niall who came to me in search of reassurance or comfort.

All through those three days I was expecting him. Every time the phone in the hall rang, or someone came to the house, I assumed, wrongly, it was him. I found his silence increasingly distracting, and as my date with you on Wednesday evening came closer I was plagued with a guilty need to see him first. At lunchtime that day I left my room and walked over to the pub in Hornsey Rise that was one of his usual haunts. Niall wasn't there, but I saw a few of the other glams and asked if they had any idea where he was. No one had heard from him since the week before.

Gradually, I realised he was deliberately staying away from me. He knew I hated not knowing where he was.

Even so, nothing would prevent me from trying to see you again. I chose my clothes carefully for the date, and took a lot of time over my face and general appearance, determined for once to make a visual impact on a man. I spent a long time in front of the mirror, assessing myself critically, and feeling a little weird for doing so. Being unseen for most of my adult life had made me careless about the way I looked.

I was ready to leave, although I was far too early, when the telephone outside my room rang. I went to answer it and at last it was Niall, speaking from a private phone. I felt a surge of relief. Only then was I certain he was not somewhere around me, hovering in his oblique invisibility.

'Susan,' he said. 'It's me.'

'Where have you been? You've really scared me, hiding like this. Why did you——?'

'I thought you'd like to know,' he said. 'His name's Richard Grey.'

'What?'

'Your friend in the pub. He's called Richard Grey.'

'Niall, how——?'

'He works for BBC News,' Niall said. 'A cameraman. He's twenty-eight years old, lives in West Hampstead, and that was his girlfriend. Do you want to know her name too?'

'No!' I said loudly. 'Niall, how the hell do you know? Are you making it up?'

'You'll find out if you see him. You're about to, aren't you?'

'That's my business,' I said.

'Mine too. Everything you do is my business. Which is actually why I'm calling you. I thought you'd like to know I'm going away for a while.'

Niall never went away anywhere, but the unexpected news made my heart lift. It would give me some time, however short, to get to know you without his interference. I waited for him to say more, and stared blankly at the wall with its noticeboard full of old handwritten messages for the other tenants. Their lives seemed so straightforward to me, so uncomplicated by unseen matters. *Anne, please phone Seb. Dick, your sister called. Party at No. 27 on Saturday night, all invited.*

'Where are you going?' I said in the end, trying to sound as if I didn't care. Or rather, that I did care but not in the way I really felt.

'That's the point. It's in the south of France. Some friends of mine have a villa down there. I don't know the exact address. It's a house near Saint-Raphaël. I'll be staying with them for a week or two.'

I couldn't think of any friends he knew who might own a house anywhere. 'All right,' I said. 'That's a good idea.'

'Wouldn't you like to come with me?'

'You know how busy I am.'

'Yes, but not too busy to see Richard Grey. That's right, isn't it? That's what you'll be doing?'

I said, 'Nothing's definite.'

'It's this evening, isn't it? That's what you agreed with him. A little private meeting between the two of you.'

I felt a familiar, wearying anxiety, that he was not going to let anything change. But even so, the fact that he knew what I was planning . . .

'Were you listening to me?'

'I might have been.'

This was the moment when with hindsight I know I should have removed Niall permanently from my life. I should have ignored him, or put down the phone on him. Maybe nothing of what was to follow would then have happened. But Niall and I had been too close too long, and I allowed his air of nonchalance to aggravate me. I could not easily forget that after the first time he had made himself deeply invisible, he had boasted that he could sustain it indefinitely. No one would ever see him. Not even other people with the glamour. Not even me. I hadn't believed him, but if he had meant it Niall could be anywhere at any time. He was implying that he had been standing there, listening undetected, when I went up to you in the pub. And how had he discovered your name and found out where you worked? He must have followed you somehow. What else had he been doing, and what was he planning?

Trying to keep my voice unconcerned, I said, 'How long did you say you'd be gone?'

'I don't think I did. Why don't I call you when I get back?'

'When will that be?'

'Why should you want to know? If I can get to a telephone I'll ring you when I arrive. Look, I'm going to hang up. We're leaving in an hour.'

I said, 'If you're thinking of interfering, I'll never speak to you again.'

'You've nothing to worry about. You won't be seeing me again for a while. I'll send you a postcard from France.'

I was born twenty-six years ago in an outer suburb of Manchester, close to the Cheshire countryside. My parents were Scots, originally from the west coast near Ayr, but they moved south to England as soon as they were married. My father worked as a payroll clerk in a large office near our house, and my mother did part-time work as a waitress. When my sister Rosemary and I were little she stayed at home to look after us.

As far as I know or can remember my childhood was normal, with no intimation of what I was to become. I was the healthy one of the two of us. My sister, three years older than me, was often ill. One of my clearest memories is of being told to be quiet, to tiptoe around the house so as not to wake or disturb my sister. Silence became a habit, because I was not a rebel. I always wanted to please, and was, or tried to be, a model daughter, every mother's dream. My sister, between illnesses, was the opposite: she was a tomboy, a risk-taker, a noisy presence about the house. I cringed and crept, wishing not to be noticed. It might seem now to be part of a pattern, but at the time the wish to shrink from prominence was only one aspect of my personality. I did the normal things of childhood: I went to school, I made friends, I had birthdays and parties, I fell down and grazed my legs and arms, I learned to ride a bicycle, I wanted to own a pony, I pasted up photographs of pop singers and film stars.

The change in me came with puberty, showing itself only gradually. I cannot remember exactly when I was aware I was different from the other girls at school, but by the time I was fifteen a distinct pattern had emerged. My family rarely took any notice of what I was doing; teachers usually ignored any contribution I tried to make in class; the other kids seemed hardly to realise I was there. I drifted away from my earlier friends one by one. I did well in class and my marks were generally good, but the term-end reports used phrases like 'average ability', 'quiet working', 'steady progress'. The only school subject in which I excelled was art, and this was partly because I had talent, but mostly because the art mistress made an effort to encourage me out of school hours.

It all sounds as if my teenage years passed meekly, but the opposite was the case. I discovered I could get away with bad behaviour. I became a troublemaker in class, emitting rude sounds at teachers, or throwing things across the room, or playing stupid pranks on other kids. I was almost never caught, and I used to enjoy the reactions my misbehaviour caused. I started to steal at school, petty objects of no value, simply because I relished the kick of getting away with it. And yet for all this I remained an averagely popular girl, accepted by everyone but never close to anyone special.

My decreasing visibility became a danger to me. When I was fourteen I was knocked down by a car, the driver claiming he had not seen me on the pedestrian crossing. Fortunately, the injuries were not serious. On another occasion I came close to being badly burned at home, when I was leaning against the mantelpiece over an unlit gas fire and my father entered the room and lit the fire. I vividly recall my feelings of disbelief as it happened, certain that he would not do it. I stood there while the flame popped into life and my skirt caught fire. Even then, my father only realised I was there when I shouted and leaped away, beating at the smouldering fabric.

Because of incidents like these, and others less serious, I developed a phobia about objects and people that could hurt me. Even today I dislike walking in crowded streets, or crossing roads, or standing on railway platforms. Although I learned to drive a car a few years ago I am never at ease when I'm driving, because I can't rid myself of the uneasy feeling that the way I operate the car will make it become unnoticed. I never swim in the sea, because if I got into difficulties I would not be able to make myself seen or heard; I haven't ridden a bicycle since I was twelve; I steer clear of people carrying liquids, after my mother once spilled hot tea on me.

Being unnoticed began to affect my health. Throughout my teens I was debilitated. I suffered one headache after another, fell asleep at unexpected moments, was prone to every infectious disease that went around. The family doctor attributed it all to 'growing up', or congenital susceptibility, but I belatedly know the real cause was my unconscious attempts to stay visible. I *wanted* to be noticed, to be thought the same as everyone else, to live an ordinary life. The wish manifested itself by forcing me into visibility, but at a price. Throughout this time I was slipping in and out, something I know now is a terrible strain.

The only relief was solitude. During the long school holidays, and sometimes at weekends, I often went off by myself into the countryside. It was only a short bus journey south from where I lived, past Wilmslow and Alderley Edge, to a still unspoilt landscape of farmland and woods. Out there, away from the main roads, I could slip happily into the world of the unseen, as if I were freeing myself of clothes or possessions or worries.

It was on one of these trips, when I was about sixteen, that I met Mrs Quayle.

It was she who first noticed me and she who made the approach. I was only aware of a pleasant looking middle-aged woman, walking along the lane towards me with a small dog trotting at her heels. We passed each other, smiled briefly as strangers sometimes do, and went on in our separate directions. It did not sink in at once that she had actually seen me, at a time when I knew I was invisible, and within a few moments I had forgotten about her. Then her dog ran past me and when I looked back I saw she had turned around and was following behind.

We spoke, and the first words she said to me were, 'Dear, do you know that you have glamours?'

Because she was smiling so naturally, and because she looked so harmless, I felt no alarm, but I suppose that had I known what she was I would have taken fright and hurried away. Instead, the oddness of her question interested me and I walked along with her, chattering about the countryside and the weather. I somehow never answered that first direct question, nor did she repeat it. She shared my love of the country, the wild flowers and the peace, and that was enough. We came eventually to her house, a cottage set back from the lane. She invited me in for a cup of tea.

Inside, the house was pleasant and well furnished, with central heating radiators, a television and video, a CD player, telephone, dishwasher and other modern gadgets. She sat down on the sofa to pour the tea, and her dog curled up beside her and went to sleep.

Then, because her first question had been hovering between us unanswered, I asked her what she meant. She had used the word 'glamour' in a way I had never heard before, so she explained that it was an old Scottish word, brought into general English before its meaning became corrupted. In the original sense a 'glammer' was a spell, an enchantment. A young man in love would approach the wisest old woman of his village and pay her for a charm of invisibility to be placed on his beloved, so that she should no longer be coveted by the other young men. Once she had been glammered, or made glamorous, she was safe from prying eyes.

Mrs Quayle asked me if I believed in magic, if I ever had strange dreams, if I could sometimes tell what other people were thinking. She had become intent, and it scared me. As soon as she saw me out there in the lane, she said, she had known that I was glamorous, that I had a psychic power. Was I aware of it? Did I know anyone else like me?

I said I wanted to leave, and I stood up. Her manner changed at once and she apologised for frightening me. As I backed away from her she told me to come to her house again if I wanted to know more, but outside in the lane I ran and ran, full of terror of her. That night I dreamed about her.

I returned to her cottage the following week. She was waiting for me as if we had arranged a time in advance. We said nothing about my running away, and we acted as if we were old friends. It was the first of many meetings, which continued for the next two years.

I now know that what Mrs Quayle told me was only a part of the story, and that it was coloured by her interest in the psychic world. Indeed, she often used the word to describe herself. Invisibility is not in fact a psychic ability, as Mrs Quayle thought, but a natural condition. Many ordinary people have talents, both positive and negative: some can sing in perfect pitch, some have a charismatic personality, some can make other people laugh, some cannot help being repulsive, some are natural leaders, some make friends wherever they go. Some people, a few, one or two like me, are inherently unnoticeable, evanescent, invisible.

I learned a lot from Mrs Quayle, but I also had to learn to reinterpret much of what she told me. For instance, she described the glamours as a kind of psychic aura, or 'cloud', similar in nature to several other mystical manifestations from the astral plane. Because my condition of invisibility was so specific, and to me so unmystical, I felt no rapport with psychic sensitives like clairaudients or spirit mediums, but even so the way she used the word 'cloud' was helpful to me. It enabled me to visualise the transition from one state to the other, a blurring at the edges, a softening of outline, a gradual reduction of detail, and this made it easier for me.

She told me of Madame Blavatsky, the spiritualist and Theosophist, who recorded many accounts of productions and vanishings through use of the cloud, and who claimed to be able to make herself invisible. Of the Ninja sect in medieval Japan, who made themselves invisible to their enemies by use of deception and distraction: a Ninja warrior would dress in clothes that blended with the physical background, then stand at the ready in total immobility for hours, before leaping out with horrid suddenness and violence to waylay and kill. Of Aleister Crowley, who declared invisibility to be a simple doctrine, one he claimed to have proved by parading around the streets of Mexico City in a scarlet robe and golden crown, while no one noticed him. And of the novelist Bulwer-Lytton, who believed himself capable of invisibility, and was often a trial to his friends. When they had gathered in his house he would move among them, fondly believing they could not detect him, then reveal himself with a loud shout, invariably to their dutiful exclamations of surprise and delight.

It was Mrs Quayle who showed me, with a mirror, that I was invisible.

I had never been invisible to myself in mirrors, because I looked in them purposely to see myself, as everyone does, and in expecting to see I noticed and *saw*. But one day Mrs Quayle tricked me, placing a mirror in an unexpected position beyond a door, and following me as I walked towards it. Before I realised what was going on I saw her reflection behind me, and for a few seconds, while I wondered at what I was seeing, I noticed no reflection of myself. Then I understood at last: I was not invisible in the sense that I was transparent, or that the science of optics was somehow being breached, but that the cloud made it difficult for me to be *noticed*.

Mrs Quayle said she could always see me, even when I was invisible to others, even, that time with the mirror, when I was briefly invisible to myself. She was a peculiar, singleminded woman, plain and ordinary in every way but the one she claimed. She was a widow, living alone, surrounded by prosaic snapshots of her family, by her everyday gadgets, by souvenirs of holidays in Florida, Italy and Spain. Her son served as an officer on an oil tanker, both her daughters were married and lived in other parts of the country. She was a practical and paradoxically down-to-earth woman who helped me understand my impractical life, and who filled my head with ideas and gave me a vocabulary for what I am and for what I am capable of doing. We became friends in an odd, unequal way, but she died suddenly of angina a few months before I moved to London.

My meetings with her were occasional and sometimes separated by several weeks. I was in the final stages of school during the time I knew her, creeping almost unnoticed through 'A' Levels, passing my subjects with medium marks, gaining a distinction only in Art. The strain to stay visible continued, and my last year at school was punctuated by fainting fits and attacks of migraine. I was only completely relaxed when I was alone or with Mrs Quayle, and her death, a few days before I sat my 'A' Level exams, made me feel isolated and helpless.

On my eighteenth birthday my parents produced a surprise. They had taken out a small endowment policy for me when I was born, and now it had matured. I had been offered a place at an art college in London, but the only grant I qualified for would cover the fees alone, not living expenses. The endowment policy was almost enough to pay for these, and my father said he was prepared to make up the rest. So, at the end of the summer I was able to leave home for the first time, and I travelled to London.

Three years followed. College is a time of transition for every student. There is the process of growing away from school friends and family, of mixing with an entirely new group of contemporaries, of acquiring skills or knowledge for use in adult life, and there is the gradual taking shape of a new mature personality, an independent human being. All these happened to me, but something that was unique to me also changed. I came to terms with the fact of my invisibility, knowing that it was a part of me and would not go away.

I shared a flat with two other young women from the art college. Although I made myself visible to them when I had to, for most of the three years they took it for granted that I was somewhere around, perhaps closed away inside my own bedroom, separate from them. This was the first change forced on me, because through these women I learned that an invisible person has a real existence in the minds of others, and is known and recognised and accepted as being there, but is simply ignored for not being fully *functional*. They noticed me when I wished them to, but for the rest of the time they acted as if I was not there.

College itself was more difficult. Naturally, I was required to attend, and to be seen to attend, and to complete my courses and assignments, and submit work and in general make my presence felt. I survived the first year by pushing myself to the limit. In this way I made the lecturers aware of me, but it was at the expense of my health. From the beginning of the second year the pressure was in theory less, because we were encouraged to work more alone. I chose a large but general course in commercial art, because here, when working with other students, I could blend with the crowd. Even so, the strain of being visible was a terrible one, and I was constantly worn out. I lost weight, suffered recurring headaches and frequently felt sick.

Living in London brought another change. At home I had grown used to eluding authority. At school it was the stupid pranks, the meaningless thievery, but outside school I had learned that it was easy for me to get away with not paying fares, that I never had to spend money in shops unless I chose to. Now that I was in London, and surviving on a tiny fixed income, it soon became a habit to avoid payment. From there it became a way of life.

Living in a big city was a part of the corrupting process, because in London it is possible even for normal people to lose themselves in the crowd. After the first few weeks, in which I was adjusting to the change, I felt more at home than I would ever have thought possible. London is made for invisible people. It deepened my state of anonymity, made my condition a natural means of survival. No one has identity in London unless they claim it.

Because I had no idea how the system worked, I bought a ticket when I used the Underground the first time, but after that I never again paid a fare. Swallowing my fear of crowds, I used the trains and buses as my free taxi service, the cinemas and theatres for my free entertainment. Invisibility refreshed me. A day in what I thought of as my shadow world, drifting unnoticed along streets and through buildings, gave me a feeling of power. This was the function of invisibility, to move on the outer limits of the world, to be undetected, unseen. I never tired of it, and fled into the shadows as a cure for the emotional and physical drain on me caused by my efforts to be real.

Because I did not know how to see, and was concerned mostly with myself, it took me several months to realise I was not alone.

There were other invisibles in London, something I should have realised was inevitable.

The first one I noticed was a young woman of about my own age. I was waiting for a train in Tottenham Court Road Underground station. As I glanced along the platform I saw her sitting on one of the benches, leaning back against the tiles of the curving tunnel wall. She looked tired, dirty and distraught. My first reaction was concern for a stranger: I thought she had been taken ill. Tube stations have large numbers of down-and-outs moving around in them, especially in winter, and many of these people are alcoholics, derelicts. Then I looked more closely and as I did so I felt there was something indefinably familiar about her. It was an insight I shrank from, because I knew I was recognising something of myself in the dishevelled, pathetic creature.

She moved suddenly, righting herself on the seat, and she stared directly at me. I saw the surprise in her face, but it faded at once and she looked away again.

She had *noticed* me! But I was invisible, secure in my shadow world!

I hurried away into one of the access tunnels, frightened at the ease with which my cloud had been penetrated. I reached the concourse at the bottom of the escalators, where many passengers were moving about, heading up to the streets above, riding down to catch one of the trains, all of them moving past me as if I were not there. The renewed anonymity reassured me, and I became more interested than frightened. Who was that woman? How could she have seen me?

Sensing the answer I returned to the platform, but a train had been in and out and she was no longer there.

The second time it happened the invisible was someone I later found out was known as a 'Harry', a middle-aged male invisible. I saw him in Selfridges, moving through the food hall, dragging a large plastic sack behind him. He was browsing along the counters, helping himself to tins and packets of food, tossing them casually into the sack. I sensed the aura of invisibility about him, but followed him unobtrusively until I was sure. I moved so that I stood before him.

His reaction, as soon as he saw me, appalled me. He looked surprised, not because I was another invisible but because he obviously interpreted my open expression and smiling face as a sexual invitation. He looked me up and down, then to my horror raised his sack and crammed it under his arm. He advanced on me, his face contorted by a dreadful leering rictus. For a moment all I could focus on was his mouth: the sight of his teeth, black and broken, and his loose, wet lips. I backed away from him, but he had fixed on me and wanted me. He said something, but the clamour of the busy store spared me from hearing the exact words he spoke, although his meaning was clear enough. He looked huge. All I wanted was to correct my blunder and get away from him. I turned to run and immediately collided with someone, another man, but he could not see me. The invisible man was almost on me, reaching out with his free arm, the hand clawing to grab me. I knew that being in a public place had no safety for me, that if he caught me he could do anything he liked in full view of everyone. I had never been so frightened. I rushed away, dodging between the shoppers, knowing he was behind me. I wanted to scream but no one would hear me! It was lunchtime, there were hundreds of people in the store, and none of them moved to get out of the way. In such a crowd there was no help for me, only obstacles against me. I looked back at him once again: no longer smiling, he was running with terrifying agility, his face nakedly angry, a predator deprived of his prey. This glimpse of him so scared me that I almost fell. My legs were weak, the fear paralysing me. I knew I was plunging ever more deeply into invisibility, my involuntary protection against danger, but useless against the man and exposing me more than ever to the peril in which he would put me. I forced myself through the crowd, aiming for the nearest exit.

When I next looked back I was in the street and the man had given up. I saw him by the store entrance, leaning against the wall, winded, watching me flee. Even then he still made me feel menaced, and I continued down Oxford Street, running until I could keep going no longer. I never saw him again.

These two encounters were my introduction to the larger shadow world of invisible people. After the incident in Selfridges I began to notice more and more invisibles around London – as if seeing the first two had opened my eyes to the existence of the rest – but I kept out of their way. I soon learned the places where they gathered: they were found where food could be stolen, or a bed found, or where crowds tended to congregate. I usually saw at least one other invisible person whenever I went to a super-market, and department stores were frequent haunts. Some invisibles lived in these large shops or in furniture stores. Others were nomadic, drifting around to sleep in one hotel or another, or breaking into people's houses to borrow unused beds or to stretch out on furniture. Later, I discovered that invisible people have a loose network of contacts and meeting places: there are concert halls, theatres and hotels where they gather, and even two or three particular pubs in different parts of London where some of them meet regularly.

Inevitably, I was drawn to them. I soon realised that the man who had attacked me in Selfridges was not typical of them all, but neither was he all that unusual. As male invisibles grow older many of them become loners, outcasts even from the outcast society of their fellows, uncaring of how they act. Most of them are in need of medical attention. Sometimes I hear about the death of one of them: a body found in a shop, or in a doorway, or on a bench beside the Thames. The authorities generally have difficulty making an identification, but the invisibles know who it is.

More usually the invisibles are young, or youngish. Their backgrounds are often like mine: an isolated childhood and adolescence, then running away from home in late teens, drawn to London or one of the other big cities. The oldest invisibles I know of are in their early or middle thirties. I don't like to wonder why so few of them survive longer.

Collectively, the invisibles are a paranoid lot, believing them-selves rejects from society, despised, feared and forced into crime. They are terrified of normal people, but they profoundly envy them. They are even frightened of other invisibles, but when they are together they brag about themselves to each other, making increasingly ludicrous claims about what they have been doing recently. There are even some who take the paranoia to the other extreme, claiming the inherent superiority of invisibility, the power that derives from the condition, the freedoms that follow in its wake.

Almost every invisible I know is a hypochondriac, and with

good reason. Health is an obsession, because illness is incurable except by nature taking its course. Many invisibles have VD and other communicable diseases, and most of them suffer from bad teeth. Life expectancy is short. A large number of them are alcoholics, or well on the way. A few take drugs, but regular supplies are hard to come by. None of them has a job, or somewhere permanent to live. Invisibles can dress well if they want to, because clothes are easy to steal, but in practice most of them wear the same clothes every day, becoming increasingly shabby and smelly until they take the trouble to steal something new. Many go around dragging huge cases and trunks stuffed with their belongings. But what they care about most of all is their health, and they talk about it endlessly. Many of them carry quantities of patent medicines, the ones they can steal most easily, and they are constantly trying out new ones.

And, like other groups of social misfits, the invisibles have their own slang. They all know about the 'cloud'. There are 'slippers' (people who sleep in department stores, which are known as 'stations') and 'homers' (people who break into houses overnight). Stolen food is called 'stuff'; money (never used) is called 'ring'; the older male invisibles are all known as 'Harry' by the women and 'sackers' by the men. Ordinary people are called 'normals' or 'fleshers' and they live in the 'hard' world, while the invisibles call themselves the 'glams'. It is part of their defensive but bragging paranoia to think of themselves as glamorous.

I was never really one of them. I knew it and they knew it. From their point of view I was only half glam, able to enter and leave their world at will. I was never trusted, never accepted, I was betrayed by my clean (but not always new) clothes, by my equanimity about illness, by my cared for, unhurting teeth. I had an identity in the hard world, a place where I lived, a college course I attended, and a GP and dentist I could visit. I went home to my parents at Christmas and Easter, escaping, as the invisibles saw it, to the world of the fleshers.

Even so, entering the glamorous world was an important step. For the first time since my early teens I was meeting people like myself. That to them my invisibility was a question of degree made no difference to me. I was more invisible than not, and it constantly affected me. The glams tried to reject me, but only because for most of them there was no escape.

Mixing with the glams had another attraction too. I found invisibility refreshing, making the next return to the hard world a little bit less of an effort, if only in the transition. Once I met the real invisibles, pathetic, frightening and isolated as I found them to be, I discovered that my option of visibility was more accessible. At first I was repelled by their hopelessness and paranoia, but later I found them a source of strength. Contact with their clouds gave me the energy to re-enter the real world, and knowing them gave me the thrill of the glamorous life. I was still young and inexperienced, and I was attracted to both versions of myself.

Then, in my last term at college, when I knew I was going to have to make decisions about the future, and when I was less certain than ever of how I wanted to live, I met Niall.

Niall was different from any other invisible I had met. He was completely unseeable by anyone who was not another invisible, his cloud an impenetrable screen against the world. He was more deeply embedded than any of the others, more remote from reality, a thin wraith in a community of ghosts.

But his separateness was also in his personality, a part of him. While most invisibles lamented their lack of identity, Niall relished his.

He was the only invisible I ever found physically attractive. He was fit, handsome, elegant, fast-witted. He bathed regularly, kept his hair tidy, smelled clean and wholesome. He was at ease in his body, and worried no more about illness than I did. He dressed rakishly, choosing stylish modern clothes and the most flowery colours. He smoked Gauloise cigarettes and travelled light, while the average glam worried too much about his health to be a smoker, and carried vast quantities of belongings wherever he went. Niall was funny, outspoken, rude to people he disliked, full of ideas and ambitions, and completely amoral. While I and some of the other glams had scruples about our parasitic lives, Niall saw invisibility as freedom, an advantage over normal people, a means of spying on them, taking from them, outdoing them.

Something else I found attractive and different was that he was actually involved in something he believed in. Niall wanted to be a writer. He was the only invisible I knew who stole books. He was forever in and out of libraries and bookshops, borrowing or stealing poetry, novels, literary biographies, travel books. He was always reading, and when we were together he would sometimes read aloud to me. Books were the only aspect of his life where he had a conscience: when he was finished with a book he would leave it somewhere it could be found, or he would even return it. Paddington Library was the place he frequented most often, conscientiously returning what he had borrowed, and sometimes pretending guilt to me if he thought the book's return was overdue.

When he was not reading he was writing. He filled innumerable notebooks with his work, writing slowly in his ornate and flamboyant handwriting. I was never allowed to see what he had written, nor did he read it to me, but I was supremely impressed.

This was Niall when I first met him and I fell under his spell at once. He was a few months younger than me, but in every other way he was wiser, more exciting, more experienced, more stimulating than anyone I had ever known. When I completed the art school course and came away with my diploma, I no longer had any doubt about what I wished to do. The glamour had become a sanctuary from the hard world and I fled into it.

The sheer excitement of being with Niall swept aside my doubts. Everything we did was heightened by irresponsibility, and because I admired him so much I tried to impress him by being like him, and more. We brought out the worst in each other, his amorality satisfying my wish for a better life.

I became thoroughly assimilated into the nomadic world of the glamorous. We lived nowhere and drifted from one overnight squat to the next, sleeping in the spare room in someone's house, or in a department store or hotel. We ate well, stealing nothing but fresh food as we needed it. When we wanted cooked food we went to the kitchens of hotels or restaurants. We had as many new clothes as we wanted, we were never cold, never hungry, never uncomfortable, never forced to sleep rough, never at risk of discovery. I feel guilty about it when I look back. I was easily led, and Niall awakened the restlessness in me, the last stirring of adolescence.

Our reckless life as invisibles continued for about three years. It all runs together in my memory, blurring into what I would like to think of as a youthful escapade. I still often remember specific incidents, when the heady feeling returns to me and I think again how clever and superior we thought we were. It was an ideal life: everything we wanted was literally within our grasp, and we never answered to anyone.

In time, inevitably, I became less dazzled by Niall. I saw that he was not so original after all, that many people in the real world affected bright colours, unusual hairstyles, French cigarettes. Niall was different only when compared with the other invisibles, and they no longer mattered to me. His interest in books, and in becoming a writer, was still admirable, but he held me at arm's length. I continued to find him attractive, but with our increasing intimacy I realised that most of what impressed me was superficial.

There was another destructive seed, steadily growing. Because Niall and I were constantly in each other's company, I drew strength from his cloud. It became increasingly easy for me to slip over into visibility, something Niall hated because he thought it gave me an advantage over him. If he ever saw me visible he would fly into a rage and accuse me of endangering us both, of risking our discovery. The reality was that he was profoundly resentful of his condition. He was jealous of me, and saw my ability to move in the real world as a freedom from him. The paradox was that the freedom emanated from him. I needed to be close to him to gain the normality I craved, and which he so feared, but the closer I grew the more dependent on him I became and the less able to enjoy or use my presumed freedom.

Other needs were surfacing. As I grew older I began to develop a conscience about all the food and property we were stealing. A defining incident occurred in the Hornsey branch of Sainsbury's: as we were leaving with our bags of food I saw an open till full of cash, and on an impulse I took a handful of ten-pound notes. It was a foolish and needless theft, because money was immaterial to us. A few days later I found out that the woman on the checkout had lost her job, and for the first time I realised that other people were being hurt. It was a sobering moment and it changed everything.

By this time I was hungering for an ordinary way of life: I wanted the dignity of a real job, the knowledge that I would earn what I lived by. I wanted to pay my way, buy food and clothes, pay to see movies, pay to travel on buses and trains. Above all I wanted to settle down, find somewhere I could call home, a place that was mine.

None of it would be possible unless I was prepared or able to be visible for long periods. While I lived rootlessly with Niall, that was out of the question.

These stirrings acquired a practical shape. I wanted to go home, visit my parents and sister, wander around in the places I remembered from childhood. I had been away too long, because since meeting Niall I had not been back to the north. My only contact with home was the occasional letter I wrote to my parents. Even this contact, hurtfully minimal as my parents saw it, was seen by Niall as a breach of our compact of invisibility. In the last twelve months I had written home only once and spoken to them on the phone only three or four times.

I was growing up at last and it was putting a distance between Niall and myself. I wanted something more than he gave me. I could not spend the rest of my life in the shadows. Niall sensed the change, and he knew I was trying to break away from him.

We came eventually to a compromise about my parents, although I knew it would be a disaster. We went to see them together.

Everything went wrong from the start. I had never before seen at close hand how normal people reacted to the presence of an invisible, and the fact that it was Mum and Dad, from whom I was already partly estranged, only added layers of emotional complexity. I was visible throughout the visit, and able to maintain it simply because Niall was with me. Niall of course remained unnoticed. As soon as we arrived I started having to cope with several different problems at once.

In the first place I wanted to behave naturally towards my parents, relax with them and show them I still loved them. I wanted to tell them something of my life in London without revealing the whole truth. And I wanted to try to put right some of the hurt I knew I had caused. But working against this, a constant distraction, was my knowledge that they did not know I had brought with me the man who shared my life, could not see him at all.

Finally, there was the behaviour of Niall himself. He callously exploited the fact that Mum and Dad did not know he was there. When they were asking how I lived, who my friends were, what work I was doing, and while I was attempting to answer with the bland lies I had used in letters, Niall was beside me, talking across me, giving them (unheard) the answers he felt they should have. When we sat down in the evening to watch television, Niall, bored with their choice of programme, started touching my body to distract me. We drove over to Rosemary's house, so I could see her new baby, but Niall, climbing into the back seat of the car beside me, whistled loudly and talked across my parents, infuriating me but leaving me powerless to do anything about it. All through that weekend I was never allowed to forget Niall was there: he stole drinks and cigarettes, yawned with exaggerated boredom whenever my father spoke, he lounged around, used the toilet without flushing it, objected to every suggestion anyone made about where we could go or who we might see, and in short he did everything in his power to remind me that he was the true centre of my life.

How could Mum and Dad not have known he was there?

Even if I set aside Niall's abominable misbehaviour it seemed impossible they could not be aware of him. Yet I was greeted and he was not. They showed not a flicker of curiosity about the unexplained young man who had arrived with me. They spoke only to me, looked only at me. They set no place for him at mealtimes. I was given the single bed in my old bedroom. Even in the cramped confines of my father's car, with Niall smoking up the interior with his cigarettes, they did not acknowledge him. After Niall lit up a second cigarette Mum opened the window on her side, but that was all.

Trying to cope with it – the blatant contradiction between what I knew was happening and how my parents were not reacting – was my major preoccupation. I well knew how they had reacted to my own invisibility in the old days, but then there had usually been ambiguities. This was different: Niall was emphatically there, but somehow they refused to see him. Even so, I was convinced that on some unconscious level they must have been aware of him. His invisible presence created a vacuum, a silent nexus of the whole weekend.

For me it made real the fact that my life in London was a rebellion against my background. I found Dad dull and inflexible, Mum prissily concerned over details that did not interest me. I loved them still, but they could not see that I was growing up, that I was not, and never would be again, the child-daughter they had known a few years before and only glimpsed since. This was Niall's influence on me, of course, and his sardonic interjections, which only I could hear, confirmed my own thoughts in continual counterpoint.

As the visit went on I felt increasingly isolated, cut off from my parents by misunderstandings, alienated from Niall by his behaviour. We had been planning to stay for three nights, but after a blazing row with Niall on the Saturday – invisible together in my bedroom, screaming angrily at each other in the cocoon of our protective clouds – I could no longer stand the strain. In the morning Mum and Dad drove me, us, to the station, and there we said goodbye. My father was stiff and white with suppressed anger, my mother was in tears. Niall was jubilant, dragging me back, as he thought, to our invisible existence in London.

But none of that would ever be the same. Soon after we reached London I left Niall. I made myself visible, I integrated with the real world. I was escaping from Niall at last. I tried to make sure he would never again find me.

He found me of course. I had been in the glamorous world too long and didn't know how to survive without stealing. Because Niall knew where I would go he found me within two months, and from that it was inevitable he would discover where I was living.

Enough time had passed, though, and something had changed. During my two months of solitude I had rented a room, the one in which I still live. It was legally mine, and it was filled with stuff I also thought of as mine, even though in those early days not everything had been paid for. The room had a door and a lock, and it was a place I could retreat into and be myself. It meant more to me than anything else, and nothing would make me surrender it. I was still surviving mostly by shoplifting, but I was full of good resolutions. I was working up a portfolio of drawings, I had contacted one of my old tutors and through his introduction I had already visited one editor in the hope of obtaining commissions. A freelance life, with all its difficulties, was my best hope of independence.

But Niall walked back into my life, assuming we were going to pick up where we had left off. He understood better than anyone what the room signified to me. I should have realised that and kept him out of it somehow, but his easygoing manner deceived me. I showed the room to him proudly. I thought it would make him accept that I had changed.

What it really meant, I quickly discovered, was that he knew where to find me when he wanted me. This was the worst of it: he would turn up at any time of the day or night, wanting company, wanting reassurance, wanting sex. My independence, small though it was, made him change. I saw a new side of him: he became possessive, sulky, bullying. I held on, knowing that the room and what it stood for were my only hope.

Through my first tenuous contacts I started to sell a little work: an illustration for a magazine article, layout work for an advertising agency, lettering for a firm of management consultants. The fees were small to begin with, but the first commissions led eventually to others and I began to build a reputation. Jobs turned up without my soliciting them, I was recommended by one editor to another, I made contact with an independent art studio who passed on freelance work to me. I opened a bank account, printed some letterheads, bought a secondhand computer, and by such tokens felt I was establishing myself in the visible world. As soon as the cheques started arriving I cut back my shoplifting to absolute essentials, and soon I was able to renounce it altogether. It became an article of faith in myself that I would never go back, and although difficult times followed, and one month in particular was extremely hard to get through, I never weakened. I derived real pleasure from making myself visible to cash a cheque in the bank, to line up with everyone else at supermarket checkouts, to try on clothes in shops and produce my chequebook for payment. As a final gesture I took driving lessons and passed the test at my second attempt.

The strain of making myself visible was also less. By working at home I could relax inside the glamour as long as I wished, only becoming visible if I ventured out. I achieved an emotional stability I had never known before. Even Niall began to realise that we had permanently changed. He eventually accepted that the old days were gone for good, but he maintained a claim on me I found almost impossible to resist.

Only I understood the profundity of his invisibility, and how impossible it was for him to function normally in the world. He played on my sympathy, blackmailing me with his pathetic condition. If I tried to insist on my independence, he pleaded with me not to abandon him. He pointed out the advantages I had over him, the stability I had achieved, hinting at the misery and insecurity he had to endure.

I invariably capitulated. He seemed tragic to me, and even though I knew he was manipulating me I let him get away with it. When I tried to resist him he used his invisibility as a weapon against me. Once I started a tentative friendship with Fergus, one of the young illustrators at the studio, and accepted an invitation out with him. Before the date Niall put on such a display of recriminations and wounded jealousy that I almost cancelled. I had never had a real boyfriend, though, and was determined to stand up for myself. I went on the date, but it was ruined by Niall. Niall followed wherever we went, Niall hung around within earshot, Niall kept interrupting every time Fergus said anything to me. The evening was wrecked before it began. It led to a furious row with Niall that night, back in my room, and my hesitant friendship was crushed.

It was Niall at his most troublesome, but it was not all of him. So long as I remained physically faithful to him, and was available whenever he chose to see me, and I did not flaunt my visibility, then he left me to live and work much as I chose.

He was not always around me. Sometimes he would vanish for as much as a week at a time, never saying where he was going, or explaining afterwards where he had been. He told me he had found a place to live, although where it was and how he managed it I never discovered. He claimed to have friends, never identified, who owned property where he could come and go as he pleased. He told me he had started writing in earnest and was submitting his work to publishers. He dropped hints that he was seeing other women, presumably hoping to arouse some sort of possessive response from me, but if they had existed nothing would have pleased me more.

Above all he allowed me to work, to live on the fringes of the real world, to build my self respect. In my distorted world, cursed by natural invisibility, it seemed to be the best I could hope for.

Then, that night in the pub in Highgate, I saw you.

I set off for our date far too early, walking quickly to burn off the nervous energy in me. I wanted to escape from the house, because that was where Niall could find me. I was still burning with anger because of his phone call, the one in which he had taunted me with your name and told me he was about to go away. I knew he was lying about that: Niall never went anywhere he didn't have to. On top of everything else it infuriated me that he would tell me that. I loathed his cleverness. Appearing to relent was a deliberate new tactic, and it had worked: as I walked along I was thinking about him, not about you.

When I reached the High Street in Highgate I started to dawdle, looking in the shop windows, staring without seeing. I was invisible, saving my energy for later. I was trying to concentrate on you and remember what you looked like, recall that feeling of excitement when I had seen you. I realised in my heart that getting involved with you would mean the end of everything with Niall, even though I knew nothing about you. The risk and novelty you presented were preferable to anything in my past.

After eight o'clock I made myself visible and went into the bar where we had met. You were not there. I bought myself a half of bitter, and sat alone at one of the tables. Because it was midweek, and still relatively early in the evening, the pub was almost empty. I let myself subside gently into invisibility.

You arrived a few minutes later. I saw you enter the bar, glance briefly around, then go to the counter. Something stirred at the sight of you, the old thrill. I thought briefly that I should stay unseen, watch you, follow you, hunt you. That was the glam way, the only genuine kick from invisibility, the voyeurism of the hidden. But as you waited at the bar while the barman served your drink, the other part of me took over: you looked so normal, exactly as I remembered you. I was not here for the hunt. I became visible and waited for you to see me.

You walked over, smiling, and stood by the table.

'There you are,' you said. 'I didn't see you when I first came in.'

'I was here.'

'Can I get you another drink?'

'No, thanks. Not yet.'

You sat down across the table from me.

'I was wondering if you'd be here,' you said.

'You must have thought I was mad, coming up to you like that.'

'What was going on?'

'It was a mistake,' I said. 'I thought I recognised you.'

'No you didn't. What was really going on?'

'Well, you know. I wanted to meet you. Don't make me spell it out. I'm still embarrassed about it.'

'OK, I'm pleased to meet you.'

I had reddened, my clumsy approach to you playing back in my mind like some terrible home movie. We talked for a while about how long both of us had been customers in this pub, then at last we exchanged names. I was both pleased and irritated to learn that Niall had been right about your name. I told you I was called Sue; everyone I had ever known called me Susan, but I liked the idea of being Sue with you.

We had a few more drinks and began to relax a little. We talked about the sorts of things I imagined ordinary people talked about when they were getting to know each other: what we did for a living, where we lived, places we both knew, possible mutual friends. You told me about the young woman I had seen you with, that her name was Annette and that she was about to go away for a month to visit relatives. You implied, without saying as much, that she was not a steady girlfriend. I said nothing about Niall.

You suggested a meal, so we went to a French restaurant across the road. You appeared to like me, and I began to be worried in case I was acting too eager. I knew I should behave more coolly, maintain something of a distance to keep your interest alive; I had read about such strategies in magazines! But I was excited. I found I liked you more than I had dared to hope, and it was nothing to do with that first attraction. I was constantly aware of your cloud, its exhilarating haze touching mine like a fingertip. I was drawing from it, holding myself visible without any strain, finding out how easy it was to relax with you and be normal. And you kept *looking* at me! I had never known anyone who looked at me so often, so frankly. I was used to a more furtive world, where invisible people avoided each other's eyes.

When you left the table to visit the toilet I had to close my eyes and breathe steadily, force myself not to overdo it. I could hardly imagine how you were seeing me, or what you must be thinking of me, and I knew I could still ruin everything through eagerness. I was painfully aware of how inexperienced I was. Twenty-six years old, and never alone with a real man before!

At the end of the meal we shared the expense, scrupulously dividing it between us. I was already wondering what was going to happen next. From my own narrow viewpoint you were such a man of the world, talking lightly of past girlfriends, of having travelled to the United States, Australia, Africa, of not having ties or any intention of settling down. Were you taking it for granted that we would go to bed together? What would you think of me if we didn't? What would you think if we *did*?

We walked to your car and you offered to run me home. I was silent in the car, watching the way you drove, thinking how self-confident you were. Niall was so different and so was I. Outside my house you switched off the engine and for a moment you seemed to be waiting for me to invite you in. Then you said, 'Can I see you again?'

I couldn't help smiling at the unconscious irony of the phrase. All your assumptions about me were entirely new. We sat there in the darkened car for several minutes, making plans for a second date on Saturday evening. I wanted more and more to invite you in for coffee or a drink, delay you, but I was scared you would tire of me. We parted with a kiss.

A heatwave broke over London that week, making it difficult for me to work. Things were already slow, because many of the firms I dealt with seemed to want less material during the summer. Hot weather anyway distracted me. Bright sunshine emphasises London's inherent scruffiness, the old buildings showing their cracks and weathering faults, the new ones looking more out of place than ever. I preferred London under grey cloud, the narrow congested streets closed in by dark stone and low roofs, softened by rain. Summer made me want to be out of the place, on a beach or cooling down in mountain passes.

You were an additional distraction, because although I knew I was acting like a teenager the fact was that I was happy. Niall had electrified me and interested me, but he had never made me happy.

The three days passed slowly, giving me plenty of time to indulge my fantasies about you. But distracting me, as before, were insistent thoughts about Niall. I was wondering how long he would be prepared to lie low. The longer he stayed away from me the more uncomfortable I felt, but I also wanted to know you well before he barged back in on me. I remembered his talk of a mysterious trip to France, and doubted again if he was really there.

I was getting ready to go out on the Saturday evening when I heard the phone ringing in the hall outside my room. One of my neighbours took the call, then banged a fist on my door. It was Niall; of course it was Niall. I was expecting you to pick me up in less than ten minutes.

'How are you, Susan?'

'What do you want? I was about to go out.'

'Yes, that's Richard Grey again, isn't it?'

'It doesn't matter who I'm seeing. Can you call back tomorrow?'

'I want to talk now. I'm in France.'

'It isn't convenient,' I said.

His voice was clear and loud in the earpiece. There was none of the usual quiet electronic background noise, the slight echo or delay, the sense of intervening miles.

'I don't care about that,' he said. 'I'm lonely and I want to see you.'

'I thought you were staying with friends. Where are you?'

'I told you. It's a place called Saint-Raphaël.'

'You sound close. Like you're in London.'

'It's a good connection. Susan, I'm missing you. Why don't you come and join me?'

'I can't. I've so much work to do.'

'I thought you said you were about to go out with Richard Grey.'

'Well—'

'It wouldn't take you long to travel here, and you needn't stay more than a few days.'

'I can't afford a holiday,' I said, feeling myself swirling around once again in his manipulations. 'I don't have any money.'

'You don't need money! Get on the first train. Or try flying. We never did that, did we, walking past the security checks and boarding a plane?'

'Niall, this is ridiculous. I can't drop everything.'

'Susan, I need you.'

I was suddenly less sure he was lying. Niall's fits of introspection and loneliness were real enough. If he actually was in London, as I still suspected, he would have abandoned the pretence of being away and come to see me. It made me feel heartless to hear the self pity in his voice, because it was a naked appeal to my better nature, one that had usually worked in the past. I wished he would leave me alone! I stared again at the noticeboard by the telephone. The same messages were there, unanswered.

'I can't think about it now,' I said. 'Call me tomorrow.'

'I know what you're up to, Susan. I know everything about you.'

I said nothing, turning away from the wall and the phone, the coiled cable stretching across my throat. Telephone conversations have an unseen quality, each speaker invisible to the other. I tried to visualise where Niall was: a shuttered room in a French villa, bare polished floorboards, flowers and sunlight, different voices in another room? Or a more prosaic truth: some house in London, one he had broken into so he could use the phone? Or had he got hold of a mobile at last? His voice was so close it was impossible to believe he was in France. If he was so paranoid about you, why had he gone away and left me?

He was crowding me. He always had, but he had found a new way.

'Why aren't you saying anything?' Niall said.

'I don't know what to say.'

139

'You'd better think of something. Grey's parked his car and he's walking towards your house.'

'*What?*' I shouted. 'Niall, where are you?'

'I keep telling you.'

'I don't believe you.'

'Why don't you come here and find out for yourself?'

Niall hung up. The line clicked, went clear, and I heard a whining sound. I was left standing there with the thing in my hand, still tangled up in the cable, listening to the petulant noise. I was turning around to replace the receiver when the doorbell went. I could see your shadow through the frosted glass window. I knew for certain then that Niall's story about being in France was untrue: he must be in one of the houses across the road, watching every movement. Or lurking somewhere in the street, using a mobile.

I stayed upset by the call for the first hour of our date. We still hardly knew each other, and so you probably weren't aware that anything was wrong. We saw a film that evening, then afterwards went for a late supper. When you ran me home in the car I did invite you in. You stayed talking until the early hours and at the end, when you left, our kisses were lingering and intimate. We made plans to meet again the next afternoon and go for a walk on Hampstead Heath.

I slept late in the morning, but still had time for a lazy breakfast and a bath before you were due to call at two thirty. The phone rang five minutes before.

I went into the hall and picked up the phone before anyone else could get to it.

'Susan, it's me.'

'Go away and leave me alone! Please!'

'I'm sorry, I'm sorry! Don't hang up on me!'

'What do you want?'

'I've rung to apologise for yesterday. It's because you made me realise you'd rather be with Richard Grey. I understand, I really do. I don't want to lose you, but I've always known I would one day.'

His voice was clear and close, almost as if he was in the next room. I was trembling. As he spoke I was leaning backwards away from the phone, craning my neck to look through the fanlight at the houses opposite. Behind which window was he standing? If he was on a stolen mobile, was he closer even than that?

'Why can't you leave me alone?' I said. 'I simply want to lead a normal life, and with you it's never going to be possible.'

'Yes, but why are you doing this to me?'

'Richard's only a friend.' It was a lie, because already you had become more than that. Perversely, I wanted Niall to be angry with me. That would make it easier.

'If he doesn't matter to you, why don't you come and see me?'

'I don't even know where you are.'

'I've told you.'

'You're still in London somewhere.'

'No, I'm not. I'm in a rented villa on the side of a hill outside Saint-Raphaël. I'd like you here with me.'

'Why do you *always* ring me just before I see Richard?'

'Are you seeing him again already?'

'I might be,' I said. 'I mean—'

'I expect he's outside your house right now,' said Niall.

'What? Can you see him?'

'I can see everything.'

'Stop it, Niall! Listen, if you will promise to stop tormenting me I'll come and see you in France.'

'All right,' he said. 'When?'

'Straight away. Tomorrow, if you like. Wait a minute—'

The doorbell had rung, and I could see your familiar shape against the glass. While the receiver swung on its cable I opened the front door. You kissed me and we embraced for a few seconds. I explained I was in the middle of a conversation and showed you into my room. I made sure the door was closed, then went to shut the front door too. Across the road, the long terrace of tall houses, dozens of windows.

I cupped my hand over the mouthpiece.

'Sorry, Niall,' I said. 'It was someone for Jenny upstairs.'

'Don't lie to me, Susan. I know Grey's there.'

'Tell me where you are in France. If I were to come, how would I find you?'

'OK, you reach Marseille somehow. There's a bus from the Hôtel de Ville in Marseille – it goes to Nice, along the corniche.

When you get to Saint-Raphaël you walk away from the village, following signs up the hill to the abbey. You'll see the house after about a mile, it's painted white, and . . .'

I let him finish, then said, 'Why are you making all this up?'

'When will you leave? Tomorrow morning?'

'I've had enough. I'm going to go now.'

'Not yet!'

'I've got to. Goodbye, Niall!'

I put down the phone before I heard anything else. I was still trembling because I was certain that the story about France was a lie. What was he up to?

I was too upset to see you straight away, so I leaned against the front door for a few moments, trying to steady myself. Something moved outside, vaguely blurred through the frosted glass. I started with alarm and backed away. I think it was only a bird, or someone walking down the road.

I thought of you, waiting inside my room, only a few feet away. All I wanted was to be with you, but Niall intruded at every step. He must know our plans! I remembered the terrible dread that Niall could achieve a level of invisibility which even I could not penetrate. He could be with me every moment I was with you!

It was madness to think he was capable of such treachery. As I stood alone in the hallway, plucking up the courage to go in and see you, I wondered, not for the first time, if invisibility itself was a form of madness. Niall himself had once described it as the inability to believe in oneself, a failure of identity. The glams led a mad life, riddled with phobias and neuroses, paranoiac in their creed, parasitic on society, predatory, vain, tragic, sexually frustrated, emotionally retarded. Their perception of the real world was distorted, a classic definition of derangement. If so, my own wish for normality would be a quest for sanity, a search for belief in myself and a sense of my own identity.

Niall's hold on me was the desperate clutching of the madman, the clawed fingers lunging through the bars of the asylum cell.

To escape I had to put the madness behind me. Not solely to cure myself, but to change my knowledge of the invisible world. While Niall made me believe he was haunting me, his grip was still tight around me. My only hope of normality was disbelief in him.

You were standing by the window in my room, glancing through one of the magazines that were on my desk.

'I'm sorry about that,' I said. 'A friend.'

'You look pale. Is everything all right?'

'I need fresh air. Shall we go to the heath?'

So we did. I collected my bag and we drove to Hampstead. It was another hot afternoon and there were people all over the heath, enjoying London's unpredictable summer. We strolled around all afternoon, arms linked, talking of this and that, looking at the other people, sometimes kissing. I loved being with you.

That evening we went to your flat and there we made love for the first time. I felt secure in your flat, believing that Niall could not find his way to it, and if he could find it then not get inside it, and if he could do even that then certainly not yet, and so I was more relaxed with you than I had ever been. A summer storm blew up while we were in bed, and we lay there in the sulphurous evening with the windows open, while the thunder rolled across the roofs and the cloudburst flooded the street litter among the cars. It felt delicious and illicit to be curled up naked with you, listening to the weather.

You dressed and went to buy some take-away food, and when you returned I put on your dressing gown and we sat side by side on the bed, chewing our way through chunky shish kebabs. I was as happy as I had ever been.

Then the phone rang and it was as if someone had thrown a damp sheet across me. I went rigid. I watched you as you left the room, and listened as you went through the doorway of the next room, heard you crossing the room, heard you pick up the receiver. There was a short silence.

You said, 'All right, Mick. No, I understand. It's OK. I knew it would be difficult. Right. See you!'

The tension drained out of me. I cursed myself again for letting Niall manipulate my feelings even when he was absent. You returned to the bedroom with a bottle of wine and two glasses, closed the curtains, switched on a lamp. I tried to look as I had been feeling two minutes earlier.

'That was about next week,' you said. 'I was supposed to be going to Turkey, but it's been cancelled. Are you OK, Sue?'

'I'm fine. So what will you do instead?'

'I'll find something. I can ring round to a few people, find out what's going on. Or I could easily take a break. I've been busy recently.' The cork came out of the bottle and you filled our glasses. 'What about you? Do you have a lot of work on?'

'There's hardly anything. Everyone's away.'

'Look, there's something I've long wanted to do, an idea for a film. I need to research something. It might not come to anything, so I've been waiting until I can make it an excuse for a trip. Would you like to go with me?'

'A trip?' I said. 'When?'

'We could leave more or less straight away, if you're not busy.'

'But where would we go?'

'That's the idea for the film. Have I mentioned my postcards yet?'

'No.'

'I'll show you.' You left the bedroom again and went into the room you called your study. You returned a few moments later carrying an old shoe box. 'I don't really collect the things. I hoard them. I bought most of them a year or two ago, but I've added a few others since. They're nearly all pre-war. Some of them go back to the last century.'

We pulled out the cards and spread them on the bed. You had sorted them into groups by countries and towns, with neat labels for each section. About half the cards were British and they were unsorted. The rest were from Germany, Switzerland, France, Italy, a few from Belgium and Holland. Almost all of them were black-and-white, or sepia-tinted. Many of them had handwritten messages on the back, conventional greetings from holidaymakers to their friends and relatives still at home.

'What I want to do is visit some of these places. Try to find the same views today, compare them with the postcards, and see how the places have changed in the meantime. As I said, it might be the basis for a film, but what I'd really like to do is go and have a look. What about it?'

The cards were fascinating. Frozen moments of a lost age: city centres almost free of traffic, travellers in plus fours parading on foreign sea fronts, cathedrals and casinos, beaches with bathers in modest costumes, strollers in straw hats, mountain scenery with funicular railways, palaces and museums and broad, deserted plazas.

'You want to go to all these places?' I said.

'No, just a few. I thought I'd concentrate on France, in the south. A lot of the cards are from there.' You took some of the postcards from me. 'It's really only since World War Two that the Riviera has been developed for tourism. Many of these cards show the places before then.'

You started going through them, pulling out a few examples to show me. I saw famous places, viewed in unfamiliar ways. One of the sets of cards was of the Mediterranean coastline around Saint-Raphaël. The coincidence was striking, and my fear of Niall suddenly hit me.

'Couldn't we go somewhere else, Richard?' I said.

'Of course we could. But this is where I'd *like* to go.'

'Not France. I don't want to go to France.'

You looked so disappointed, the cards spread out on the bed around us.

I said, 'What about some of the other places? Switzerland, for instance?'

'No, it's got to be the south of France. Well, I can go another time.'

I found myself running through the same excuses I had used on Niall. 'I'd love to, really I would. But I'm broke at the moment.'

'We'd go in my car. I could pay for everything. I'm not hard up and I can probably claim it against tax.'

'I don't have a passport.'

'That's easy. I can get you one overnight. There's an office in the BBC—'

'No, Richard. I'm sorry.'

You were picking up the postcards, restoring them to their meticulous order.

'You're not telling me the real reason, are you?'

'No. OK, the truth is there's someone I know, someone I don't want to run into. He's in France at the moment. Or I think he is, and—'

'Is he the boyfriend you've gone out of your way never to mention?'

'Yes. How do you know?'

'I assumed there must be someone else.' The postcards were all put away now, restored to their neat row in the shoe box. 'Are you still seeing him?'

Again, your innocently ironic choice of words. I started to tell you about Niall, trying to put the reality into terms you would accept. I described him as a long-time boyfriend, someone I had known since I was young. I said that we had grown away from each other but that he was reluctant to let me go. I characterized him as possessive, childish, violent, manipulative. Niall was all of these, but of course they were only a part of what he meant to me.

We discussed the problem for a while, you putting the reasonable case that there was practically no chance we would see him, and anyway in the unlikely event we did then Niall would be forced, by seeing us together, to acknowledge that I had left him. I was adamant, saying that you could not conceive the influence he had over me. I wanted to run no risk of meeting him.

Even as we were saying all these things, I was thinking about my own doubts about where Niall might actually be. I still had to confront that problem. To believe that Niall was anywhere *other* than Saint-Raphaël was to court madness.

'If you're finished with him, Sue,' you said, 'he's going to have to live with the idea sooner or later.'

'I'd rather it was later. I want to be with *you*. We could go somewhere else, anywhere else.'

'All right. Where do you suggest?'

'What I'd really like is a spell out of London. Couldn't we simply get in your car and drive somewhere?'

'In Britain, you mean?'

'Maybe it sounds dull to you, but I've lived mostly in towns. There are whole areas of Britain I've never seen. Couldn't we tour around?'

You seemed surprised, your offer of a trip to the French Riviera exchanged for my rather limp idea of a drive around Britain, but that was what we finally agreed to do. When you took the cards back to your study I went with you, looking at the oddments of film equipment you had collected. You seemed embarrassed about them, complaining they took up space and collected dust, but for me they gave an insight into you before we met. Your

146

awards were in the study too, half-hidden behind a stack of film cans.

'You didn't tell me you were famous!' I said, taking down the Prix Italia and reading the inscription.

'That was luck. Anyone could have won it that year. There were good stories all over the place.'

I read it aloud, finding it difficult to make out the words in the dimly lit corner in which it was kept. '*Richard Grey, camera operator, BBC Television News. Special Award. News filming in circumstances of extreme personal danger.* What happened?'

'Nothing special. It was the sort of thing news crews get into from time to time.' You took the trophy from me and returned it to its shelf, even further in the background and out of sight. You led me back into the bedroom. 'I need another drink.'

'Tell me,' I said.

'It was a riot in Belfast. The sound recordist was there too. It was nothing special, whatever the award people said later.'

'Richard, please tell me about it.'

You were looking uncomfortable. 'I don't often talk about it.'

'Go on.'

'It was part of the job. We all took it in turns to go to Northern Ireland. I didn't mind being there. You get paid extra because it's fairly difficult work. I've never been put off by that sort of thing. Filming is filming, and you find problems with every job. Well, that day there'd been a Protestant march and we'd been out on the streets for that. In the evening we were at the hotel having a few drinks. Then word came in that the army were sending in some Saracens to sort out some kids who were throwing stones in the Falls Road. We talked about whether we should go down there; we were all tired, but in the end Willie and I – Willie was the sound man – decided to go and have a look. The reporter had already gone to bed, but we got him up. I loaded the camera with night stock, and one of the army Land-Rovers gave us a lift.

'It didn't look like much when we got there. A bunch of teenagers were hurling stuff around. We were behind the troops, fairly well shielded, and nothing much seemed to be going on. These incidents generally fizzled out around midnight. But then it suddenly got worse. They started throwing petrol bombs and there were obviously some older men out there too. Am I boring you?'

'No, of course you're not! Go on!'

'The army decided they had to break it up and they fired plastic bullets. Instead of scattering, the kids kept on pelting us. When the troops rushed them, Willie and I went forward with them. That's generally the safest place, behind the troops. We ran about a hundred yards and came straight into a Republican ambush. There were snipers in houses, and the side street had a whole gang of people waiting with petrol bombs.

'Everything went mad. Willie and I were separated from the reporter, and didn't see him again until later. The soldiers were dashing about and we were in the thick of it. I filmed all the way through. I suppose I got a bit carried away. Nothing hit us, but we had a couple of near misses. Somehow, we got in among the people who were shooting at the troops, and we were filming right in front of them. They were too busy to notice us. But then the troops came back with plastic bullets, and everyone scattered at last. We were still there in the middle of it all. Well, we got away in the end and we had some good footage.'

You grinned, trying to minimise the story. The description suddenly reminded me of a particularly horrifying sequence on TV, one that had been shown several times before being with-drawn for use as prosecution evidence.

I said, 'Was that the famous bit of film where the woman's hair caught fire?'

'Yes.'

'And the one where you see the face of the man who shot the soldier?'

'Yeah. That was my film.'

I said, 'When you were there, actually filming, what did it feel like?'

'I can't remember much about it now. It simply happened.'

'You said you got carried away. What did you mean?'

'Sometimes you're so involved with the filming that you stop thinking about it. You don't notice what's going on, except what you can see through the viewfinder.'

'Were you excited?'

'I suppose so.'

'And no one noticed you?'

'Not really, no. It was as if I had become . . . You know, as if they couldn't see me.'

I asked no more questions, because I knew by then what had happened. I could see it in my mind: you and the sound man, running and crouching, linked by the film equipment, in the thick of the action, filming by instinct. You said you had had a few drinks, that you were tired, that no one seemed to notice you. I could identify the feeling exactly, imagine how you must have felt. For those few moments your cloud had defensively thickened around you and the other man, and taken you through the danger invisibly.

We spent three more days in London, ostensibly preparing for our trip but in reality using the time to get to know each other better, and to spend many hours in bed. Your bachelor existence made me feel domestic. We talked about redecorating your flat, I made you buy kitchenware, and as a present I gave you a huge houseplant for your living room. You seemed bemused by it all but I had never felt more blissful.

We left London on the Thursday morning, driving north on the M1 motorway with no destination in mind, just a shared wish to be on our own together. I was still nervous that Niall might be somewhere around. Only when we were in your car, speeding away, did I finally feel safe from him.

We stopped for the first night in Lancaster, checking into a small hotel near the university. We rested after the long drive, feeling happy, anticipating the holiday together. That evening we made plans for the next day, touring around the Lake District. We discovered we were both lazy about sightseeing. We were content to drive to a place, walk around briefly and take a few snapshots, perhaps have a meal or a drink, then drive to somewhere else. I liked being driven by you and found your car smooth and comfortable. With our things in the luggage space at the rear, the back passenger seat was empty, and so we used it as a dump for the tourist guides and maps, the food we bought to eat on the way, a bag of apples and chocolate, souvenirs, and all the other litter you accumulate when travelling. For three days we followed an erratic route, crossing and recrossing the north of the country: from the Lakes we went to the Yorkshire Dales, then briefly visited the hills of southern Scotland before returning to the north-east coast of England. I loved the contrasts in the British scenery, the swift transitions from low to high ground, from industry to open countryside.

We left the north country and headed down the flat eastern side. You said you had never been to this part of the country before, so it was new to both of us. You still seemed puzzled by me, but were clearly cheerful enough on your own terms. The longer we were together the more I felt I was breaking out. An unhappy, inadequate life was behind me at last.

But then, on the fifth day, came the first of the intrusions.

We had arrived in a village called Blakeney on the north coast of Norfolk, and were staying in a bed-and-breakfast in the narrow street that led down to the shore. I disliked the look of the village as soon as we arrived, but we had been driving for several hours and all we wanted was a place to stay for the night, before visiting Norwich the next day. As soon as we had taken our luggage to our room we went straight out to find dinner, leaving the bags unopened. When we returned, all my clothes had been removed from my bag and were laid out in neat piles on the bed. Each garment had been carefully folded.

'It must be the woman who owns the place,' you said.

'But surely she wouldn't come in and interfere with our stuff?'

I went down to find her, but she had already gone to bed.

The following night, in a Norwich hotel, I was woken up in the small hours by the sudden and unpleasant feeling of having been hit by something. You were asleep. I reached over to switch on the lamp and as I did so something moved quickly down the pillow and on to the mattress. It was hard and cold. I sat up in fright, twisting away from whatever it was, and got the light on. What I found in the bed beside me was a cake of soap, quite dry, perfumed, the brand name engraved into its surface. You stirred but still did not wake. I climbed out of bed, and almost at once discovered the coloured foil wrapper. It had been neatly opened and laid flat on the carpet. I stared dumbly at it, wondering what on earth it meant. Finally, I climbed back into bed, switched off the light, then lay deep under the covers, holding on to you. I did not sleep again that night.

In the morning you suggested driving westwards, right across the widest part of the country, to visit Wales. I was preoccupied with the event in the night and simply agreed. We had left the road map in the car, so I offered to go down and collect it.

The car was where we had left it the night before, in the hotel park. There was a key in the ignition and the engine was running.

My first thought was that you must have left it running all night by mistake, but when I tried the door I found it was locked. The same key was used for both. Trembling, I opened the driver's door with the key you had given me, and reached in for the one in the ignition. It was brand new, as if recently bought, or stolen.

I hurled it as hard as I could into the shrubbery surrounding the car park. Back in the room, when I handed you the road map, you asked me what the matter was. I did not know what to say, so I told you my period was due to start, as in truth it was, but the real reason was a growing dread of the inevitable.

I was silent all through breakfast, and stayed deep inside my terrified introspection as we drove along the straight roads that crossed the Fens.

Then you said, 'I'd like an apple. Do we have any left?'

'I'll look,' I managed to say.

I turned around in the seat, something I had done many times in the last few days, but this time I was shaking with fear.

The paper bag containing the apples was on the part of the passenger seat directly behind you. Everything else was there, heaped into a pile on that side: the maps, your jacket, my holdall, the shopping bag with the food for our picnic lunch. It was all on one side of the bench seat: every time we put the stuff behind us we instinctively placed it there, leaving the other side empty.

Leaving room for another passenger.

I forced myself to look at the place, behind my seat. The cushion was indented, bearing weight.

Niall was in the car with us.

I said, 'Stop the car, Richard!'

'What's the matter?'

'Please! I'm going to be sick! Hurry!'

You pulled the car over at once, running it up on the verge. The moment it stopped I scrambled out, still holding your apple. I staggered away from the car, feeling weak, shaking all over. There was a rising bank, a low hedge, and beyond was an immense flat field of crops. I leaned forward into the hedge, the thorns and sticks prodding into me. You had switched off the engine and you came running to me. I felt your arm round my shoulders, but I was shuddering and crying. You were saying soothing things but the horror of what I had discovered was throbbing through me. As you held me I thrust myself forward and down against the hedge, and vomited.

You brought some tissues from the car and I wiped myself clean with them. I had moved back from the hedge, but I could not turn to face the car.

'Shall we try to find a doctor, Sue?'

'I'll be all right in a minute. It's my period. It sometimes happens like this.' I couldn't tell you the truth. 'I needed some air.'

'Do you want to stay here?'

'No, we can drive on. In a while.'

I had some antacid tablets in my bag, and you brought me those. The prosaic chalky mint taste was comforting. I sat down in the dry grass, staring at the tall stalks of cow parsley nodding around and above me, insects drifting in the heat. Cars rushed by on the road behind us, their tyres making a sucking sound on the soft tarmac. I could not make myself look back, knowing Niall was there.

He must have been with us from the start. He had probably stayed to listen when I spoke to you in the pub, had been with us on our first dates, had been with us in the car from the time we left London. He had been there, silent behind us, watching and listening. I had never been free of him.

I knew that he was forcing me to act. To live the normal life I craved I had to put Niall behind me for ever. I could not go back to the morbid, vagrant life of the glams. Niall wanted to drag me back, by making unworkable anything that threatened him.

I had to fight him. Not at that moment – the shock of what I had discovered was too fresh – and preferably not alone. I needed you to help me.

I waited in the grass while you crouched beside me. A few

minutes earlier the thought of getting back in the car with Niall still there would have been out of the question. I knew, though, that it would be the first necessary stage in facing up to him.

'I'm feeling better,' I said. 'We can drive on.'

'Are you sure?'

You helped me up and we embraced lightly. I said I was sorry to cause a fuss, that I'd probably be OK from now on, that as soon as the period actually started I would feel better. Over your shoulder I was looking at the car. Reflected sunlight glinted from the rear passenger window.

We walked back to the car, took our seats and strapped ourselves in. I tried to listen for the sound of the door behind me, in case Niall too had been outside while we halted, but an invisible can use a door without being detected.

When we were back on the road I steeled myself and turned to look at the back seat. I knew he was there, could feel the presence of his cloud, but it was impossible to *see* him. I could look at our untidy pile of maps and food, could see the luggage compartment behind, but when I tried to look directly at the seat behind mine, my eyes would not settle, my sight was diverted away. There was just the unseen presence, the suggestion of weight depressing the seat cushion.

After that I stared straight ahead at the road, constantly aware of him behind me, looking at me, looking at you.

We stayed overnight in Great Malvern, the hotel built in a beautiful position on the edge of town, standing on the side of the Malvern Hills. The Vale of Evesham spread away beneath the window of our bedroom. As soon as we arrived I took you to bed, trying in the only way I knew to make up for the oddness of my behaviour during the day. How could I ever begin to tell you about Niall? But what kind of future would we have if he continually followed us around?

The short term decision I came to was to act as if Niall was not there, suppress the thoughts of him. But it was impossible to act on such a decision: all through the evening, as we walked in the hills, then drove into the town for a meal, I deliberately steered the conversation away from anything personal. Naturally, you were aware of it.

Later, when we returned to the hotel bedroom, I took the room key away from you and opened the door myself. You walked in first. I followed with a quick, intentionally surprising movement, pushing the door closed sharply behind me. I was rewarded with the feeling of weight pressing against it from outside, but I shoved the door into place and locked it. There was no bolt. Locked hotel doors never presented a barrier to Niall: he could easily steal a master key, and later enter the room without either of us noticing, but that would take him at least several minutes. That was as much as I thought I would need.

I said, 'Richard, I've got to talk to you about something.'

'What's going on, Sue? You've been acting strangely all evening.'

'I've got to be frank with you. I told you about Niall. Well, he's here.'

'What do you mean, he's here?'

'He's in Malvern. I saw him this evening when we were walking.'

'I thought you said he was in France.'

'I never know where he is. He told me he was going to France but he must have changed his mind.'

'What the hell is he doing here? Has he followed us?'

'I don't know. It could be coincidence. He often travels around to see friends.'

'What are you saying?' you said. 'Do you want him to join us for the rest of the trip?'

'Of course not! But he's seen us together. I'll have to talk to him, tell him what's happening.'

'No, I'm not with that. If he's seen us together, he already knows everything he needs to know. What would be the point of saying anything more? We're leaving in the morning, so we won't have to bother about him again.'

'You don't understand! I can't do that to him. I've known him for too long. I can't walk out on him.'

'You already have, Sue.'

I knew I was being unreasonable, but the only way I could describe Niall to you was as a possessive ex-lover, accidentally encountered. We argued on for an hour or more, both of us becoming entrenched in our positions. Niall must have entered

154

the room at some point during it all, but I would not allow the fear of him to influence me. At last we went to bed, worn out by the impasse. I felt safer in the darkness and we held on to each other under the sheets. Because my period had actually started that evening we did not make love, nor did we wish to.

It was another restless night, the problem churning away in my mind. As with all obsessive problems, no solution presented itself, and in the loneliness of the night I felt an overwhelming sense of despair.

Nevertheless, I was awake at half past six, with a resolution formed. I knew I would have to confront Niall directly, and I decided to do it as soon as possible. I left you asleep in the bed, dressed quietly, then told Niall to follow me. I went down through the hotel and let myself out through the main door.

It was already a fine, warm morning. I walked along the road, up the hill, to where it took a sharp turn to the right and cut through two steep cliffs to the other side of the hills. You and I had walked up there the evening before, shortly after making love. I scrambled up one of the mounds and walked across the broad summit. Small rocks stuck out from the grass. It was utterly still and quiet.

I found a flat rock and sat down on it, staring across Herefordshire.

I said, 'Are you here, Niall?'

Silence. Sheep grazed on the slopes beneath me. A solitary car drove up the road and cut through the gap towards Malvern.

'Niall? We should talk.'

'I'm here, bitch.' His voice came from a short distance away, somewhere to my left. He sounded out of breath.

'Where are you? I want to see you.'

'We can talk like this.'

'Make yourself visible, Niall.'

'No. *You* make yourself invisible. Or have you forgotten how?'

I realised that I had been continuously visible for more than a week, the longest time since my early teens. It had happened so naturally with you that I had simply not thought about it.

'Suit yourself.'

He had moved. His voice came from a different direction each time he spoke. I tried to see him, knowing that there was always a way to find the cloud if only I knew how to see. But I had been with you too long, or Niall had retreated too far into his glamour. I imagined him prowling around, circling as I sat on the rock. I stood up.

'Why won't you leave me alone, Niall?'

'Because you're fucking with Grey. I'm trying to make you quit.'

'Leave us alone! I'm finished with you. I'm never going to see you again.'

'I've already arranged that for you, Susan.'

He was still moving around, sometimes behind me. If only he had stayed still I would not have felt so frightened.

I said, 'Please don't interfere, Niall. It's over between us!'

'You're a glam. It'll never work with him.'

'I'll never be like you! I hate you!'

It was then that he struck me, a hard fist coming out of the air, banging against the side of my head. I had no way of bracing myself or dodging, and the blow threw my head to the side. I lurched backwards, reaching behind me as my foot struck the rock on which I had been sitting, and I fell heavily on the ground. An instant later Niall kicked me, high up on my leg by my hip. I shouted with pain and curled up desperately in a foetal position, my arms over my head. I braced myself against more blows. But I heard him right beside me, leaning down so that his invisible mouth was close by my ear. I smelt the familiar sourness of old tobacco on his breath.

'I'm never going to leave you, Susan. You're mine and I don't intend to lose you. I'm helpless without you. Stop it now!'

He pushed his hand past my arm and grabbed a handful of the front of my blouse. He jerked me into a sitting position, the fabric straining and pulling under my armpits. He pushed his other hand roughly under the blouse, and tore and scratched at my breasts. I hunched myself tighter and twisted away from him, forcing him to let go but ripping the thin blouse at the front.

He said, still crouching down beside me, 'You haven't told him about me yet. Tell him you're an invisible, tell him you're half mad.'

'No!'

'If you don't, I will.'

'You've done enough harm already.'

'I've hardly started. Would you like me to grab the steering wheel next time we're going fast enough to make it interesting?'

'You're crazy, Niall!'

'No more than you, Susan. We're both mad. Make him understand that, and if he still wants you then maybe I'll leave you alone.'

I sensed him move away from me but I stayed huddled on the ground, terrified of more invisible blows. Niall had often hit me in the past when he was angry enough, but never like this, never from within the cloud. I was still dazed from being struck on my head, and my leg and back were aching. My left breast felt as if it had been cut, but when I explored gently I found it looked all right. I let a few minutes pass and then sat up slowly, looking around for him. How close was he?

I was desperate to talk to you, craved your comfort, but how could I explain and what would you say if I did? Squatting painfully on the grass I gingerly explored the damage to me: there was a sore area on my lower back and a bruised lump on my thigh. I had a grass graze on my elbow. My head was aching. The front of my blouse was hanging open and two buttons were missing.

I must have been dazed. I wandered around on the hill for a while, but soon my need to be with you became paramount. I limped slowly down the road to the hotel, holding my blouse together with my hand. I saw you the moment I entered the hotel grounds. You had opened the rear hatch of the car and were putting your suitcase inside. I called out to you but you did not hear. I realised that in my wretchedness I had slipped back into invisibility, another of Niall's victories over me. I forced myself out of the cloud and called to you again. This time you heard and turned towards me. I ran to you, sobbing with relief and misery.

You knew at once that I had been with Niall. I had no hope of concealing it from you. I tried to minimise what he had done, but I could not hide my torn clothes and bruises. I think I would have understood if you had been angry with me, but you were as upset as I was. We stayed on all morning in Malvern, discussing Niall, but in terms you would understand, not true ones.

We left Malvern after an early lunch and drove into Wales. Niall was in the car, sitting behind us silently.

We stopped somewhere to buy petrol, and for a few moments I was alone in the car with Niall.

I said, 'I don't owe you anything, but I'll tell him tomorrow.'

Silence.

'Are you there, Niall?'

I had turned around to look back at the empty half of the rear seat, but again I was unable to see him. Instead, I could see *through*, to where you were standing next to the car, holding the petrol filler, looking back at the pump. Electronic digits were flickering orange in the sunlight. You saw me apparently looking at you, and you smiled briefly.

When you turned away again, I said, 'It's what you want, isn't it? I'll tell Richard tomorrow.'

Niall said nothing but I knew he was there. His silence intimidated me, probably on purpose, so I opened the door and left the car. I went into the filling station shop and browsed through the magazines while you paid the cashier.

After a long drive we arrived in the village of Little Haven, on the far western coast of Dyfed. It was a small and pretty place, with a long rocky foreshore, and in spite of the time of year was not crowded with visitors. In the evening we walked on the beach to watch the sunset, then called in at the local pub before returning to the hotel.

There was a distance between us. You could not understand why I had gone to meet Niall, and I could not explain. Because he had beaten me up you wanted me to renounce Niall forever, but I would not or could not. I knew you were hurt, puzzled, angry; I was desperate to mend everything.

Niall's way, to tell you of my invisibility, was probably the only solution, because it would satisfy him and explain myself, but I was exhausted by the subject. A better, more enjoyable method was on my mind. When we were back in our room I slipped away to the bathroom. Although my period was still on, I put in my diaphragm to halt the bleeding temporarily.

In bed you wanted to talk about Niall again, but I deflected you. There was nothing I could say to make amends. I held you, kissed you, tried to arouse you. At first you resisted but I knew what I wanted. We were lying on the top of the covers, the elderly double bed creaking as we moved around. You responded at last and I felt my own arousal growing. I wanted to make love to you more excitingly than ever before, and I kissed and fondled you with great intimacy. I loved your body, the solidity of it and its hard curves.

We rolled over so that you were above me, and you were caressing me with your hands and tongue. I raised my parted knees, ready for you, but you appeared to change your mind and rolled to the side. I felt your hands pulling me around and against you, pushing my shoulders down against your chest. I wanted you inside me, but your hands pulled my rear away from you, twisting my haunches awkwardly. We were kissing mouth to mouth, and I could not understand what you were wanting to do. Your fingers were digging into the flesh around my hips, thrusting me away. I realised that both your hands were on my breasts, lightly fingering my nipples.

Other hands were reaching from behind, pulling at my hips!

I was entered from behind, a pushing intrusion. Pubic hair prickled against my buttocks. I gasped, turned my head, felt an unshaven chin beat into the curve of my neck, and knees kicked into the crook of mine. The weight of the man behind me thrust me forward against you, and one of your hands slipped down to stroke me. I grabbed your wrist to stop you finding what was already there and in desperation brought your hand up to my mouth to kiss it. Niall's sexual thrusting against me was violent, making me gasp in outrage and distress. You were growing more excited, wanting to enter me. I had to stop you somehow and so I curled away from Niall, pushing my backside more acutely against him in a desperate effort to twist free. He gasped with lust, as I tightened on his member. I took you into my mouth to suck. Niall shifted position, moving forward so that he was kneeling between my legs, his hands under my belly and holding me while he rammed at me. His movements grew more urgent, and he took a handful of my hair and wrenched it painfully, pushing my face down, harder on you, taking you further in. I could not breathe, began gagging. You were lying back, your arms somewhere away from me, while the rape went on. I was swinging my elbows upwards and back, trying to beat Niall away from me.

I managed to get you out of my mouth, but Niall continued to push my face into your groin. I heard you groaning with pleasure, while Niall hammered mercilessly at me. I felt him climaxing at last and he grunted audibly, expelling his breath noisily. You said my name, your voice full of desire for me. Niall slumped across my back, releasing my hair and playing his hands across my breasts. As he relaxed I was able to shift my weight, but I still could not wriggle him out of me. He was monstrously possessing me, his weight forcing my face down against you. You said my name again, wanting to make love. I managed to turn my face to see you. Your eyes were closed, your mouth was open. I had to get Niall out of me, but I was pinned beneath him. Repeated jabs with my elbow had no effect. His frantic breathing was close by my ears and his fingers were still pressing into me. I could feel him softening inside me, so I made another effort to twist my hips, raising my body as I did so. At last I managed to slide away from him, but he was still there holding on to me. I loathed the touch of his hands! I elbowed him again and he loosened his grip on me. As soon as I was free I crawled across your body, hugging your chest, bringing my face to yours. You kissed me with great passion, and pulled me over you with a smile of desire and affection. I could feel Niall beside us on the bed, some part of him pressing against my side.

You entered me at last and we made love. Because I was squatting above you we were looking at each other. I kept my face expressionless, knowing that if I allowed myself to show what I was really feeling then I could only moan with horror. I moved my body with yours, hoping it would be enough. Niall was still there. I could feel the heat of his body against my lower leg.

How could you not be aware of him? Was Niall so profoundly invisible to you that you could not hear his rasping breath, smell his sated body, feel his weight on the bed? How could you not have understood the cause of the violent physical contortions he had forced on me?

As soon as you had finished I lay beside you, and we pulled a sheet over us. I whispered that I was exhausted, and we lay in each other's arms with the light out. I waited and waited as your breathing steadied and you fell asleep. When I was sure I would not disturb you I slipped out of the bed and went to the bathroom. I showered as quietly as I could, scrubbing myself clean.

When I returned the room smelled of French cigarettes.

In the morning I said to you, 'Do you remember the puzzle they used to print in children's books?'

I took a piece of paper and made two marks:

X   **O**

'If you close your left eye,' I said, 'and look with your right eye at the cross, then move your face closer to the paper, the circle seems to vanish.'

You said, 'That's a physical failure of the eye. The retina has only a limited amount of peripheral vision.'

I said, 'But the brain compensates for what the eye cannot see. No one believes the circle has *actually* vanished. A hole does not appear in the paper, where the circle used to be. Only the circle disappears, or becomes invisible.'

You said, 'What are you getting at?'

We were sitting on the rocks of the shore near Little Haven. It was low tide and the sands were gleaming in the sunlight. Holiday makers were all around us. Far away a number of children were splashing in the shallows.

I said, 'Do you see those women over there, with the dog, walking by the edge of the sea? How many of them are there?'

'Are you serious?' you said.

'Yes. How many women are walking the dog?'

'Two.'

'There were three of them a few moments ago. Did you notice?'

'No. I wasn't looking.'

'Yes you were. All the time we've been sitting here, you've been staring over there.'

'Yes, but I wasn't paying attention,' you said.

'That's the point.'

'What point?'

I said, 'People see without noticing, look without seeing. Nobody sees everything. Imagine you've been invited to a party where you know hardly any of the people. No one greets you and

161

you feel selfconscious. You take a drink and stand at the edge of the room, hoping to see a friendly face. As you look at the people you begin to notice some of them. You make quick judgements of their appearance, and if they are women you wonder if they might be alone. If they are with men, you notice them too. Gradually, the ice breaks and you speak to some of the people; as you do, each one becomes the focus of your attention. The evening goes on, and although you no longer feel a complete stranger at the party there are still many people you never actually speak to. Maybe you notice one of the men who is too drunk, a young woman wearing a daring dress, someone else who laughs too loudly. The rest remain in the background of your attention. Every person in the party is visible to you, but there is a sequence, an order, in which you become aware of them. Always, at every party, there will be someone you *never* notice.'

You said, 'How do you know?'

I said to you, 'How do you know you do not? Now suppose you are at another party. You go into a room and there are ten men and one woman. As you enter the room the woman, who is beautiful and voluptuous, starts to dance. She removes all her clothes. As soon as she is naked you leave the room. How many of the men would you be able to describe afterwards? Would you even be sure there were ten of them, and not nine, or an eleventh you did not notice at all?'

I said to you, 'Richard, suppose you are walking down a street and two women come towards you. One of them is young and pretty, and is wearing attractive clothes. The other is an older woman, perhaps the girl's middle-aged mother, and she is wearing a plain, shapeless coat. As you pass they both smile at you. Which one do you notice first?'

You said, 'You're talking about sexual responses!'

'Sex comes into it,' I said. 'But not every time. Suppose you have a group of ten people: five men and five women. A sixth woman approaches. What she will usually notice first is the other women, and she will look at them before she looks at the men. Women notice women, just as men notice women. A child will notice other children before seeing the adults. Some women notice children before they notice adults. Most men see women before they see children, and then they notice the other men.

162

There is a hierarchy of visual interest. In any group of people there is always someone who is noticed *last*.'

I said to you, 'A friend rings you up and you agree to meet. You haven't seen him – this time we'll make it a man – you haven't seen him for five years. You go to meet him in a busy street. There are crowds of people, all strangers, and they are thronging around you. You have to look at them all because you are trying to spot your friend. You look at women as well as men. After a while you begin to wonder if you can remember accurately what your friend looked like, the last time you saw him. You start looking more closely at the faces going past. Then at last your friend appears. He has been delayed, but you meet him and that's all right. You instantly forget all your worries about recognising him. Afterwards, if you think about it, you will realise that while you were waiting you looked directly at hundreds of faces and were aware of thousands of others. You looked at most of them, but in fact they did not register on your mind. Within a few seconds you cannot remember what a single one of them looked like.'

You said, 'But there's nothing unusual in any of that. What does it prove?'

'It proves nothing about you and your friend, but about the other people. It's normal *not* to notice most people. What you see is what you choose to see, or what interests you, or anything that's drawn to your attention. I'm trying to tell you that there are some people you will *never* see. They are too low in the hierarchy, they are the ones who are noticed last, or not at all. Ordinary people do not know how to see them. They are never noticed. They are naturally invisible.'

I said, '*I* am naturally invisible, Richard, and you only see me because you want to.'

You said, 'That's ridiculous.'

So I said, 'Watch me, Richard.'

And I stood before you and allowed myself to slip into invisibility.

We walked back to the hotel in silence. To my amazement you seemed more discontented than ever. You said nothing about the invisibility I had just proved to you, and I was wondering what more I would have to do. I had exposed the deepest secret of my life, and given you the explanation you demanded of me. Yet your reaction to it was indifference. You seemed not to believe, not to understand, nor even to care. Surely there could be few greater revelations than human invisibility? I had made myself vanish in front of you, and you appeared not to have noticed! I could hardly believe it possible!

I wondered if I had done something wrong, perhaps touched on some buried trauma from childhood, or confronted you with internal conflicts about your own glamorous ability. Your rejection of what I had done was so total that I couldn't see any way of raising the subject a second time.

We liked being in Little Haven and so we stayed on for three more days. During most of this time the subject remained unspoken between us. Because I did not know what more I could say I left it unsaid, and in the interests of harmony between us it was probably a wise strategy: our mood eventually lightened and we began once more to enjoy each other's company. It at least gave me more space in which to think about what had happened, and in the end I came to the conclusion that I had somehow blundered. I had not explained clearly enough, or you had not understood, or you had thought I was not speaking literally.

Yet I was convinced that when I made myself invisible before you, I had seen a *clouding* of your eyes, a revelation of your understanding.

I did want you, Richard, and your glamour attracted me, but I realised you were in denial about it. I came to believe I had tried to rush you. The feeling was confirmed by something that happened on the evening before we returned to London.

You had said you wanted to look at the road map for the journey the next day and walked off to find the car. We had left it in the visitors' long-stay park on the edge of the village. I went with you some of the way, then decided instead to visit the tiny bookshop in the main street. After browsing through the titles for about fifteen minutes I walked back to the sea front, vaguely expecting to meet you there when you returned from the car park. Instead, I saw Niall.

Or I thought I did. I saw a young man of Niall's general appearance standing by the top of the steps that led down to the beach. It was a warm summer evening and there were still many people about. As a group of teenage girls went noisily past I temporarily lost sight of him.

I had hardly thought about Niall for the last three days, and although I knew that he must still be following us around I had closed my mind against him. But suddenly I had seen him. That is, he was visible to me! Without really thinking why I was doing it, I walked across to where I had seen him, but by the time I reached the flight of steps he was no longer there. I looked on the beach and in each direction along the front, but I could not see him.

When I turned away from the front I saw him again. This time there was no doubt who it was. I recognised his clothes: a light-blue jacket, dark-blue slacks, the collar of a pink shirt visible under the lanky hair at the back of his head. I had been with him when he stole those clothes, and he had worn them many times since. I also knew the way he walked: he had a mannered, upright gait, a spring in his step, almost like that of a fashion model. For someone who was never seen, Niall always acted as if he were acutely aware of his appearance.

I followed him up the main street but as he went past the entrance to the Red Lion public house he disappeared again. Thinking he must have dodged inside I went towards the door, but I had covered only half the distance when I realised Niall was in sight again. He was a few yards away and walking straight towards me.

I was shocked by his appearance now that I could see him head-on. Many days' growth of beard shadowed his face, his hair was uncombed and his clothes were dirty and crumpled. His eyes had a wild, desperate look, and all the self-confidence had gone from him. He was so close to me that he passed me almost as soon as I saw him, and in his wake I smelt sweaty armpits and unwashed underwear. I had never known him to be like this before. Niall was always a neat dresser, fastidiously clean and groomed.

'Niall?' I called after him, because he was striding so quickly that he was already retreating from me. He gave no sign of having heard me, and walked on.

I followed him again and almost at once I lost sight of him. He was on the fringe of visibility, slipping in and out. I kept walking in the direction he had been going, trying to visualise where he might be, even though I could not actually see him any more. Without warning, he appeared on the other side of the street, further along, walking in the *opposite* direction, as if by some miracle he had transported himself some distance away before walking back so that I was able to see him again. How could he have done that?

I called his name across the street, but once again he gave no sign of having heard me. We were not separated by much: the street is narrow and what traffic there was at that time was moving slowly. I dodged through the cars and caught up with him.

'Niall, what are you doing?'

He ignored me as if I wasn't there and strode onwards. Again I followed him, mystified by his behaviour, but also starting to feel uncertain of what I was actually seeing, what might really be going on. Niall was acting as if he was unaware of me, as if I were invisible to him!

It was such a total reversal of everything I knew about him, and for that matter about myself, that it was frankly incredible.

Suspecting that he was about to vanish again, I darted forward and caught his arm, saying his name again insistently. I felt the solidity of his body, the soft burring feeling of the corduroy material of his jacket, but he walked on, staring moodily at the ground. A few moments later he disappeared again.

People were staring at me. A group of three middle-aged couples on the other side of the narrow street had halted, and were peering inquisitively at me. Two of the women were laughing together. I knew how strange my behaviour must look in this small holiday resort, full of ordinary people in ordinary lives. I ducked away from their gaze and hurried down the pavement, not looking to either side. I came in a moment to a small square in front of the parish church. In the centre was a patch of lawn, and I went over and sat down on a wooden bench. I hated it when Niall suddenly left me; now that he apparently could not see me I hated it more. It all confused me and made me feel uncertain. I remembered the awfulness of his intrusions, the neurotic state he could induce in me.

Worst of all, it made me question whether or not he had really been there. His sudden manifestations were those of a visitant, a voice, a fist, striking out of the air, conscience of my past.

Until I met you Niall had never used his profound invisibility against me. Why?

If he cannot be seen, is he really there?

When he materialises from nowhere, what is it that I appear to see?

Such thoughts lay close to the madness I feared, and my body was stirring with physical frustration. I felt an overwhelming need to resolve everything, no matter what the cost. To clear my mind, to ease my body, I headed for our hotel. I wanted to see you again, irrespective of the consequences, or the possible outcome. I never felt more sure that only in you lay sanity and certainty.

You had returned to the hotel room before me and were sitting on the bed reading the morning's newspaper. You pretended not to notice me.

I said, 'Richard, something's happened!'

'Not Niall again,' you said, looking up for a fraction of a second, then turning back to your paper.

'Yes. How do you know?'

'I can see it in your face. You said he was in Malvern. Now what the hell's he doing here? Is he following us around?'

'All that matters is that he's here.'

'That's not how I see it. I've had enough. Tomorrow we go back to London, and we're finished. If you want to be with your damned boyfriend you stay here.'

'Richard, I love you.'

'I don't think that's true.'

I had been diverted from what I wanted to say. Everything was too complicated and charged with emotion, and with potential for hurt and misunderstanding. I wanted to simplify it, start again from what I saw as the central truth: that you were the only one I wanted to be with. But you threw it in my face, and that made me angry too. The arguing became illogical, until we both abandoned it.

We were hungry so we went out to a restaurant, but we sat in silence through most of the meal. The few words you said to me were sarcastic and critical. Back in the hotel you would not calm down. You paced about the room, as unwilling in your own way as I was to let the subject drop.

You said, 'Sue, what in hell's going on with you? Half the time we're together your mind's on something else. When it's not you suddenly start that crap about invisibility!'

Startled, I said, 'It's not crap to me.'

'Yes it is.'

'I'm naturally invisible, Richard. And so are you.'

'No you're not, and neither am I. It's a load of bullshit.'

'It's the single most important fact in my life.'

'All right. Do it. Make yourself invisible.'

'Why?'

'Because I don't believe you.' You were staring at me with cold dislike.

'I've already shown you.'

'So you said at the time.'

'I'm upset now. It's difficult.'

'Then tell me why you came out with all that crap.'

'It's not crap,' I said. I concentrated on intensifying the cloud. After a few moments' uncertainty I felt myself slip into invisibility. 'I've done it.'

You were staring directly at me. 'Then why can I still see you?'

'I don't know. Can you?'

'Plain as daylight.'

'It's because – because you know how to *look*. You know where I am. And because you're the same as me. Invisible people can be seen by others.'

You shook your head.

I deepened the cloud, and within it I moved away from you towards the side. It was a small room, but I stood as far away from the bed as I could go, pressing myself against the polished veneer of the wardrobe door. You were looking at me.

'I can still see you,' you said.

'Richard, it's because you know *how*! Don't you understand that?'

'You're no more invisible than I am.'

'I'm scared to go deeper. You look so angry.'

168

'I don't know what's going on,' you said. 'Is it a joke? Are you trying to make a fool of me?'

I tried again, staring back at your angry face from within my cloud, wondering how I could ever convince you. I was trying to recall the disciplines Mrs Quayle had taught me. I knew how to intensify the cloud, but for many years my fear of the shadows had pushed me the other way. I was terrified that once I entered the deepest levels of the glamour I would become, like Niall, stuck for ever.

For a moment you frowned, looking away, as if watching me cross the room. I held my breath, knowing you had lost sight of me. But you looked back.

'You're no more invisible than I am,' you said, looking me in the eyes.

The cloud dispersed and I slumped on the bed. I began weeping. There was a pause and then you were sitting beside me, your arm around my back. You held me close and neither of us said anything. I let the tension drain out of me and I sobbed against you.

We went to bed at last, but there was no lovemaking that night. We lay beside each other in the dark, and although I was exhausted I found it impossible to sleep. I knew that you too were awake. How much could I tell you about Niall? If you disbelieved my demonstrations of how I could slip in and out of invisibility, what would you think of a man you would never be able to see at all?

Like you, I knew we could not go on like this, but no matter what I did I felt I was going to lose you. Niall would haunt me for the rest of my life.

Out of the dark you said, 'This evening, when I was walking back to the car, I saw you in the High Street. What were you doing?'

'What did it seem I was doing?'

'You looked as if you had gone out of your mind. You were dashing about all over the place, apparently talking to yourself.'

'I didn't know you were there.'

'Was Niall something to do with it?'

'Of course.'

'Where is he now?'

'Somewhere around. I'm not sure any more.'

'I still don't understand how he followed us here,' you said.

'When he wants something, he's persistent.'

'He seems to have power over you. I wish to God I knew what it was.'

I lay there silently, wondering what to say. Nothing made sense that was not *my* sense, but you would not believe that.

'Sue?'

'I thought you would realise,' I said. 'Niall's glamorous too. He's invisible.'

We spent the whole of the next day driving back to London. There was a barrier of resentment and misunderstanding between us, and I no longer had any idea what I could do or say to repair the damage. You were hurt and angry, unapproachable by reason, or with loving intent. I still wanted only you, but now I was losing you.

Niall travelled back with us, sitting silently and invisibly in the rear seat of the car.

We arrived in London during the evening rush hour, and after we left the motorway it was a slow and tiresome drive to Hornsey. You took me to my house and parked the car outside. I could see the fatigue in your eyes.

'Would you like to come inside for a few minutes?' I said.

'Yes, but I won't stay long.'

We unloaded my stuff from the back of the car. I was watching to see some sign of Niall, but if he climbed out of the car he did so without my noticing. I let us into the house and closed the front door quickly, just in case. It was a senseless precaution, because he had had a key for years. I picked up the small stack of mail waiting for me on the hall table, then opened my room door. As soon as we were both inside I closed the door quickly and bolted it, the only way I could be sure of keeping Niall out if he was not already there. You noticed, but said nothing.

I opened the window at the top and pulled back the half-drawn curtains. You sat down on the end of my bed.

You said, 'Sue, we've got to sort this out. Are we going to go on seeing each other?'

'Do you want to?'

'Yes, but not with Niall hanging around.'

'It's all over, I promise you.'

'You've said that before. How do I know he isn't going to turn up again?'

'Because he told me that if I talked to you about him, so that you know what he thinks he's losing, he would accept that.'

You thought for a moment, then said, 'All right, what's the great sacrifice?'

'I've been trying to tell you. Niall and I are both invisibles, and it's what has kept—'

'Not that again!' You stood up and moved away from me. 'I'll tell you what I think of all that. The only invisibility I'm aware of is this damned ex-boyfriend who follows you around. I've never met him, never seen him, and as far as I'm concerned he doesn't exist! You know, I've started to wonder—'

'Don't, Richard!'

'You've got to get him out of your system.'

'Yes, I know.'

'All right. We're both tired. I want to go back to my place and get some sleep. It was probably a mistake to have been away for so long. We'll feel different after some sleep. Shall we have dinner tomorrow?'

'Do you want to?'

'I wouldn't suggest it if I didn't. I'll telephone you in the morning.'

On that, after a brief kiss, we parted. I watched you drive away, with a superstitious feeling that I would not be seeing you again. It felt as if we had reached a natural end, one I had been incapable of preventing. I was helpless in the face of your doubts about invisibility. Niall had undermined everything.

I returned to my room and closed the door, bolting it behind me.

I said, 'Niall? Are you here?' A long silence followed. 'If you're in the room, let's talk. Please! If you're here, say something!'

His absence unnerved me almost as much as his invisible presence. I walked quickly around the room, thrashing my arms about, moving in sudden, unpredictable spurts of activity. He seemed not to be there but I was still not sure. I stood over the kettle while it boiled, then made myself a cup of tea. I placed it on the table next to my chair. I then found one of the candles I kept in case of power failure, stuck it to an old saucer, and lit it. I placed it on the table next to the cup of tea, and sat down in my chair. I sat completely still, cradling the cup in my hands, and watched the candle flame.

After five minutes the air in the room was still tranquil, the sun was beating down warmly on my legs, and the flame had not flickered once. I was as certain as I could be that Niall was not there. I blew out the candle and put it away. I opened my suitcase and hung up my clothes, making a heap on the floor of the ones that needed washing. There was no food in the place, but because you and I had stopped for lunch on the way I was not seriously hungry. I changed my clothes, putting on a pair of jeans and a clean shirt. Then I remembered the pile of mail, and sat cross legged on the bed to look through it.

In the middle of the stack of envelopes was a picture postcard.

The postcard was unsigned, but I recognised the handwriting as Niall's. The message simply read, *Wish you were here*, and underneath was an X. The picture was a modern reproduction of an old black-and-white photograph: a quay in Saint-Tropez with a warehouse in the background. I tried to decipher the postmark, but it was smudged and illegible. The postage stamp was French: the green head of a goddess, *France Postes, €1.60.*

It had unquestionably been sent by Niall. He never signed his name, and anyway I knew his handwriting. Even the X was flamboyant.

I opened the other envelopes, skimming through their contents, barely registering them. When I had finished I tipped the envelopes and circulars into the wastepaper basket. The picture postcard lay on the bed.

I still had the bruise on my thigh where Niall had kicked me. My back was still feeling stiff from when I was pushed to the ground. I vividly remembered the rape, the car with the engine running, the bar of soap dropped on me in the night. I had *seen* Niall the previous evening, dipping in and out of visibility in the narrow streets of Little Haven.

How could he have been in France?

The postcard, with its mocking message, its showy anonymity, denied everything I had experienced in the last few days.

Either Niall had been shadowing me during my holiday with you, or he had been in France, where in fact he had claimed to be from the outset.

Was I imagining everything?

I remembered the decision I had taken: Niall *had* to be in France, otherwise I was accepting the madness of the invisible world. I had wanted to act on that, but Niall had appeared in England. So the decision shifted: Niall was not in France. To believe anything else meant the same madness.

Throughout our trip Niall's presence had been beset with uncertainty. Passers-by thought I was talking and gesticulating to myself; you never saw him; he could rape me while I made love to you and you never knew. He entered and left rooms without my seeing the door open, he was in the car and not in the car, sitting behind us, invisible to us both. When I saw him he had seemed like a figment, an image from a nightmarish dream: moving silently, appearing and disappearing, ignoring me, taunting me.

But there were odd and plausible details. He had been out of breath after we climbed the hill behind Malvern, I had felt the rasp of his pubic hair as he raped me, there was the clarity of those oddly close-at-hand phone calls, the distinctive smell of his cigarettes in the room.

The postcard was an objective disproof of everything like that. It had been posted in France, and it had turned up in the anonymity of a bundle of other letters.

I tried to think of an explanation for the card, however wild. Niall had bought the card in England and talked one of his friends into posting it to me from France. But where would you come across a card like this in England? (Printed vertically in tiny letters, next to the line dividing the address space from the message were the words: *DIRA – 31, rue des Augustines, 69100 VILLEURBANNE.*) Perhaps he had found it in a shop somewhere, and thought of sending it to me as a way of disorientating me? Niall was capable of something like that, but it was over-elaborate. Then he had said he was in Saint-Raphaël, not Saint-Tropez. Why the inconsistency? Maybe he had indeed travelled to

France when he said, sent the card, then immediately returned? But why? It was implausible, too much trouble to go to when he had other ways of getting at me.

Anyway, I had *seen* him. He looked like someone who had been trailing us, unshaven, pale, wearing dirty clothes. He had seemed plausible and realistic.

Had I imagined him into existence, an embodiment of guilt, or of my past, or of my conscience?

If I could make myself invisible to the world, was I equally capable of summoning another presence into being? Had Niall come from my unconscious? A visitation of what I wished on myself, what I expected, what I most dreaded?

As I sat there, these turbulent fears whirling through me, I realised I had slipped into invisibility without noticing. My cloud had intensified because of my terror. I pushed the postcard under the covers of the bed, out of sight.

My invisibility – curse or talent, whichever it might be – was the only area of my life of which I was certain. I knew what I was and what I could become. It might be my madness, but it was all mine.

I walked across the room and opened the long wardrobe door. I stared into the mirror inside. My reflection came back at me: my hair was untidy, my eyes were dilated. I swung the door to and fro, trying to confuse the image, trying to make myself not see, but I was always there. I remembered the trick Mrs Quayle had played on me, concealing a mirror so that in my surprise I failed to see myself. Only Mrs Quayle had believed in my talent more than I did.

Both Niall and you eroded my self-confidence in different ways: Niall by his behaviour, you by your disbelief. I had thought that by bringing you into the world of the invisibles you would see me as I really was, and by sympathy and understanding would show me the way out of it. Niall, for converse reasons, held me back, or tried to. You were complements of each other, suspending me between you.

Whichever way I turned I seemed to be losing my mind.

I stared at the reflection of myself, knowing I could not trust even that. It made me look as if I were there, when I knew I was not.

You said you saw me, when I knew you could not.

Only Niall knew me for what I really was, and I could not trust him at all.

I hurried out to the hall and picked up the telephone. I dialled your number; there was no answer. Back in my room the post-card from Niall was still to be explained. I stared at it for a while, thinking of its consequences, then propped it up on the shelf over the gas fire. It was safest, easiest, to treat it as just another postcard, sent by a friend on holiday.

I went through the rest of my mail again – one letter enclosed a much-needed cheque, and another a commission for some art-work – then I undressed and went to bed.

The first thing I did in the morning was telephone you. You answered after a few rings.

'Richard? It's me. Sue.'

'I thought you might have called last night.' Your voice sounded throaty, and I wondered if I had woken you up.

'I did try, but there was no answer.' You said nothing, and I couldn't remember if we had made a firm arrangement that I would phone you. 'How are you?' I said.

'Tired. What are you doing today?'

'I'm going in to visit the studio. There's a job for me. I can't afford to let it go.'

'Will you be out all day?'

'Most of it,' I said.

'Shall we meet this evening? I'd like to see you and I've got some news we should talk about.'

'News? What is it?'

'I've been offered some work. I'll tell you about it later.'

We made our arrangements about when and where to meet. While I was talking to you I had a mental image of you sitting on the floor by the phone. I imagined you with your hair mussed from the bed, your eyes still half closed. I wondered if you slept in pyjamas when you were alone. The thought made me feel affectionate towards you, and I wished I could see you at once. I wanted to visit your flat again, be with you in your home, not endlessly travelling around from one hotel to the next, never sure if Niall was watching. For some reason I thought of your flat as safe from Niall, although there was no reason why it should be.

Thinking of you there reminded me of the day of the storm, when we had planned our holiday.

I said, 'While we were away, someone sent me a postcard. It wasn't you, was it?'

'Postcard? Why should I do that?'

'Whoever sent it didn't sign it.' I thought of Niall's distinctive handwriting. 'It was an old card, the sort you collect.'

'Well, it wasn't me.'

I said, 'When I see you this evening, would you bring some of your cards along? The places you wanted to go to, in France. I'd like to look at them again.'

I visited the studio in town and collected the brief for the work they wanted me to do. I made a start on it at home in the afternoon, but my mind was elsewhere. I left early for our date and had to hang around outside the Tube station for twenty minutes before you arrived. As soon as I saw you, walking up from the direction of your flat, I was so glad and relieved that I ran towards you. We stood for a long time kissing and holding each other as the traffic went by.

We walked back to your flat, arm in arm, and went to bed as soon as we were there. To be together again made everything right. Afterwards, we walked up the hill to Hampstead and found a restaurant. During the meal I told you about the work I had been given.

'They want some posters designed, probably for the Underground. I'm glad to be doing them.'

'What are they advertising?'

'An exhibition at the Whitechapel. It's the sort of thing I like. What about you? You said you'd been offered something.'

'I'm in two minds about accepting it,' you said. 'It'll mean going away for a while. Maybe two or three weeks. One of the American cable news channels needs a British crew to cover the military situation in Costa Rica. They can't get one of their own crews into the country. Political reasons.'

'I don't like the sound of that.'

'Filming war-zone stories is what I'm good at, what I know how to do. Shall I take the job?'

'Not if you're likely to get killed.'

You made a dismissive gesture. 'I wasn't thinking about that. What about you? If I'm away for a couple of weeks, will you still be here when I get back?'

'Of course I will!'

'What about Niall, Sue? Is that all over?'

'I'm sure it is.'

'People say that when they're not sure.'

'Richard, I'm certain. Yes, it's *over*.'

'You see, I don't want another row. But when we were away something was going on. I wanted to know the truth about you and Niall, and instead you came up with all that stuff about being invisible.'

'It's the same thing to me,' I said.

'It wasn't what I wanted to hear.'

I took your hand across the table. 'Richard, I love *you*. I'm sorry about all that, about everything. You've nothing to worry about.'

I meant it then, as I always had, but I knew in my heart that the problem of Niall was not yet completely solved. I changed the subject. I told you to take the job, and promised I'd still be here when you came back. I sincerely meant this too. You told me a little more about the work: the other men you would be working with, where you would be going, the sort of stories you were supposed to be covering. I wished it were possible for me to go with you.

You had brought some of your postcards to the restaurant, and gave them to me to look at. I glanced through them quickly, trying to give the impression that my curiosity was idle. There were pictures of Grenoble, Nice, Antibes, Cannes, Saint-Raphaël, Saint-Tropez, Toulon, all of them depicting the places as they had been before World War 2. There were only two pictures of Saint-Tropez: one showed a beach near the village, the other was a view of one of the streets, with a glimpse of the harbour through the houses.

You said, 'What are you looking for?'

'Nothing. I wanted to see them again.' I stacked the cards together and passed them back to you casually. 'Maybe we should have had our holiday in France, as you suggested.'

We decided to spend the night at your flat, but I needed to

return to my room first so I could pick up a few things. We drove over there, and while I stuffed a change of clothes into my overnight bag you stood by the old iron fireplace. Niall's postcard was still there on the shelf, propped up against the wall. I saw you staring at it, so I took it down and gave it to you.

You read the message aloud. ' "Wish you were here." But not signed. Do you know who sent it?'

'I think it must have been Niall. It was in the heap yesterday.'

'But you said he was—'

'I know. It doesn't make sense, does it? Exactly as you said. There he is, following us around, and there he is, sending me postcards from France.'

'So now you say he was in France all along?'

'Looks like it. I can't explain it either. Let's go to your place.'

But we were back in well trodden territory. I could see the dread in your eye, and feel it in my heart.

You said, 'This Niall business isn't over, is it? Whatever you say, whatever you promise, he's still lurking around!' You slammed the card face down on the shelf. 'Sue, the thing is, when you first meet someone you realise there's almost certainly going to be a lover from the past, someone who might still be on the scene, or who still means a lot to the person you've met. It's happened to me before and I see it as inevitable. It's always been something that I could deal with. But you and Niall, that's different. It goes on happening, whatever you say.'

'It's only a picture postcard, Richard.'

'Then why did you point it out to me, why does it still matter?'

'Because I've tried to tell you. You wouldn't understand.'

'You've told me nothing that makes sense. I know you think I'm being unfair, but it's got to stop! You're the only woman I've ever loved. I'm damned if I'm going to put up with this any more. I'll be away for a couple of weeks, and that should be enough time for you to make up your mind.'

'You mean I have to choose between you and Niall?'

'Got it in one.'

'I've already chosen, Richard. Niall won't accept it.'

'Then you'll have to make him.'

In the end we went back to your flat and spent another angry night, with fitful sleep. In the morning I went home, feeling desolated. As soon as I was back in my room I tore up Niall's card and flushed the pieces down the lavatory. The following day you telephoned to say you were flying out to San José that evening, and promised you would get in touch as soon as you were home.

Two days after you left, Niall returned.

I am entirely to blame for what followed. I felt I was being forced to make a decision, and I made it. I realised what the consequences would probably be, and accepted them. You wanted me to choose between you and Niall, and I chose Niall.

The plain fact was that Niall was haunting me and would go on doing so until he had his way. Whether he did it by following me around invisibly, or more simply by being who he was, he was not letting go. Everything in my relationship with you was constantly at risk. You were sick of it, and so was I. I loved and wanted you, but I was finally understanding that I could never have you.

Described in such a way my decision probably sounds more calculated than it really was. When you left to work in Central America I had every intention of holding on, and I was doing so, in suspense until you returned. Then Niall turned up at the door of my room, and as soon as I saw him I realised what I was going to have to do. To be free of him I had to convince him of what I wanted. I could only do that when you weren't with me.

He had let himself into the house using his key, but my bolted door prevented him from going any further. He knocked and called my name. I slid back the bolt and he walked in. He looked well. He was clean shaven, had cut his hair, was wearing new clothes, and exuded some of his old air of self-confidence. He was in good spirits, and when I told him you were away he said only that he knew it would never have worked. He talked amusingly about the supposed unreliability of people who worked for TV, or who went on long working trips abroad. It was not malicious, although it had something of the same effect, sowing a few seeds of doubt about you. Niall moved back in on me as if nothing had changed, and although I would not let him stay with me that first night, afterwards we were sleeping together again.

Where had he been? It was on my mind, because so many questions had been raised, but it was not in Niall's nature to be candid about anything. Now I had him alone I wanted to hear what he had been hoping to achieve, why he had acted so badly, what he had been up to that afternoon in Little Haven. Typically, though, when I tried to ask him direct questions about the last two weeks he easily diverted me.

For instance, his second visit. The weather was still sultry and it was stuffy and airless in my room. Sitting up in my bed, Niall said, 'I'd like a drink. Do you have anything?'

'There are a couple of cans of lager, I think. In the fridge.'

'Lager's not what I want,' he said. 'Pass me my bag, would you? I brought you some of the local plonk.'

I took the bottle from the bag and read the label. ' "Côtes de Provence, 1991".'

'Where's your corkscrew?' Niall said.

'Behind you, in the drawer. Did you buy the wine in France?'

'Sort of.'

'They sell this in the off-licence down the road,' I said. 'They had it on offer at the weekend. I saw it in the window.'

Niall was using the corkscrew, leaning down over the side of the bed to get leverage. With the cork out he wandered over to the table, and came back with two glasses.

'Well, cheers!' he said.

'Niall, what did this wine cost in, what was the village called?'

'I can't remember exactly. A few euros.'

'You went into a shop and paid for it?'

'You know. I saw it there, helped myself. The usual.'

'I thought you said you bought it.'

'I never buy anything. You know that. Drink up!'

He lit one of his Gauloise Caporal cigarettes, tossing the match carelessly on the carpet. It left a thin trail of smoke in the air, but was out before it hit the ground. I took the blue cigarette pack away from him and looked closely at it. The paper seal over the top said *Exportation*, which looked French enough, but underneath it said *Made in France*. The health warning was also in English. Nothing was proved.

'While you were away, what was the weather like?'

'Hot. Why do you want to know?'

'Hot and sunny?' I said. 'Mediterranean sun?'

'Yeah, that sort of thing. So what?'

'You don't have a sun tan.'

'Neither do you.'

'I haven't just come back from the south of France,' I said.

'Did I say I had?'

'As good as. You sent me a postcard from Saint-Tropez.'

'I did? I must have been missing you.'

I slapped my hand down on the bed in frustration, slopping some of my wine. The stain spread into the sheet.

'For heaven's sake, Niall! Tell me the truth! Were you here in England, following me around when I was on holiday with Richard?'

He grinned infuriatingly.

'So that's what you were up to!' he said. 'I thought you sounded funny on the phone.'

'You haven't answered me,' I said.

'What do you think?'

'I don't *know*!'

'Were you sleeping with Richard Grey?' Niall said.

'This is impossible!'

'Don't worry about it. It's all over isn't it? He's gone, I'm here, bygones are bygones. I won't ask what happened, if you don't ask me.'

His sheer cheek made me laugh, in spite of everything. 'Niall, you're hopeless! You went off in a sulk, you wouldn't let me see you, you made all those weird phone calls—'

'Bygones?'

I never asked him again about France or the postcard, or about the beating he had given me that morning, or about the rape. At best he would scoff away my questions with his easy ambiguity, while at worst any serious reply would once again open up the contradictions. Anyway, I had decided by then to put all that behind me, and make the most of what I had. And the reward was that I soon found the best of Niall: funny, reckless, capricious, stimulating, sexy. I knew it would not last, but I was determined to enjoy it while I could. I was glad of the respite, the freedom to concentrate on one matter at a time. I *would* convince him we were finished, and I *would* get him out of my hair for good, but as the days went by I realised it was not going to happen straight away. On the contrary, Niall and I were getting along better than we had done for months.

The worst possible thing happened, from your point of view. You returned from your trip to Costa Rica at least three days earlier than I expected, and arrived at the house without telephoning first. I was in bed with Niall when I heard the house bell ring. Only five minutes earlier we had been making love, and we were still slumped in each other's arms in sweaty calm. One of the neighbours went to the door. I heard the sound of your voice.

'Oh God!' I said, scrambling out of the bed and pulling on my dressing gown.

Niall, naked on the bed behind me, sat up to lean on one elbow. 'Expecting someone?'

'Please! Keep your voice down!'

'If that's who I think it is, he won't be able to hear me.'

'It can't be Richard! I thought he'd be away until the end of the week.'

'Get rid of him and I'll sit here quietly until he's gone.'

I went to the door and opened it, and you were standing there. I was too shocked by your sudden arrival to know what to say. I backed guiltily into the room, clutching the untied dressing gown across my naked body. The instant you saw me you frowned suspiciously and stepped forward into the room.

You said, 'What's going on? Why are you in bed?'

'I was working late last night,' I said. 'I was having a lie in.'

'Are you on your own?'

'On my own! Can you see anyone here?'

'For God's sake, don't start that again! Didn't you get the telegram I sent?'

'No, I never saw it.'

'I tore it up yesterday,' said Niall, lighting a cigarette.

'*What?*' I swung around in amazement. Niall was sitting up, pouring himself a glass of wine. I turned back to you. 'No, I had no idea. How was the trip? Have you finished early?'

'Niall's been here, hasn't he?'

'Tell him I'm here now,' said Niall behind me. He had a hard, determined expression. Knowing the worst of him, what he was capable of, I stepped between the two of you.

'Can you see him?' I said to you.

'Of course not. What did he do: leap out of the window when I knocked?'

'Hey, that's pretty funny!'

I glared at Niall, who was now standing beside the bed, stretching his arms with his cigarette between his lips.

When I looked back at you, you said, 'Don't try to explain, Sue. You don't have to. I suppose I asked for it.'

'Richard, it's not what you think.'

'It's exactly what he thinks. He's not as thick as that.'

'I'm still on Central American time,' you said, looking at your watch with a dazed expression. 'My watch is wrong. What's the time?'

'It's half past eleven,' said Niall. He took my clock from the shelf and shook it in front of your face. I tried to elbow him back.

'It's late morning. I was about to get up.'

'But you have seen Niall, haven't you? While I was away?'

'Yes,' I said.

'Is that all? "Yes"?'

'I felt . . .' Suddenly, all the resolve I had been so sure of seemed like a betrayal of the worst kind. I said lamely, 'Richard, I felt you were forcing me to choose.'

'Sue, the hell with this. You promised me it wouldn't happen.'

'Why does he keep calling you Sue, Susan?'

'Shut up!' I shouted. 'Richard, not you. I'm sorry.'

'I've had it up to here. I'm not taking any more of this shit. Goodbye.'

'Richard! Look, we have to talk. Please!'

'You've talked me to death, lady.'

'No, I'd like to hear it, Susan,' Niall said.

'I can't . . . can I see you this evening?'

'No. No more. I'm sorry.' You looked totally destroyed by this exchange.

'Right then, bugger off!'

'Is that man going to run your life for ever?' you said.

'I tried to explain to you, Richard,' I said. 'I can't get away from him. Niall won't let me! He's glamorous too.'

You looked impatient. 'Don't start that again. Not now.'

'This man's a cretin, Susan. What do you see in him?'

I could no longer attempt to control the three-way conversation. I retreated and went to sit on the edge of the bed. I stared hopelessly at the floor.

'Sue, what has glamour to do with any of it?'

'Not glamour,' I said. '*The* glamour. Niall has the glamour. All three of us have the glamour! It's the most important thing in my life, and in yours too if only you knew it. We're all invisible. Can't you get that into your head.'

In my misery I knew I was sinking into invisibility. I no longer cared, no longer wanted anything but to be rid of you both. Niall was standing beside you, ludicrously naked, his face set in that unpleasant combination of arrogance and inadequacy that showed when he felt threatened. You had a stupid look, as you stared round the room.

You said, 'Sue, I can't see you! What's happening?'

I said nothing, knowing that even if I spoke you would be unable to hear. You stepped back, placed your hand on the door and opened it a few inches.

'That's right, Grey. Time to fuck off.'

I said, 'Shut up, Niall!'

You must have heard, because you looked sharply towards me.

'He's here, isn't he?' you said. 'Niall's here now!'

I said, 'He's been with us ever since I met you. If you had learned how to look when I tried to show you, you would have seen him.'

'Where is he? Where *exactly* is he?'

'I'm here, you stupid prick!' Niall said, waving his arms, moving around. His voice was suddenly stronger than ever before. I realised that for the last few seconds his cloud had been thinning. It was more dispersed than I had ever seen it. He kicked out at you with his foot, catching you on the shin. You reacted in surprise, and looked intently at Niall. He was closer to genuine visibility than I had thought was possible for him, and I knew you could see him, or something of him. You whirled around, shoving Niall out of the way, snatched the door open and went out, slamming it behind you. Moments later the street door slammed too.

I sprawled across the bed and started to cry. Long minutes passed. I could hear Niall moving around, but I closed my mind to him. When I next looked he was standing with his peacock clothes on, looking both defiant and shaken.

'I think I'll call back later, Susan,' he said.

'Don't bother!' I cried. 'I never want to see you again!'

'He won't come back, you know.'

'I don't care! I don't want to see him and I don't want to see you! Now get out of here!'

'I'll call you when you've calmed down.'

'I won't answer! Get to hell out of here and don't come back!'

'I'm going to fix Grey!' he said, in a low and peculiarly menacing voice. 'You too, probably—'

'For God's sake, *get out!*' I ran from the bed, opened the door and shoved him through, pushing it against his weight. I bolted it. He banged on the door and called something to me, but I didn't listen. I was utterly sick of everything, blaming myself, blaming you, blaming Niall.

A long time later, when I dressed and went out for a walk, I discovered I had become visible.

I had grown used to the feeling of being visible when I was with you, but now I was alone. There was no other cloud near me from which I could draw strength. Visibility had become my normal state. It felt odd and a little encouraging, like wearing new clothes.

When I was back in my room I tried to return myself to invisibility. It was more difficult than I would have believed. As soon as I relaxed I slipped into visibility again. By the time evening came I knew that everything I had sought was mine. It seemed ironical, but deserved, that I had had to lose you to gain it.

That was the day of the car bomb, but I did not hear about it for some time. Working backwards I think that it probably went off while I was out for my walk, but I don't remember hearing it. London is full of noises, and the high ground of Hampstead Heath lies between our two parts of the city. I had no television and I read no newspapers, and anyway my preoccupations were flooding everything. I worked at my drawing board until late into the night.

I went into the West End the next day to visit the studio, and learned from newspaper placards and headlines that there had been a big car bomb. It had gone off outside a police station in north-west London. Six people had been killed, and several more had been seriously injured. It did not occur to me that you might have been one of them. None of the victims was named in the newspaper I bought, and I wasn't expecting to hear from you. Apart from the usual shock and disgust about such an outrage, felt by everyone, I thought little more about it.

I saw nothing of Niall for almost a week, then one day he turned up at the house. He made no attempt to enter with his key, but rang the bell at the street door. When I went out I found him in a subdued, defensive mood. I felt no shock at seeing him. By this time I had almost forgotten about the car bomb.

He said, 'I won't come in, Susan. I wondered how you were taking the news.' I told him I didn't know what he meant. He had a guilty look about him. 'I was passing and thought I ought to see you. In case you wanted to say anything to me.'

'No, there's nothing. What news are you talking about?'

'You obviously haven't heard. I wondered if you would. You'd better read this.'

He passed me a copy of *The Times*, rolled up tightly. I started to unfurl it.

'Not now,' Niall said. 'Read it when I've gone.'

I said, 'Is it about Richard? Is it bad news?'

'You'll see what it is. And there's something else. You often said you wanted to read what I've been writing. Well, I've written something for you. When you've read it you can either keep it or throw it away. I don't want it back.'

He passed over a manilla envelope, sealed with transparent tape.

'What's happened to Richard?' I said, the newspaper already half open.

'It's all in there,' Niall said. He turned and walked quickly away.

I tucked the envelope under my arm, and read the newspaper as I stood in the doorway. It was on the front page, continued on inner pages. I found out at last what had happened to you. The edition of the paper Niall had given me was dated two days after the bombing, so the event itself was no longer the dominant news. The story by this time was the aftermath: the police hunt for the terrorists, political news about extra security measures being introduced by the Home Office, and on the second page the latest bulletins about the casualties. I learned that you and several other surviving victims were in intensive care, under

186

police protection. It turned out that one of the terrorists had also been injured in the blast, and the others had issued a macabre warning that surviving members of the public, whom they called 'witnesses', would be eliminated. Because of the threat, even the identity of the hospital in which you were being treated was kept secret.

I bought every newspaper I could find, and followed the story for as long as it was reported. You were the worst injured of all the surviving victims and the last to be removed from the critical list. I know that if I had really tried I would have been allowed to visit you earlier, but I sincerely believed that after our last confrontation seeing me might have done you more harm than good.

Eventually, only one of the tabloid newspapers was carrying occasional bulletins about your progress, following what they called your 'story'. From this paper I learned that you had been moved to the convalescent hospital in the West Country, and that you were still suffering from loss of memory. At long last I plucked up the courage to try to see you, thinking I might at least be able to help you with that. I telephoned the newspaper and they arranged everything.

This is what happened to you, Richard, in the weeks before the car bomb. Do you now remember?

PART SIX

Three weeks after he returned to London from Devon Richard Grey was offered filming work in Liverpool. It was a four day assignment, operating the camera for a television documentary about urban renewal following the Toxteth riots during the 1980s. Because of his injuries the work would be physically demanding, but the unit would be crewed to union levels, including camera assistants. He hesitated for less than an hour before accepting, and caught the train to Liverpool the following day.

The job temporarily solved the problem of what to do with his time. He was frustrated by the continuing stiffness of his body and he was keen to be working again. Anyway, money was at last beginning to run low. There was the likelihood of compensation being paid by the Home Office and correspondence was going to and fro between a solicitor and the Criminal Injuries Compensation Board, but it was not something on which he could count.

Until the job came along Grey had been hobbling through the days, learning again how to go shopping, to the movies, to the pub. Everything had to be taken slowly. Once a week he attended the physiotherapy department at the Royal Free Hospital in Hampstead. He was steadily improving, but it was gradual progress when he wanted dramatic advances. He walked as much as he could, because although immediately afterwards he felt tired and uncomfortable the long-term effect was a steady easing of his left hip. The stairs outside his apartment were an obstacle, but he found he could manage. Driving was still difficult because of the strain the clutch pedal put on his hip. He was thinking of changing to a car with automatic transmission, but it would have to wait until he was better off.

Leaving London would mean a break from Sue, something which a few weeks before he would never have dreamed he wanted, but which had become essential. He had to have time away from her to think about other things, to clear his mind a little.

Grey wished fervently that she had turned out in reality to be what she had at first appeared to be: an attractive girlfriend from his lost weeks who would help him through the period of recovery, leading perhaps to something more, perhaps to something less. But it was not working out that way. When he first met Sue he had found her oddness intriguing and provocative, hinting at layers of buried complexity which patience might unravel. He still found her physically attractive, she interested him and a great deal of tenderness existed between them. As his body healed their physical relationship became more exciting and satisfying. But the real difference was that she said she loved him, while in his innermost self Grey knew he did not love her. He liked her and he wanted to know her better and more intimately, but he did not love her. He was emotionally dependent on her, missed her when they were apart, felt protective of her, but still he did not love her.

The problem was their past together.

He did not *feel* about it. Memories of sorts now came from his lost weeks, but they were fragmentary and disconcerting, confusing rather than elucidating.

Real memories are a cocktail of remembered and overlooked experience. Odd and irrelevant facts lurk in the mind, stubbornly unforgotten after many years, while crucial dates and facts get lost in the muddle of everything else. Snatches of forgotten tunes, old jokes, childhood games, arrive unsummoned in the mind, while the result of an important meeting can be forgotten within a few days. Inexplicable associations exist: a smell will evoke a particular event, a fragment of music will remind you of a town, a colour will be linked imperishably with a mood. Grey had such memories for most of the years of his life, but his amnesiac period was both incomplete and regulated.

What memories he had were not good enough. They came with a superficial accuracy that made him instinctively distrust them. His mind told him stories and sequences of events that had a shallow plausibility, but they did not feel as if they had really happened. The analogy he made with it was a film that had been edited, so that all the inconsistent bits, the unexplained, the half-forgotten, had been removed for the sake of narrative continuity.

The rest of his memories, his old life, were like uncut rushes, unsorted, unassembled, hanging around randomly in his mind.

He was recognising at last that his memories of France were mostly false, projected on his mind from some quirk of the unconscious, and nudged along by Dr Hurdis's attempts to hypnotise him. He was fairly certain he had not been to France, or not, at least, at the time he remembered. There were no entry or departure stamps in his passport, for instance, although EU border rules meant that that did not prove much any more. More significantly, perhaps, there was nothing in his bank or credit card accounts that suggested he had been abroad, nor were there receipts, old tickets, or anything similar. His heavy withdrawals of cash suggested he had been spending money on something unusual, but within the UK. Some parts of the story were apparently true. He had met Sue, of course, and there was the business with Niall. There had been a holiday together. He had been filming in Central America. There was a final, disruptive row.

But there was also Sue's account of their past together and here the real gap appeared.

While she indirectly confirmed his edited memories, her story was something he had only *heard told*. He could accept and believe what she said in the way he might read and believe a book or a newspaper. She obviously thought that once she told her story some buried unconscious memory would be triggered, and his real memories of the same incidents would be magically restored. He wanted to believe that too and throughout her story had waited for some resonant image with which he could identify, some moment of psychological conviction, opening the way to the rest. It had not come. Sue's story remained a story and it was remote from him.

If anything, it had deepened the problem of his forgotten period. Using the same analogy, she had shown him another edited film, ready made, complete in itself, using some of the same material but otherwise different.

The muddle of real memories still eluded him.

His present misgivings, though, were centred on two other

areas. There were Sue's repeated claims about invisibility, and there was her obsessive and destructive relationship with Niall.

Once before Grey had been briefly entangled in a triangular sexual situation. Although he had genuinely cared for the woman at the centre of that, and had tried not to put pressure on her, the constant indecision, the wavering of loyalties and his own unavoidable feelings of sexual jealousy, had ultimately poisoned the affair. He had sworn afterwards never again to become involved with someone leading a double life, yet it was exactly what he appeared to have done with Sue. Something powerful must have drawn him to her.

Sue said that Niall was no longer bothering her and that she had not seen him since the day she described, when he came to the house and gave her the copy of *The Times*. It certainly appeared to be true that there was no one else around at the moment.

Niall remained a factor, though.

It was as if she was holding something in reserve about him. Grey felt that should Niall suddenly choose to make his presence felt, he would again cause trouble between them. Niall had by consent become a subject they never discussed, but by his very absence he remained omnipresent.

Sue's claims about invisibility only deepened the division.

Grey was a practical man, trained to use eye and hand. His vocation was with visual images, deliberately lit, carefully photographed. What he saw he believed in; what he could not see was not there.

Listening to Sue's account, he thought at first that her endless talk of invisible people was allegorical in some way, a description of an attitude, or of a kind of recessive personality. Maybe that was so, but he knew she also meant it literally and physically. She maintained that some people could escape notice through the failure of others to see them.

Grey found it unconvincing in itself, while her further claim, that he himself was of the same condition, was frankly incredible to him.

Yet Sue's account was that she had recognised in him the talent he had, and that he had already used it many times without knowing it. Now, she claimed, the talent was dormant in him, shocked out of him by the assault of his injuries. If he could remember *how*, she said, he would allow it to reawaken.

Listening to her, the doubts she frequently expressed, her inadequacies, the talk of madness and delusion, he wondered if the explanation lay there. The sheer obsession of Sue's insistence was itself close to delusion, a mad jargon, the desperation of a persistent but illogical belief.

His was the sort of outlook that believed surprising claims should be proved, or, failing that, have convincing evidence produced in support of them. It seemed to him it would be simple to settle the matter one way or another, but Sue was maddeningly imprecise. Invisible people were *there*, they could be *seen*, but unless you knew how to see they would not be *noticed*.

They went out one day to Kensington High Street, mingling with the crowds of shoppers on a busy afternoon. Sue told him that this was the kind of situation where you would find glams. She duly pointed out a number of people, claiming they were invisibles. Sometimes Grey could see who she meant, sometimes he could not. Misunderstandings happened all the time: that man by the entrance to the shop, not that one, *that* one, he's moved, too late.

He began taking photographs, pointing the camera wherever Sue told him an invisible person was present. The results were inconclusive: when they looked at the prints the photographs of crowds were simply photographs of crowds, and he and Sue could only argue whether this person had been visible at the time, or that couple had been invisible.

'Make yourself invisible,' Grey said. 'Do it while I watch.'

'I can't.'

'But you said you could.'

'It's different now. It's not easy for me any more.'

'You can still do it, though?'

'Yes, but you know how to see me.'

Nevertheless, she tried. After much frowning and concentration she declared herself to be invisible, but as far as Grey was concerned she was still there, easily seen by him. She accused him of disbelieving her, but it was not as straightforward as that.

He believed, for instance, in what he thought of as the neutrality of her appearance, something he had found attractive from the start. In some ways it disguised her with ordinariness. Everything about her appearance was simple, plain and regular. Her skin was fair, her hair was light brown, her eyes were hazel, her features were even, her figure was slim. She was of average height and her clothes hung naturally on her body. When they were not wrangling about their love life, and spent quiet hours together, her manner was lenitive, emollient. When she moved she did so quietly. Her voice was pleasant, but unremarkable. A disinterested glance at her might find her dull and mousy, but to Grey, interested in her and involved with her, she was exceptionally attractive. What he perceived in her was merely disguised by the plainness of the surface; something electric came from within. When they were together he was constantly wanting to touch her. He liked the way her face changed when she smiled, or became preoccupied, or when she was concentrating on her work. To him she was beautiful. When they made love he felt that their bodies blended without touching, an imprecise sensation that he experienced every time but which he could never define. It was as if she were a complement to him, his equal and opposite in everything.

She claimed that by disbelieving in her invisibility he was rejecting all that she had told him, but in fact it was the concealed quality of her that intrigued him, and which made her invisibility convincing to him emotionally, if not in practice. She was not invisible to him, or not in any way he understood the word, but she was for all that an inexact person. He believed he was a long way from rejecting her.

Even so, the trip to Liverpool gave him an opportunity to reflect on her from a distance.

The sea could always be sensed in Liverpool: the great river front with the view across to Birkenhead, the glimpse of the Irish Sea to the west, the self-confident architecture of the Victorian shipping offices, the smell of water on the gusting wind. Away from the centre, but not far away, where the buildings were meaner and the streets were narrower, the sea evinced itself differently. Here was a grim red-light district of slum houses, empty warehouses where bonded goods had once been stored, pubs with maritime names, cleared areas fronted with advertising placards selling Jamaican rum and airlines to America.

This was Toxteth, where belated government intervention was trying to impose community spirit on a place where transience was the norm.

It was good to be working with an Arriflex again, feeling its lumpy weight on his shoulder, the moulded eyepiece against his brow. Grey greeted the workaday camera with a sense of quiet reunion, amazed to discover how natural it still felt in his hands, how his vision was narrowed and sharpened by seeing and thinking through the viewfinder. But he was used to working with a smaller crew, and the large numbers of people around him disconcerted him at first. He felt he was on trial, that they were waiting to see if he still knew what to do, but he soon realised that he was only imagining his own fears and that everyone else was too busy with their own jobs to be thinking about him. He settled to the work.

The first day's shoot exhausted him because he was out of practice in other ways, and during the morning of the second day his leg and shoulders were painful. The work absorbed him, though. He knew that these few days were worth a hundred hours of physiotherapy.

The director was an experienced documentary maker, and they kept easily to the schedule. They always finished filming by late afternoon, leaving the evenings free. The crew were staying at the Adelphi Hotel, and each evening most of them stayed in to drink in the large, palm-filled mezzanine bar. For Grey it was a valuable opportunity to talk shop, swap stories about old assignments, catch up on gossip about people he knew. There was talk of more jobs coming up, a chance to work on contract in Saudi Arabia, a political story developing in Italy.

It was all so different from the last few weeks, obsessed with himself and Sue, her bizarre story and claustrophobic relationships. He telephoned her from his room one evening, and hearing her voice on the line gave him the sense of drilling a long tunnel back to something he had already left behind. She said she was lonely without him, wanted him back with her soon, sorry about everything, different now. He uttered reassurances, feeling glib, trying to make them sincere. He still wanted her, yearned for lovemaking with her, but while he was away it all felt as different as she said.

They shot the last sequence on the fourth evening. The location was a working men's club, the barn-like interior of a former warehouse. Grey arrived early with his assistants, set up the lights for the interviews, and widened two of the gangways for the camera to dolly along. To one side there was a small platform with a number of spotlights overhead, musical amplifiers stacked unused under covers at the back. The acoustics were bright, and the sound man winced at the amount of echo when he took a level. Most of the club members were men, wearing suits without neckties, and the few women kept their outdoor coats on. Everyone drank from straight glasses, talking noisily over the band music coming from the loudspeakers. As the place filled up, and a couple of bouncers took up their position by the door, Grey was reminded of a pub in Northern Ireland where he had filmed a few years before. That had had the same Spartan décor: plain tables and chairs, bare floorboards, beer mats and ashtrays from breweries, overhead lights with cheap lampshades, the bar itself lit by fluorescent tubes.

They started filming with a few establishing shots of the crowded room, then close-ups of a few drinkers, and a number of interviews: how many people were unemployed, the levels of violent crime, what prospects there were of moving away, jobs vanishing everywhere.

The main entertainment of the evening was a stripper, who came on the platform wearing a gaudy sequinned costume which had obviously seen much use. Grey took the camera on his shoulder and moved in to film her act. Seeing the camera, the woman put on an elaborate show, grimacing sexily, grinding her backside, stripping off her costume with exaggerated gestures. She looked as if she was in her middle thirties, she was overweight, had a bad complexion under her make-up, had stretch-marks on her belly, and pendulous breasts. When she was naked she jumped down from the platform. Grey followed her with the camera as she went from table to table, sitting on laps, spreading her legs, letting her breasts be fingered, wearing a look of grim gaiety on her face.

When she had gone, and the camera was being reinstalled on the dolly, Grey stood to one side, remembering.

There had been a stripper in that bar in Belfast. He and the sound man had gone there in the middle of the evening, after a sectarian shooting. They arrived as the ambulances and police were leaving. All there was left to film was bullet holes in the wall and broken glass on the floor. Because it was Belfast the blood was soon mopped up and the commotion died down, and even as they were filming the drinking resumed and new customers arrived. A stripper came on and went through her act, and Grey and the sound man had stayed to watch. As they were about to leave the gunmen abruptly returned, pushing through the crowd near the door and shouting threats. Both carried Armalite rifles, pointed upwards. Without thinking what he was doing, Grey hefted the camera to his shoulder and started filming. He forced his way through the crowd, going right up to the gunmen, filming their faces. He was there when they opened fire, killing a man at point-blank range before pumping a dozen rounds into the ceiling, bringing the plaster down in flakes and lumps. Then they left.

Grey's film was never transmitted, but it was later used by the security forces to identify the men, and they were arrested and convicted. Grey's reckless act of courage won him a cash bonus from the network, but the incident was soon forgotten. What no one could understand, including Grey himself, was why the gunmen had let him film them, why they had not shot him.

Standing there in the racket of the drinking club in Liverpool, Grey thought about what Sue had said. She had reminded him of the story he must have told her, about filming the street riot. She said: In the heat of the moment you made yourself invisible.

Had that happened in the bar in Belfast too? Was there after all something in what she said?

He completed the rest of the filming in the club, feeling selfconscious, thinking himself an intruder into the depressing lives of these people, and was glad when they had packed up the equipment and could return to the hotel.

As soon as he was awake in the morning Grey telephoned Sue at the house. She came to the phone sounding groggy with sleep. He told her that the shoot had been extended and that he would not be back in London for two more days. She sounded disappointed but did not question him. She said she had been doing some thinking and wanted to talk to him. Grey promised her he would contact her as soon as he was back, and they hung up.

After breakfast the crew met in the lobby before dispersing. Grey noted down a few phone numbers, and provisionally arranged to meet the producer in London the following week. When they had all said their farewells he hitched a lift in the car of the assistant director, who was driving to Manchester. Grey was dropped off a short bus ride away from the suburb where Sue had said she was born.

He located the address in a telephone directory, and walked through the residential streets to find it. The house was a pre-war detached villa, standing in a short cul-de-sac.

A woman answered the door, smiling at him but looking cautious.

'Excuse me, are you Mrs Kewley?'

'Yes. Can I help you?'

'My name's Richard Grey and I'm a friend of your daughter Susan.'

The smile disappeared. 'It's not bad news, is it?'

'Not at all. I've been working near here. I thought I'd call on you and say hello. I should have telephoned first. Susan's fine, and she sends her love. I didn't mean to alarm you.'

'You said you name was . . . ?'

'Richard Grey. If it's inconvenient . . .'

'Would you like to come in for a few moments?'

There was a corridor inside, with a glimpse through to a kitchen at the far end. Carpeted stairs rose from the hall, with small framed paintings hanging from the wall. He was shown into the front room, where chairs and ornaments were set out with neat precision. Mrs Kewley bent down to light the gas fire, then straightened slowly.

'Would you like a cup of tea, Mr Grey? Or I could make some coffee.' Her accent was northern, with no detectable trace of the Scottish he had expected.

'Tea, please. I'm sorry to turn up on your doorstep without warning.'

'I'm always interested to meet Susan's friends. I won't be a moment.'

There was a photograph of Sue on the mantelpiece: her hair

was long and tied back with a ribbon. She looked much younger, but her awkward way of sitting when she knew she was being looked at was the same. The photo was mounted in a frame, and the name of the studio was inscribed in gold foil in one corner. He guessed it had been taken shortly before she left home.

Grey prowled quietly around the room, sensing that it was not often used. At the end of the corridor he could hear voices and the movement of crockery. He felt like an intruder, knowing that Sue would be furious if she found out what he was doing. He heard voices approaching, so he sat down in one of the chairs by the fire. Outside, he heard a woman say, ''Bye now, May. I'll pop in again tomorrow.'

''Bye, Audrey.' The front door opened and closed, and Sue's mother came into the room with a tray.

They were uncomfortable with each other, Grey because of his uncertain motives for being there, and Mrs Kewley presumably because of his unannounced arrival. She looked rather older than he had expected, with hair already white and a slight stiffness in her movements, but her face was unmistakably like Sue's. He was pleased by glimpsing similar gestures.

'Aren't you the friend who is a photographer?' she said.

'That's right. Well, I'm a film cameraman.'

'Oh yes. Susan told us about you. You were in an accident, weren't you?'

They talked for a while about the car bomb, and his spell in hospital. Grey was relieved to have something he could talk about so easily, but he was surprised to learn that Sue had mentioned him to her parents. She gave the impression she had little contact with her family. Realising that what people say to their parents is often a guarded form of the whole truth, he was cautious about what he said of Sue's present life, but Mrs Kewley told him that Sue wrote many letters home. She knew all about Sue's career and even had a scrapbook of cuttings, many of which Grey himself had never seen. It was a small insight into Sue, discovering how much work she had sold, how excellent most of it was, also to realise that she was obviously well established in her field.

When the scrapbook had been set aside, Mrs Kewley said, 'Is Susan still going out with Niall?'

'I'm not sure. I don't think so. I didn't know you had met him.'

'Oh yes, we know Niall well. Susan brought him home with her one weekend. A nice boy, we thought, though rather quiet. I believe he is a writer, but he wouldn't say much about it. Is he a friend of yours too?'

'No, I've never met him.'

'I see.' Mrs Kewley suddenly smiled nervously and glanced away, like Sue. She obviously realised she had made a gaffe, so Grey quickly assured her that he and Sue were simply friends. The moment off-guard broke the ice, and Mrs Kewley was more talkative after it. She told him about her other daughter, Rosemary, married and living a few miles away in Stockport. There was a granddaughter, whom Sue had mentioned once.

Grey was thinking about the account Sue had given him of the one occasion she had brought Niall to this house. It had sounded markedly different from the scene of indulgent parental approval that Mrs Kewley described, and according to Sue had led directly to her first separation from Niall. Yet Mrs Kewley had obviously met him, found nothing unusual about him and had even formed a favourable opinion of him.

'My husband will be home from work soon,' she said. 'He works part-time at present. Will you stay and meet him?'

'I'd like to,' Grey said. 'But I do have to catch a train to London this afternoon. Maybe I'll be able to meet your husband before I leave.'

She started asking innocent questions about Sue and her way of life in London: what her room was like, the sort of people she worked with, whether she took enough exercise, and so on. Grey answered her, feeling apprehensive, aware that he could easily blunder into some minor contradiction with Sue's own version of herself. The revelation about Niall underlined how little he really knew or understood Sue. To avoid the problem he started asking questions of his own. It was not long before Mrs Kewley produced a photograph album. Feeling more like a spy than ever, Grey looked with interest at the pictures of Sue's childhood.

She had been a pretty child, and the plainness that he found so intriguing developed later. In her teens Sue began to look gawky and sullen, posing obediently for the photographs but averting her face. Mrs Kewley passed quickly over these pictures, obviously reminded of particular moments.

At the back of the album, not mounted like the others but slipped loosely inside the pages, was a colour snapshot. It slid to the floor as Mrs Kewley was putting away the album. Grey picked it up. It was a more recent picture of Sue, looking much as he knew her. She was standing in a garden next to a flower bed, and beside her was a young man with his arm around her shoulders.

'Who is that?' Grey said.

'Sue's friend Niall, of course.'

'*Niall?*'

'Yes, I thought you knew him. We took that picture in the garden, on his last visit.'

'Oh yes, I recognise him now.'

Grey stared at the photograph. Until this moment his unseen rival had possessed a minatory quality in Grey's mind, but to see him at last, even in a slightly blurred snapshot, made him immediately less of a threat. Niall was young looking, slight in build, had a shock of fair hair over a high forehead, and wore an expression that was both surly and arrogant. He was frowning, and he looked up resentfully from beneath his eyebrows. His mouth was turned down with disdain. The way he stood, the set of his shoulders, evinced contempt and condescension. He looked like an ambitious, intelligent man, impatient of the failings of others. He was smartly if colourfully dressed, and had a cigarette in his mouth. His face was turned towards Sue. He held her possessively, but she was standing ill at ease and she looked tense.

Grey returned the photograph to Mrs Kewley, and she slipped it back inside the album. Not realising the effect the picture had on him, she began chattering about Sue and the years in which she was growing up. Grey kept his silence and listened. What emerged was a story supported by neither the pictures he had just seen nor Sue's own version. According to her mother, Sue had been a contented girl, clever at school, popular with the other girls, talented at drawing. She had been a good daughter, close to her sister, considerate of her parents. Her teachers spoke well of her, and friends in the neighbourhood were still asking after her. Until the two girls grew up and left home they had been a happy, intimate family, sharing most things. Now they were proud of her, feeling that she was fulfilling the promise she had shown. Her parents' only regret was that she could not visit home more often, but they knew how busy she was.

Something was missing, and after a while Grey sensed what it was. Parents who spoke well of their children usually told amusing stories about them, harmless anecdotes about childish foibles, to round out the picture. Mrs Kewley spoke in generalisations and platitudes, soft on detail, but her enthusiasm was genuine and she smiled often at her memories, a kind woman, a nice woman.

Soon after midday her husband arrived home. Grey saw him on the path outside the window, and Mrs Kewley went out to meet him. Moments later he entered the room and shook hands with Grey.

'I'm going to put lunch on,' Mrs Kewley said. 'You will join us, won't you?'

'No, I really must be leaving soon.'

The two men were left together, standing facing each other, an awkward silence between them.

'Perhaps you'd care for a drink before you leave?' said Mr Kewley at last, still holding the morning's newspaper he had brought in with him.

'Yes, thank you.' The only alcohol in the house turned out to be sweet sherry, a drink Grey disliked, but he accepted it with good grace, sipping it politely. Soon afterwards, Mrs Kewley returned and the three of them sat in a semicircle in the little room, talking about the firm Mr Kewley worked for. Grey finished his drink as quickly as he could, and said he really must be getting along to the station. The other two seemed relieved, but they all went through the motions of renewed invitations to stay to lunch, and thankful refusal. Grey shook hands again with Sue's father, and Mrs Kewley saw him to the door.

He had walked only a short distance from the house when he heard the front door reopen.

'Mr Grey!' Sue's mother came quickly towards him. In the daylight she looked suddenly much younger, more like Sue herself. 'Just something!'

'What is it?' he said mildly, trying to reassure her because unexpectedly she had a different look, a new urgency.

'I don't want to delay you.' She glanced back at the house, as if expecting her husband to be following. 'It's about Susan. Please tell me! How is she?'

'She's fine, really.'

'No, don't say that. Please tell me how she really is! What is she doing? Is she well? Is she happy?'

'Yes, she's both. She enjoys herself. She's doing well. She seems contented.'

'But do you *see* her?'

'From time to time. Once or twice a week.' Noticing that her expression had not changed, Grey added, 'Yes, I do really see her.'

Mrs Kewley was close to tears. She said, 'My husband and I, well, we don't really know Susan any more. She was our little one and at first we lavished so much attention on her, but then later Rosemary, her sister, was often unwell and we rather neglected her. I think Susan never forgave us, or understood why we seemed to turn against her. It wasn't like that, there was nothing we could do . . . I'd love to see her again. Please tell her that. Use those words: see her again.'

She sobbed once but controlled it quickly, turning her head up and away, her chest heaving.

'I'll tell her as soon as I see her.'

Mrs Kewley nodded, then walked quickly back to the house. The door closed softly and Grey stood silently in the street, aware that Sue's account had oddly been confirmed. He wished he had not called.

Grey had promised Sue he would phone her as soon as he was in London, but he was exhausted when he arrived back from Manchester. He went straight to bed. In the morning he realised he had a day in hand and decided to contact her that evening.

He was sorry he had visited her parents. Nothing had been achieved by the trip. Now it was over he acknowledged that his real motive had been curiosity about her invisibility, proof or disproof, whichever might have emerged. All he had found was more ambiguity. A difficult adolescence, recalled by her parents in a synoptic way, partially suppressed, accounted for normally. If she had been invisible to them it was the more familiar failure of parental vision: an inability to accept she was growing up and changing, seeking independence and her own identity, rejecting her parents' lives and background.

The pressure of domestic needs grew on him. Returning home from a working trip inevitably involved the same routine: a backlog of mail, a shortage of clean clothes, food to be bought. He was out for most of the morning, attending to these chores, and while he was around the shops he called in at the newsagent who was still delivering the tabloid newspaper every weekday morning. He loathed the paper for many reasons, not least because it was a daily reminder of his long stay in hospital. Grey was told that the newspaper was being delivered on the instructions of the newspaper distributors, but he persuaded the newsagent he wanted it no more.

Returning with a laundry bag containing his clean clothes and two carrier bags of groceries, Grey discovered someone walking away from his front door. It was a striking looking young woman with short dark hair. As soon as she saw him she smiled expectantly.

'Mr Grey? I thought you must be out. I was about to leave.'

'I've been shopping,' he said redundantly.

'I tried to telephone you yesterday, but there was no answer.' She saw his frown and added, 'I don't suppose you remember me. I'm Alexandra Gowers. I'm a student of Dr Hurdis.'

'Miss Gowers! I'm sorry, I didn't . . . Would you like to come in?'

'Dr Hurdis gave me your address. I hope you don't mind.'

'Not at all.'

He opened the door, went in first with his bags, then tried to stand to one side to let her go first. She squeezed past him in the narrow hallway, bending down to pick up a slip of paper. 'I had left a note for you,' she explained, and crumpled it.

He followed her up the stairs at his usual slow pace.

He was trying to think what he remembered of her from before: his mental image was of a rather severe face, heavy and shapeless clothes, spectacles, overlong hair. She had obviously been putting in some work on her image in the meantime, to good effect. He showed her into his living room.

'I must put the shopping away,' he said. 'Can I make you some coffee?'

'Yes, please.'

He moved about in the kitchen, getting the cafetière ready, switching on the kettle and dumping his selection of convenience foods in the freezer. He remembered Alexandra being there when he was hypnotised the first time, but she hadn't been present at later sessions. Since leaving Middlecombe he had heard nothing from Dr Hurdis.

She was sitting on his ancient sofa when he took the coffee in to her. He poured cups for them both, then settled on the chair opposite her.

'I was calling in the hope I could make an appointment with you,' she said. 'I'd like to interview you.'

'Is it likely to take long? I have the rest of the afternoon, if that's any good.'

'It could take a whole day. It would be for my dissertation. I'm doing postgraduate research with Dr Hurdis at Exeter University, and my subject is the subjective experience of hypnosis.' She looked at him, waiting for a response. Not getting any, she added, 'There's been a lot of work recently on hypnosis as a clinical tool, but there's almost nothing about what the subject experiences.'

'I don't think I'd be much use to you,' Grey said, after a moment's thought. He was distracted by the sight of her crossed legs, and was in conflict with himself over noticing them. 'I've put all that behind me. Anyway, I'm afraid I can't remember much about it.'

'That's actually the main reason I'd like to interview you,' she said. 'If you're willing, can you suggest a suitable day and time?'

'I don't know. I'm not sure I want to talk about it.'

She said nothing, stirring her coffee and looking candidly at him. Grey was deep in mixed feelings about her, unreasonably. It was as if once you became a case history they would never leave you alone afterwards. She was reminding him of what it had been like in the wheelchair, constantly in pain, totally dependent on other people, unable to do anything for himself. He had thought that once he left hospital all that would be behind him.

'So you won't do it?' she said in the end.

'There must be other people you could talk to.'

He noticed that she had returned her notebook to her bag.

'The problem is that Dr Hurdis will only let me approach

patients whose sessions I've actually been present at, the ones who gave their permission. The only other people I have access to are experimental subjects. Other students, mostly. Clinical cases are vital to my kind of research and your case is especially interesting.'

'Why?'

'Because you're articulate, because of what happened under hypnosis, because the circumstances—'

'What do you mean, what happened?'

She shrugged, picked up her coffee for a sip. 'Well, that would be the point of interviewing you.'

Grey was already regretting his unexpressed hostility and was starting to enjoy her forthright and unembarrassed way of getting his interest. He knew she was dangling a morsel of curiosity towards him, just as her elegant legs in their sheer black stockings were being deployed in another area.

'All right,' he said. 'We can talk about it if you wish. But look, I was planning to have lunch in a few minutes. Why don't we go to the pub and have something?'

A few minutes later, as they walked slowly down the road together, Grey suddenly identified the teasing memory he had of her. Recollections of her physical appearance were vague, but the opposite, her seeming disappearance, had amazed and impressed him. There had been that moment, under the hypnosis, when Dr Hurdis instructed him to look at this young woman, and he had known she was there but he had been unable to *see* her. It was an uncanny echo, pre-existing, of everything Sue had said.

They found the pub only half full. They sat in one of the booths by themselves. With the food and drink set before them, Alexandra told him a little more about herself. After graduating from Exeter she had been unable to find a job, and so had stayed on to do research, postponing the problem of a career and aiming for higher qualifications. She was surviving on a shoestring, living with her brother and his wife in London, and when in Exeter stayed in a grubby house shared by a number of other students. She thought the research would probably continue for a few more months, but after that she'd have to look for a job. She was thinking she might go abroad.

She told him about her research. She said the phenomenon

that interested her was spontaneous amnesia: the experience of the hypnotic subject who, without instructions from the hypnotist, could not afterwards recall what had happened. It was apparently fairly common, but took on extra significance in clinical cases where the subject was being treated for loss of memory.

'The special feature of your case is that you seemed to recover some of your memory under hypnosis, but afterwards you couldn't remember remembering.'

'That's about right,' Grey said. 'It's why I can't be much help to you.'

'But Dr Hurdis said that you have since recovered your memory.'

'Only some of it.'

She reached into her bag and brought out her notebook. 'Do you mind?' Grey shook his head, smiling, as she put on her spectacles and turned the pages quickly. She said, 'You were in France, before the accident?'

'No, I *remember* being in France. I don't think I was ever actually there.'

'Dr Hurdis said you were emphatic about it. You were speaking French, for instance.'

'That came up in later sessions too. I think what happened was that I was cobbling together something, a kind of fake memory. At the time it was important to remember anything, no matter what.'

'Paramnesia,' Alexandra said.

'Yes. Hurdis told me about that.'

'Do you remember this?' She produced a piece of paper, curled at the edges and obviously folded and unfolded many times. 'Dr Hurdis asked me to return it to you.'

Grey recognised it at once: it was the passage he had written during the first hypnotic session, when Alexandra was present. Gatwick Airport, the departure lounge, the crowds of waiting passengers. It was familiar and banal to him. After a glance at it he refolded it and slipped it into his jacket pocket.

'Not interested?' Alexandra said.

'Not now.'

He went to the bar to buy some more drinks. Another memory

from their first meeting was tugging at him. As they parted she had made an ingenuous remark about stage hypnotists and the trick they could play on their subjects, making them see members of the opposite sex without their clothes on. Sue had been uppermost in his mind at the time, but for a few moments Alexandra had shamelessly teased him. It was refreshing to be with a woman who was not Sue, because with Sue there was a constant undercurrent of what could be said, and what could not. Alexandra had the attractive quality of being straightforward. He hardly knew her, so it was all he saw. He liked her seriousness and her singlemindedness, also the way she intimidated him, apparently without meaning to, and the way she came on at him, apparently with that intent. She was mature, lacked selfconsciousness and clearly had a formidable mind. Grey sneaked a quick look back at her, and found her staring at him. She had been reading through her notebook. Her short dark hair was swept back behind an ear, obviously a habit from the time when it fell over her eyes as she leaned forward.

Back at the table, Grey said, 'What else happened that day?'

'You told Dr Hurdis you couldn't remember the trance.'

'Some of it came back afterwards. But there was a sort of gap. He told me to go deeper, but the next thing I knew he was waking me up.'

'I think it's safe to say it went a bit out of control. I'd never come across anything like it before. I don't think Dr Hurdis was ready for it either. It began when you were speaking French. You were mumbling and it was difficult to hear, so we were both standing close to you, looking right at you. What happened next is difficult to describe. Our attention must have wandered, something distracted us. It *felt* as if we had finished, that the session was over, and that for some agreed reason you had left the room.

'We both straightened, and Dr Hurdis said, "I'm going into Exeter after lunch, so would you like a lift?" I specifically remember the words. I thanked him, put away my papers and picked up my coat. Dr Hurdis said he had to speak to one of the other doctors, but would meet me for lunch in a few minutes. We left the office together and I followed him out of the door. I looked back into the room the way you do, glancing round to make sure I hadn't forgotten everything. Everything was as it should be. The chair you had been in was vacant. I'm certain of this: you weren't there any longer.

'So I closed the door, caught up with Dr Hurdis and we walked along the corridor towards the stairs. Then Dr Hurdis stopped dead. He said, "What on earth are we doing?" I had no idea what he meant, but he clicked his fingers sharply in front of my eyes, and it startled me. It was like being woken out of a dream. For a moment I couldn't think where I was. Dr Hurdis said, "Miss Gowers, we haven't finished the consultation!"

'We went straight back to the office and you were there, sitting in the armchair, still in the trance and mumbling away.'

She paused to take a drink. Grey was staring at the table between them, thinking about that day.

'I assume you don't remember any of this?' Alexandra said.

'I had vanished?'

'As far as we were concerned, yes. Just for a moment.'

'But long enough for you both to think the session was over,' Grey said. 'Isn't that unusual?'

'You can say that again! But let me tell you the rest of it, because we think there's a possible explanation. As soon as we were back in the office Dr Hurdis was obviously shaken up by it. He can be difficult when he's angry and he started ordering me around as if it had been my fault. I took out my pad again and tried to listen to what you were saying, but he pushed me out of the way. He spoke to you in the trance, telling you to describe what you were doing. It was then that you asked for something to write with. Dr Hurdis snatched my notepad and pen from me and gave them to you. You wrote that.'

She indicated the pocket where he had put the slip of paper.

'While you were writing, Dr Hurdis took me to the side of the room and said, "When the patient comes out of the trance we must say nothing of what happened." I asked him what that was, and he said we could discuss it later. He repeated that we must not under any circumstances talk about it in front of you. You were still writing, and Dr Hurdis was obviously still rattled by what had happened. He was as rough with you as he had been with me, and grabbed the pen away. He gave me back my pad. You called out that you wanted to go on writing and sounded distressed. Dr Hurdis said he was going to bring you out of the trance. Again he warned me not to say anything. He calmed you down, then started waking you. You can probably remember the rest.'

'When I opened my eyes I had the impression something had gone wrong,' Grey said. 'But obviously I wasn't able to tell what.'

'Now you know. We had temporarily lost you.'

'You said you thought you could explain it?'

'It's only a guess, but Dr Hurdis suggested it might have been a form of negative hallucination. The process of hypnosis can sometimes affect more than the subject. The repetition of words, the soothing suggestions, the quiet room. All these sometimes lull the hypnotist himself into a light trance and make him as suggestible as his subject. It happens fairly often, although hypnotists usually take precautions. What we think must have taken place with you is that Dr Hurdis and I became hypnotised. We're both good subjects. If that happened, it's possible that we had the same negative hallucination, in which we were unable to see you. There have been other cases. The few I've been able to trace have been when the hypnotist was working alone. As far as I know there's no precedent for both the therapist and an assistant sharing an hypnotic experience.'

Grey was thinking of something Sue had said, that invisibility depended as much on the observer as the observed. Some can *see*, some can not. Was her invisibility caused by an induced negative hallucination, and therefore explicable in terms that clinical psychologists already used and could confirm? Alexandra had mentioned the soothing methods of the hypnotist, the quiet repetition of words, and this reminded him unavoidably of the effect Sue's appearance and mien often had on him. Her quietness, her calming manner, the sense of contentment she induced in him when they were left to themselves and not wrangling about Niall.

He also remembered the day they had been out in the street trying to prove invisibility one way or the other, photographing the people Sue claimed were natural invisibles. He thought of the snapshot he had seen of Sue and Niall together. The camera could not suffer a negative hallucination.

'So you think that's what really happened?' he said.

'Unless you actually made yourself invisible,' Alexandra said, smiling. 'There's no other explanation.'

'All right, what about genuine invisibility?' Grey said on an impulse. 'Isn't that possible? I mean—'

'Actual, corporeal invisibility?' She was still smiling. 'Not unless you believe in magic. You yourself had a negative hallucination that day. Dr Hurdis made it impossible for you to see me, so you know how it works. I wasn't *really* invisible, except to you.'

'But I don't understand the difference,' Grey persisted. 'I couldn't see you, so you were to all intents invisible. In what way would corporeal invisibility be different? And then you say that I became invisible to you and Hurdis. Was I still really there?'

'Of course you were.'

'What if you had put your hand out, tried to put it into the chair where I had been sitting? Would you have been able to touch me?'

'Yes. But I wouldn't have *felt* you, because the hallucination is complete. It's not only the eyes that cease to see. The whole conscious mind loses the ability to perceive.'

'That's surely the same thing, though. You made me invisible.'

'Only subjectively. We made you invisible to us because we failed to notice you.'

Alexandra began to tell him of another case history, a woman who spontaneously hallucinated negatively and who was treated with hypnosis. Grey listened to the story. But he was also thinking in parallel, trying to reinterpret in these terms everything Sue had told him.

If what she said was true, and she apparently believed it was, this might be a plausible explanation. As Alexandra said, however unlikely it was it remained the only possible rational answer, even though the extent of Sue's claims increased the unlikelihood. She said Niall was invisible to everyone, presumably meaning that he was able to make everyone hallucinate at once.

It was difficult to think about this and listen to Alexandra at the same time, so he put it aside for the time being. Their conversation became more general and personal. She asked him about his recovery, how he was adapting to normal life, what problems remained. He told her about his recent filming work, and said he had briefly visited Manchester. Somehow, he never mentioned Sue.

Afterwards, they walked together back to his flat. Outside the door, Alexandra said, 'I must be getting back to my brother's. But thanks for talking to me.'

'I think I've learned more than you.'

They shook hands formally, as they had done on their first meeting.

Grey said, 'I was wondering. Shall we meet again? Perhaps one evening?'

'Not for an interview, I presume.'

'No, not for that.'

'I'd like that.'

They made a date for the following week. She wrote her address and phone number on a page of her notebook, then tore it out and gave it to him. He noticed that she wrote the numeral '7' with a dash through the stem.

Grey visited Sue in the evening. As soon as he arrived he knew something was wrong. It was not long before he found out what it was: Sue's mother had telephoned her and told her of his visit.

At first he tried to lie.

'We had to go to Manchester for some filming,' he said. 'I decided on an impulse to look them up.'

'You said you were working in Toxteth. What the hell does that have to do with Manchester?'

'All right, I went specially. I wanted to meet them.'

'But they don't know anything about me! What did they tell you?'

'I know you think I was spying on you, but it really wasn't like that. Sue, I had to know.'

'Know what? What could they possibly tell you about me?'

'They *are* your parents,' Grey said.

'But they've hardly seen me since I was twelve years old!'

'That's why I went. Something happened while I was on the shoot.' He told her about the stripper's act in the club and the memory it had prompted of the Belfast pub. 'It made me see everything you had said in a different light. That there might be some truth in it after all.'

'I knew you didn't believe me.'

'It's not that. I have to know for myself. I'm sorry if you think I've been snooping, but the idea came to me on the spur of the moment. I wanted to talk to someone else who knows you.'

'I've been invisible to Mum and Dad since I was a kid. The only times they've seen me have been when I've forced myself into visibility.'

'That's not the impression they gave me,' Grey said. 'You're right that they don't know you well, but that's because you've grown up and left home.'

Sue was shaking her head. 'That's the way they account for it. It's how people deal with someone around them who's invisible. They come up with a rational version to explain to themselves what's happened. It's a way of coping.'

Grey thought of Alexandra, her rationalisation.

'Your mother said she had met Niall.'

'That's impossible!' But she looked surprised.

'You told me yourself that he went home with you for a weekend.'

'Niall was invisible the whole time. Richard, they *think* they saw him. They know about Niall, I told them about him years ago. The only time he's been home with me was that one week-end, but they couldn't have seen him because it's simply not possible.'

'Then why does your mother think she knows him? She's even got a photograph of him. I saw it. You and Niall together, in the back garden.'

'They took several. Niall's probably in most of them. Don't you see, though? That's how she explains it to herself! When they had the pictures developed there was Niall, the young man they'd sensed without noticing. Thinking back, they would seem to remember him.'

'Yes, but it's just as likely that they did see him. It doesn't prove anything one way or the other.'

'Why do you need proof?'

'Because it's coming between us. First it was Niall, now it's this. I want to believe you, and I do believe you, but everything you tell me can be explained two ways.'

Throughout all this they were in her room, Sue squatting cross

legged on her bed, Grey in the chair by her d
and paced about the room.

'All right,' Sue said. 'While you were away I gav
thought. If you're right, and this is what's standing betw
we've got to solve it. We're drifting apart, Richard, and I d
like that. If you want proof I think I can give it to you.'

'How?'

'There are two ways. The first is simple. It's Niall. He's in-
fluenced us from the moment we met, and he's actually been with
us, physically present, yet you've been totally unaware of him.'

'That's not proof to me,' Grey said. 'It works either way. He's
here with us, as you say, lurking around invisibly. Or the other:
he's never been near me, and the reason I've never seen him is
that he's never been close enough for me to see him.'

'I knew you'd say that.' Sue looked agitated but determined.

'For a long time I seriously wondered if Niall really did exist,'
Grey said. 'You've only ever *told* me about him. And since I left
hospital you've only ever told me about him in the past tense.
Even you say you haven't seen him for a long time.'

'That's true.'

'What's the other proof?'

She halted her prowling. 'That's more complicated. I'm hungry
now. I've bought some food for dinner. I can't afford to keep
eating out.' She produced a supermarket carrier bag, and took
down a couple of pans.

'Tell me while you're cooking,' he said.

'It's something I have to show you. Sit there, and keep out of
the way.'

Grey did as he was told, swivelling to and fro in her office chair.
She had only cooked for him once or twice, but he liked the way
she went about it. It was pleasant to watch her doing something
ordinary. They spent so much of their time obsessed with themselves.

But while she was cooking, Grey said, 'As a matter of interest,
where *is* Niall these days?'

'I was wondering when you'd ask me that.' She had not turned
to look at him. 'Does it matter?'

'From everything you said, he was never going to leave you
alone.'

pping vegetables, scooping them a
r. 'He could be here in the room with
know. There's nothing much I can do
at I can do, and have done, is change
make it matter to me. Now I don't care.
possible to be and he can do anything he
at it doesn't matter whether he's actually
wledge that he has that ability is the same as
. These days I assume he's everywhere I go. I
take it ... he's watching me, listening to me. It makes no
difference whether he is or isn't. He leaves me alone and that's
what I wanted all along.' She turned down the cooking rings to
their lowest setting, and covered the pans. 'OK, dinner will be
ready in about ten minutes. After that we're going for a walk.'

It had been raining earlier but now the night was clear. Traffic
went by, car engines sounding loud against the shiny wetness of
the streets. Richard and Sue passed several pubs, a late-opening
newsagent, an Indian restaurant with a blue neon sign. Soon they
were walking down a wide residential road which ran along the
side of Crouch Hill. The lights of north London glittered below
them. Overhead, an airliner with brilliant strobe lights crossed the
sky, heading down towards Heathrow, miles to the west.

'Are we going anywhere particular?' Grey asked.

'No, you choose.'

'What about once round the block then back to your place?'

Sue came to a halt beneath one of the streetlights. 'You say you
want proof, and I can give it to you. After that, will you accept it
for what it is?'

'If it's proof.'

'It will be. Look at me, Richard. Do I seem any different?'

He looked at her in the orange radiance from the sodium lamp.
'The light doesn't do anything for you.'

'I've been invisible ever since we left home.'

'Sue, I can still see you.'

'No one else can. What I'm going to do is make you invisible
too, and then we'll go into one of these houses.'

'Are you serious?'

'Totally.'

'All right, but the problem is me.'

'No, it isn't.' She stretched out a hand and took his. 'You're invisible now. Anything I choose to touch becomes invisible.'

He could not help but glance down at himself: chest and legs, solidly there. A car went past, its blinker indicating a left turn. Spray flew briefly around them.

Sue said, 'No one can see us. The only thing you must do is hold my hand. Whatever happens don't let go.' She tightened her grip. 'OK, pick a house.'

Her voice had taken on an earnest note, a charge of excitement, and Grey felt a tingle of the same.

'What about that one there?'

They both looked at it. Most of the windows were dark, but a pale red glow came through curtains on the top floor.

'It looks as if it's been converted into apartments,' Sue said. 'Let's find another.'

They walked along, holding hands, staring at the houses. They went to a few front doors, but where there were several bell-pushes and a list of names Sue suggested finding somewhere else. Too many self-contained apartments meant too many locked doors inside. At the end of the terrace the house had a darkened porch and a single bell. Behind the curtains of the front room they could see the glow of a television screen.

'This will do,' Sue said. 'Let's hope there's a door open.'

'I thought you would break a window.'

'We can do anything we like, but I'd rather not cause damage.'

They went through the garden and along the narrow pathway against the side of the house, pressing past rain-sodden trees and bushes. The ground floor room at the back was brightly lit by a fluorescent tube. When Sue tried the door it opened easily.

'We'll only stay long enough,' Sue said. 'Don't let go of my hand.'

She pushed the door fully open and they went inside. Grey closed the door behind them. They were in a kitchen. Two women stood with their backsides leaning against a working surface, one of them holding a sleeping baby against her shoulder. On the table in front of them were two cheap glass tumblers containing beer, and an ashtray with a cigarette smouldering. A slightly older child, wearing a soiled disposable nappy and a filthy T-shirt, was playing on the vinyl-tiled floor with a plastic car and some wooden blocks.

The woman holding the baby was saying, '. . . but when we gets in there they treats us like rubbish, so I says to him don't you go talking to me like that, and he looks at me like I was dirt . . .'

Grey felt huge and selfconscious in the cramped room, wanting to edge past the two women, but Sue went to the sink where she turned on the cold tap. The water splashed down noisily on the unwashed crockery stacked below, several large droplets spraying up and falling on the floor around the child. He yelped and ducked away. Still listening to her friend, the woman walked around the table and turned the tap off. On her way back she picked up the cigarette and put it in her mouth.

Sue said, 'Do you want to see what they're watching on television?'

Grey winced because her voice was so loud, but neither of the women appeared to notice. Still clutching Sue's hand he followed her out of the kitchen and into the passage leading to the front of the house. Here, a couple of old bicycles leaned against the staircase bannisters. Three large cardboard boxes containing bottles were stacked one on top of the other. Sue opened the second door and they went inside.

A soccer match was being shown on television, the volume turned up loud. The room was full of men and youths, sitting forward with their arms resting on their knees, holding beer cans or smoking cigarettes. The air was thick with smoke, and the men were responding noisily to the commentary and the match. England were playing Holland and apparently losing. Derision and scoffing poured out whenever the England side lost control of the ball, but the catcalls were louder when Holland took possession.

Sue said, 'Let's have a look at them.'

She turned on the overhead light and led Grey across the room. There were three adults and four youths.

'Knock that bleeding light off, John!' one of the older men said, not looking away from the screen. One of the teenagers got up and switched off the light. Returning to his seat he had to push past Grey, who instinctively eased himself to the side to make way. Sue gripped his hand again.

'Shall we sit down?' she said.

Before he could answer she led him to the sofa, where two of the men were sitting. Neither of them looked up, but one shuffled forward so that he sat on the floor and the other moved up to make room for them. Sue and Grey sat down, Grey feeling certain that their presence must register at any moment. The match went on, and England missed another chance. Contemptuous noises roared out in the room, and a beer can hissed wetly open.

'How do you feel?' Sue said, raising her voice over the noise.

'They're going to see us in a moment.'

'No they're not. You wanted proof and this is it.'

He noticed how her voice had changed. It had a thick, sensuous quality, reminding him of her lovemaking. The palm of her hand was sweaty against his. 'Want to see more?'

She got up from the sofa, dragging Grey with her. To his surprise she stood in the centre of the room, standing between the TV set and most of the men. Grey tried to pull her away to one side, but she stayed put.

'Surely they can see us?'

'They can sense we're here but they can't see us. Has any of them looked at us?'

'Not directly, no.'

'They can't.' Sue was looking flushed and her lips were moist. 'Watch this.'

With her free hand Sue quickly unbuttoned the top of her blouse. Pulling Grey after her she went towards the man who was making most of the noise. She leaned down in front of him, and with a deft movement reached inside and pulled down one of her bra cups to reveal a breast. She leaned closer to the man, holding the breast a few inches from his face. He leaned to one side to see past her, to keep watching the match.

Grey tugged Sue back by the hand.

'Don't do that!'

'They can't see me!'

'OK, but I don't like you doing it.'

She faced him, her blouse open and her breast still exposed. 'Doesn't this turn you on?'

'Not like that.' But he could feel himself becoming aroused.

'I always feel randy doing this.' She pressed his hand to her

217

breast, where the nipple was a firm bead of excitement. 'Do you want to make love?'

'You're kidding!'

'No, come on. Let's do it! We can do anything we like.'

'Sue, it's impossible.' He was too frightened, too aware of the roomful of men.

'Let's fuck now! On the floor, in front of them!'

There had often been an incongruous coarseness in Sue when she made love, but it had never before been as blatant. Her free hand was at the front of his trousers, pulling at his zipper. She got her hand inside and began to release him.

'Not in here,' he said. 'Outside.'

They went quickly into the hall. Sue saw the stairs and rushed up them, still clasping his hand. They found a room with a bed, and threw themselves on it. They loosened their clothes and coupled almost at once. Sue, when she came, let out a shriek of pleasure, taking his hair in handfuls and tugging at it painfully. He had never known her as sexually abandoned before.

They were lying on the bed, still conjoined, when the door opened and one of the women they had seen in the kitchen came in. Grey tensed and turned his face away, a desperate attempt to hide. Sue said in a normal voice, 'Keep still. She doesn't know we're here.'

Grey looked back and watched as the woman opened a wardrobe door. She stood looking at herself in the full-length mirror, then began to undress. When she was naked she stood in front of the mirror again, turning from side to side. Her buttocks were heavy with dimpled cellulite, her swollen belly sagged, and her breasts fell flatly down her chest, the nipples turning outwards. The woman leaned forward, looking at the reflection of her eyes, pulling down the lower lids. She let off an uninhibited fart, then scratched her anus with her fingernails. When she stood back again she tried to shape her hair with her hands, still turning to and fro, looking critically at herself. Grey could see Sue and himself reflected in the mirror behind her. He felt a deep sense of revulsion, knowing they were violating an intimacy. As his sexual desire drained away he recoiled from Sue, letting himself slip out of her.

She wrapped her arms round his shoulders, holding him down against her.

'Don't move, Richard! Stay until she's gone.'

'But she's going to get into bed!'

'Not yet. She can't while we're here.'

After a few more seconds the woman sighed and closed the wardrobe door, shutting away the mirror. She took a dressing-gown from the back of the door and put it on. Before leaving the room she lit a cigarette, tossing the match box on to the bedside table. Her cloud of smoke swirled by the door when she had gone.

'Let's get out of here, Sue. You've proved your point.'

He moved away from her and swung himself off the bed, pulling up his underpants and trousers, tucking his shirt away. He knew that because Sue was no longer touching him he was visible again, but all he wanted was to get out of the house and leave these people alone. Revulsion still filled him.

Sue finished tidying her clothes and took his hand again.

'You used to do this with Niall, didn't you?'

'I used to *live* like this. I slept in other people's houses for three years. We ate their food, used their lavatories, watched their TVs, slept in their beds.'

'Didn't you ever think about the people you were invading?'

'For God's sake!' She snatched her hand away from his. 'Why do you think I tried to get out? I was only a kid. I'm trying to put it behind me. This is how Niall lives and how he'll live for the rest of his life. We're only here because you wanted proof.'

'All right.' He kept his voice low, knowing he could probably be heard. Thinking of her sexual excitement, he said, 'But the truth is you still get a kick out of it.'

'Of course I do! I always did. It's better than a drug.'

'I think we should leave. We can talk about it back at your place.' He held out his hand.

She shook her head and sat down on the bed.

'Not now.'

'We've been here long enough.'

'Richard, I'm not invisible any more. It started to go after we made love.'

'Then get back into it,' Grey said.

'I can't. I'm drained. I don't know how.'

'What are you talking about?'

219

'I can't make it happen on demand any more. Tonight was the first time in more than a week.'

'Can't you do it long enough to get us out of the house?'

'No. It's gone.'

'What the hell are we going to do?'

'I suppose we'll have to run for it.'

'The house is full of people.'

'I had noticed,' she said. 'But the front door's at the bottom of the stairs. It might be all right.'

'Let's go. That woman will be back at any moment.'

Sue did not move.

She said, quietly, 'I was always terrified this would happen. In the old days, with Niall. That we'd be in someone's house and the glamour would suddenly leave us. That was the kick, the danger of it.'

'We can't sit here and wait for it to come back! This is crazy!'

'You could try, Richard. You know how.'

'What?'

'Make yourself invisible! You've done it before.'

'I don't remember!'

'What about that pub in Belfast? Imagine you're filming. We're in a corner, but you've got the camera and you can go on using it.'

'I'm too scared of being discovered! I can't concentrate on that!'

'But that's when you did your best work, when you were stuck, when people were throwing petrol bombs.'

Grey narrowed his right eye, half closing it to approximate the narrow field of a viewfinder. He imagined the familiar press of the sponge-rubber eyepiece, the faint vibration of the motor transmitted to his brow. He hunched his right shoulder, taking the weight of the Arri, and cocked his head slightly to the side. There was a battery pack around his waist, a cable looping down and behind him, resting on his shoulder blade. He imagined the sound man beside him, cans on his ears, the Uher resting on his waist, holding up the grey windsock mike so it prodded up and above him from behind. He thought of the Belfast streets, a mass picket outside factory gates, a surging crowd on the collapsing terraces at Maine Road football ground in Manchester, a CND demonstration in Hyde Park, a food riot in Somalia, all vivid in his mind, moments of surging and unpredictable danger glimpsed through the lens. He squeezed his finger on the tit, and the film slid silently through the gate.

Sue put her hand on his shoulder. 'We can go now.'

They heard the sound of the toilet along the corridor flushing, followed by footsteps on the landing outside. A moment later the woman they had seen undressing walked into the room, the half-burned cigarette dangling from her lips. Grey swung the camera to follow her, pulling focus as she stepped around them to go back to the mirror in the wardrobe.

Grey led the way to the top of the stairs then walked slowly down, one step at a time. They could hear the sounds of the televised soccer match coming through the open door of the front room. Grey panned to the room, glimpsing the backs of the men's heads. Sue reached past him and unlatched the front door. Once they were both outside she pulled it to behind them.

Grey continued filming until they were out on the street, then slumped, feeling weary. Sue took his arm and brought up her mouth to kiss the side of his face, but he turned away from her, angry, worn out and repelled.

There was always a next day, a waking to the realities of the present. Richard Grey rarely remembered his dreams when he woke up, although he was usually aware of having dreamed. He understood them as a reorganisation of actual daytime memories into a kind of symbolic code stored away in the unconscious. Each morning was therefore a fresh memorative start. As he muddled sleepily through the first two or three hours, glancing at his mail, reading the headlines of the newspaper, sipping black coffee, he was aware of a kind of oneiric stew in his mind, an amalgam of mostly forgotten dreams and snatches of the day before. Conscious memories rarely came to him until he forced himself to think properly. Only after he had drunk a second cup of coffee, and dressed and shaved, and was beginning to wonder how he would spend the rest of the day, would he start seeing the new day in the context of the old. Continuity returned slowly.

The morning after the visit to the house, Grey found it more difficult than usual to wake up. He had not been especially late to bed, but there had been a long and mostly grumpy conversation at Sue's before he left. Somewhere in it was a conflict over sex: Sue had wanted to make love again and he had not.

He felt disagreeable on waking. There was nothing in the mail and the newspaper depressed him. He fried an egg and made a greasy sandwich of it, then drank coffee and stared through his window at the street below.

When he dressed he put on clean clothes and transferred the contents of his pockets. Amongst the litter of coins, keys and banknotes he found the slip of paper Alexandra had given him, stuffed negligently in his jacket pocket.

He opened it carefully, smoothing it with his hand on the table, and read it through. It began with the words:

The board was showing that my flight was delayed, but I had already gone through security and passport control and there was no escape from the departure lounge.

The passage continued with a description of the lounge, and concluded:

There was nowhere left to sit, nothing much to do except stand or walk about and look at the other passengers. As I crossed the lounge for the third or fourth time I no—

It was at this point that Hurdis had interrupted him. The last word, which Grey knew was 'noticed', was only half written and there was a line scored lightly beyond it. Everything began and ended with being noticed.

He knew the rest, a familiar story. Staring idly through his apartment window Grey remembered the long train journey across France, the meeting with Sue, their falling in love, their conflict and separation because of Niall, then their reunion and eventual return to England. The memories ended with his chance involvement in the terrorist bombing, the one event apparently no one disputed.

It was all real to him still, his only knowledge of the period he had subsequently lost. Whenever he dwelt on the story, images came starkly and convincingly from it. The first time he and Sue had made love. How it had felt to be in love with her. How it felt to miss her. The long and fruitless wait in Saint-Tropez and the brief consolation of the young woman from Hertz. The enervating Mediterranean heat. The taste of the food. These memories had inner conviction, a sense of story and of events unfolding. Earlier he had thought of it as a piece of film already edited, but thinking again it occurred to him that a closer analogy was that of seeing a movie in a cinema. A cinema audience accepted on trust that the whole thing was fiction, that it was written and directed and acted, that a large technical crew was somewhere out of sight behind the camera, that the film had been edited and synchronised, and music and sound effects had been added, but they nevertheless suspended their disbelief and went along with the illusion.

Grey felt that while he was inside the cinema watching the film his real life had been lived *outside*, but that his memory of the film was an acceptable substitute for what he had missed.

This fragment of his confabulated past had another importance to him. It had sprung unbidden from his subconscious, the product of an inner need, a desperation to *know*. As a result it was now a part of him, as valid as reality itself even though it was not what had really happened to him. It dealt explicitly with his lost period, with the events leading up to the explosion. It gave him continuity.

And it excluded Sue, except as a secondary figure. It did not admit of her invisibility. The real Sue demanded a primary position and insisted that he accept her claim to be invisible.

Thinking of Sue, Grey was suddenly reminded of the events of the night before. Since waking he had not thought about the visit to the house, although in a vague way it had been at the back of his mind.

He had found it a disturbing experience, burdened with feelings of intrusion, violation, voyeurism, animal lust, trespass. The sex with Sue, satiating her frantic physical need, had provided only neurotic relief, lacking pleasure. He recalled the urgent undoing of clothes, of thrusting himself into her while they both still wore shoes, while their jeans tangled around their knees, while Sue's unhooked bra and unbuttoned blouse lay flatly over her half-bared breasts. Afterwards, the innocent woman, overweight and narcissistic, standing in her own room while strangers appraised her, and then their fear of being caught, trapped in someone else's house like thieves.

This morning, while he stumbled around the flat in his customary early stupor, it had all the quality of a half-remembered dream, as if the reality of it had been resorted symbolically during the night, encoded and despatched to his unconscious. Grey thought of something that happened a few years before: he had dreamed that a friend of his had died. For most of the following day he had felt a vague sense of sadness and loss, until, mid-afternoon, he realised that it had been indeed only a dream, that his friend was still alive. The feeling about his invisible intrusion with Sue was similar, although its cause was opposite: until reminded of it Grey had remembered it in a dreamlike manner, his mood subtly affected by it, until his conscious realisation that it had really happened.

Failure of memory surrounded all this talk of invisibility.

Sue's account of his lost weeks spoke of his own natural ability as an invisible, and his subliminal recognition of hers. But because of the bomb he had forgotten it all. Invisibility was a past, unremembered condition: Sue said that he no longer knew how, that her own talent had receded. Even Niall, supremely and terminally invisible, was not around any more.

And last night's adventure, supposedly Sue's conclusive proof, had gone half forgotten until now.

Was amnesia inherently related to invisibility? Alexandra told him he had become invisible to her and Dr Hurdis, but it had happened during the period of hypnotic trance he could not remember. Then there were the lost weeks, invisible to him, which he had replaced with spurious, confabulated memories. Weren't those exactly like the way in which ordinary people accounted to themselves for the presence of invisibles? Sue's parents, bringing up a child they could hardly see, explained the mystery as a difficult daughter growing up and moving away. The unseen Niall, selfishly disrupting Sue's visit home, was afterwards given the benefit of the doubt, and thought to be a nice young man. The soccer fans, presented with a randy female standing between them and the screen, merely leaned to one side to keep watching. The woman in the house acted as if the kitchen tap had turned itself on, and later failed to see two strangers fornicating on her own bed.

It sounded increasingly like the confabulation he had gone through, when he tried to account to himself for the weeks he had lost.

Sue had said people were *made* invisible by the failure of those around them to notice them. Was it spontaneous amnesia on a grand scale?

After lunch Grey went for a walk by himself. Exercise for his hip was still essential, so he drove his car up to the West Heath near Hampstead and walked for a couple of hours through the oaks, beeches and hornbeams of the small but beautiful park. As he was heading back to his car he came across a film crew from the BBC, who were shooting some exterior action for a play. He recognised the cameraman, so he walked over and they talked briefly between takes. Grey was actively seeking work, and was not averse to letting it be known. The two men agreed to meet for a drink in a few days' time.

He watched the unit at work for a while, wishing he were a part of it. The story was an episode from a thriller series. The scene they were shooting involved two men chasing a terrorised young woman through the trees. The actress was wearing a flimsy yellow dress, and between takes she stood with her boyfriend, shivering inside her coat, muttering about the chilly weather, and chain-smoking. She looked, off-camera, utterly different from the frightened and vulnerable character she was playing.

Walking on, Grey thought about the one incident from the night before that had fundamentally affected his outlook. This was the discovery that Sue, when she thought herself invisible, became sexually aroused and voracious in her lust. Because he had been there, had seen the change coming over her, he had felt it too and responded. But it was an insight he had not expected. What he found attractive about Sue was what he thought of as her shyness, her modest dislike of being stared at, her physical restraint, her soothing manner, her neutral looks and demure way of speaking. Sometimes she made love tenderly and hesitantly, sensitive to his needs, but at other times she had been uninhibited and wild, and he assumed that it was another aspect of what he induced in her. Sexual knowledge is frequently revealing and surprising. But she had never been sexually aggressive in that way before. He was not repelled by it, but it did make him feel that until that incident he had perceived her wrongly.

The actress back there was in real life unlike the part she was playing. Sue, thinking herself unseen, switched from the role she habitually played to another character. She was two people: the woman he usually saw, and the one he had never seen until last night. In her invisibility, her concealment from the world, she revealed herself.

To Grey, it felt as if his other doubts coalesced around the revelation. If it had come earlier it might have made no difference, but at such a late stage he felt unable to cope with yet another reversal.

Sue had always been trouble to him, and she showed no sign of changing. By the time he was back in his car Grey had resolved not to see her again. They had a date to meet in the evening, but he decided to telephone her as soon as he was home and cancel it. He drove back to his flat, thinking of what he was going to say to her. She was waiting for him, though, sitting on the steps of the small porch outside his front door.

In spite of the decision he had made only minutes earlier, there was a part of him that remained pleased to see her. She kissed him warmly before they went inside, but Grey felt resistant to her. Reluctantly he led her upstairs, wondering how to broach the subject face to face. A phone call would have been easier, more cowardly. All his resolve was fading. He felt like a drink, so he took a can of lager from the fridge, but made some tea for Sue. He could hear her moving about restlessly in the front room as he swallowed some of the beer and waited for the kettle to boil.

When he took her the tea she was standing by the window, looking down into the street.

'You don't want me here, do you?' she said.

'I was about to phone you. I've been thinking—'

'I've come about something important, Richard.'

'I'd rather not talk about it.'

'It's about Niall.'

Somehow he had known it would be, as soon as she used the word 'important'. He put down her cup by the spare chair, noticing that she had brought with her a large manilla envelope stuffed with papers. It was lying on the cushion of the chair. Outside in the street someone was trying to get a car going, the starter motor making a repeated nagging, whining sound as the battery lost power. Such a noise always made Grey think of a sick beast of burden, flogged endlessly by its unforgiving driver.

'There is nothing on earth I need to know about Niall,' Grey said. He felt remote from her, the distance between them lengthening.

'I've come to tell you Niall's left me for good.'

'That's not what you said yesterday. Anyway, Niall's not the problem any more.'

'Then what is?'

'Everything that happened last night, everything you've ever said. I've finally had a gutful and want no more.'

'Richard, what I've come to say is there's nothing left to come between us. It's all over. Niall's gone, I've lost the glamour. What more do you want?'

She stared at him across the room, looking helpless. Grey remembered suddenly how it had felt to love her, and he wished it were possible again. Outside, the irritating sound of the fruitless attempts to start the car came to an end. Grey walked across to where Sue was standing, and looked down into the street. He was invariably distracted by the sound of a car being started, because he could never free himself of the idea that somebody might be interfering with his own. He could see no one around, though, and his car was standing where he had parked it.

Sue took his hand. 'What are you looking for?'

'That car being started. Where is it?'

'Haven't you been listening to me?'

'Yes, of course I have.'

She released his hand and went to sit down, moving the large envelope to her lap. After looking up and down the street once more, Grey went to his chair. Two people, rapidly becoming estranged, facing each other across a room.

Sue said, 'What we did last night was a mistake. We both know that. It'll never happen again. In fact, it *can't* happen again. I have to explain. Please listen.' Grey was making no effort to conceal his impatience with her. 'While I believed Niall was somewhere around,' she went on, 'I could still feel able to make myself invisible. But last night was wrong. Something failed. I thought I was trying to prove invisibility to you, but really I was trying to prove to myself that Niall's influence had left me. Now I'm certain of it.'

She held up the envelope for him to see.

'What's that?' Grey said.

'It's something Niall gave me, the last time I saw him.' She drew a breath, watching him. 'He came to see me and gave me a newspaper which listed the names of the people injured by the car bomb. This was a few days afterwards. You were still in intensive care in Charing Cross Hospital, long before you were transferred to Devon. At the same time as he gave me the newspaper he handed this envelope to me. I didn't know what it was and I didn't care. I never even opened it. I knew it was something of Niall's, but by that time I was alienated from him. It was almost as if he had been responsible in some way for that car bomb. Everything that went on shortly before the bomb seemed, afterwards, to be building up to it. But this morning I was thinking about last night, and why it had gone wrong, and I knew Niall must be somehow behind it. It was as if that part of my life, the invisibility, no longer made sense without him. I remembered him giving me this envelope, so I searched through my stuff until I found it. You've got to see what it is.'

'Sue, I'm not interested in Niall.'

'Please at least look at it.'

He took the envelope from her and with an irritable movement pulled out what was inside. It was a sheaf of papers, handwritten, torn from the sort of A4 writing pad found in any stationery shop. The top of each page was corrugated where it had been ripped off. The first page was a brief note, written in the same hand as the rest.

It said, *Susan – Read this and try to understand. Goodbye – N.*

The handwriting was neatly crafted and regular, but it was distracting to try to read it because of the use of extravagant loops and curls. Full stops, and the dot above the letter 'i', were drawn as minute circles. It was written in a variety of coloured inks, as different pens were used, but mostly in radiant blue. Grey knew nothing about graphology, but everything about the handwriting bespoke selfconsciousness and a misguided wish to seem prestigious.

'What is this? Did Niall write it?'

'Yes. You should read it.'

'While you're sitting there?'

'I suppose. At least look through it long enough to realise what it is.'

Grey set the note aside and read the first few lines at the top of the next page. They said:

The house had been built overlooking the sea. Since its conversion to a convalescent hospital it had been enlarged by two new wings built in the original style, and the gardens had been relandscaped so that patients wishing to move around were never faced with steep inclines.

'I don't understand,' Grey said. 'What's it all about?'

'Look further on,' Sue said.

Grey put several of the pages on one side, and read at random:

But she tossed her hair back with a light shaking motion of her head and looked straight at him. He regarded her, trying to remember or see her as he might have done before. She held his gaze for a few moments, then cast her eyes downwards once more.

'Don't stare at me,' she said.

Grey said, beginning to feel confused, 'It's a description of you, I think.'

'Yes, there's a lot of that. Read more of it.'

He started turning the pages, picking out odd sentences and reading them, constantly dazzled by the extraordinary handwriting and its elaborate curlicues. It was easier to skim than to read, but at another random place he found:

Grey felt comfortable and relaxed and drowsy, listening to Hurdis with his eyes closed, but none the less he was still aware of everything around him. It was as if his senses had somehow been made more acute than normal, because he found he could discern movements and noises not only inside the room but from further afield. Outside in the hall two people walked past, talking to each other in quiet tones. The lift motor grumbled. Somewhere in the room Alexandra Gowers made a clicking noise, as if with a ballpoint pen, and started writing on her notepad. The sound of the pen was so delicate, so deliberately contrived by her hand, that Grey suddenly realised that by listening closely he could follow what she was writing: he sensed that she had written his name in capital letters, then underlined the words. She wrote the date next to his name. Why had she put a line through the stem of the '7' . . . ?

Saying nothing else to Sue, Grey turned quickly through the rest of the pages. He knew what the writing said. The sense came across to him without him having to read closely because it was all intimately familiar to him. These were his experiences, his memories.

There was not much further to go. The text ended with the words:

The day went slowly by, the evening came, and as her lateness became apparent he found hope turning to apprehension. Late in the evening, far later than he had expected, she called him from a payphone. The train had been delayed but she was at Totnes station and was about to hire a taxi. She was with him half an hour later.

When she saw he had finished, Sue said, 'Do you understand what it means, Richard?'

'I understand what it says. What is it?'

'It's Niall's way of dealing with the inevitable. He knew I'd leave him for you. It's a story he wrote about that.'

'But why should he give it to you? This is what happened! How the hell could he have *written* it?'

'It's only a story,' Sue said.

Grey slowly rolled the papers in his hand, making them into a short truncheon.

'But how did he *know?*' he said. 'When did Niall give this to you? You said it was shortly after the car bomb, but it couldn't have been. None of it happened until much later!'

'I don't understand it either,' Sue said.

'Niall didn't make this up! He couldn't have made it up! He must have been there – all the time I was in hospital Niall was there too! That's what it means. Don't you see that?'

'Richard, that story's been in my room for weeks.'

Suddenly Grey moved in his seat, looking wildly from side to side.

'Is Niall following me? Is he *here*?'

'I told you. Niall is anywhere he wants to be. If he's here, it doesn't matter.'

'He's here now, Sue! He's in this room!'

Grey stood up, lurching on his weak hip, and took a clumsy step to the side. He flailed at the air with the papers in his hand. The beer can at his feet fell on its side, the frothy lager pouring in gulps on the carpet. Grey swung about, groping with one hand at the air around him, prodding and punching with the rolled-up pages in his other fist. He moved awkwardly to the door, snatched it open to peer outside, then slammed it closed. He reached blindly for me as the air swirled about us both.

I stepped back, keeping my distance, not wishing to be whacked with a truncheon of my own making.

'Hold it, Grey!' I shouted, but of course you did not hear.

I heard Susan say, 'Richard, for God's sake! You're making a fool of yourself!'

Neither of us paid her any attention, for the conflict is solely between you and me. You were directly in front of me, balancing your weight on your good leg, your fist raised against me, your eyes in their desperation seeming to stare straight at me. I turned away from your disconcerting cameraman's gaze, even though without your camera you would never be able to see me.

It has gone far enough. Here it ends.

Hold that position, Grey! Nothing more is going to happen. You are strong. You force your arm around, moving fractionally, like the frames of a film being inched through the gate. Keep still!

That's better. Susan too: stay still!

I pause.

My hands are trembling. See what you do to me, Grey? You scare me so easily. We are a threat to each other, you with your blundering insensitivity to other people's pain, I with my freedom to orchestrate you. But I am back in control, if only for a while, and you may stay there as you are.

All right, now I shall tell you what you least wish to hear:

I am your invisible adversary and I am somewhere around you. You can never see me, because you do not know how or where to look. I have been everywhere with you. I watched you at the hospital, I was there when Susan came to see you. I saw what you were up to and I listened to what you said. I was in the south of France, and gave you the words. I followed you about Wales, and gave Susan the words. I am with you in London, and the words are mine. You have never been free of me. I have looked at you and listened to you. I know everything you have done and everything you have thought. Nothing is private to you, nothing is yours.

I said I would fix you, Grey, and that is what I have done.

I am everything you have ever feared. I am invisible to you, but not in the sense Susan meant, nor in the way you think.

Consider the room in which the three of us find ourselves. This is your living room, in the apartment you think of as yours. We are all here, confronting each other again, and as ever failing to see or notice.

I know the room intimately, although in reality I have never visited it. I can *see* it. I can move around it, walking on the floor, or drifting in the air, look at it in its generality or inspect it in its closest detail. Here are the white painted walls that Susan so dislikes, covered with the cheap emulsion paint used by the builders who converted the house into flats. Here is the carpet, slightly worn, and the furniture, rather better, once the property of your parents, left to you by them and held in storage for some years before you found this place. There is a television set in one corner, with a layer of pale dust over the screen. Underneath is a video recorder set to BBC 2, with a half-recorded tape sticking out of the slot. The digital clock is showing *00:00:00* and is blinking on and off because you have never bothered to set it properly. I see bookshelves attached to one wall. They sag in the middle because you or whoever put them up did not measure the distance between the brackets. I scan along the shelves to look at your choice of books, and I find you an uninteresting, even philistine, reader. There are technical manuals about cameras and lights, books of photographic theory, guidebooks and maps, a stack of glamour magazines, no doubt for use in the long evenings before you met Susan, and a selection of best-selling paperback novels, the sort sold in airports. We should not have much to talk about, you and I, were we to meet. You are practical, unimaginative, you want proof of everything. You need to touch, need to look twice.

On the sill against the window are marks on the white paint where your houseplants stood: the sunlight has yellowed the paint except for five circular patches, themselves marked by grains of dried potting compost. There is a faint smell of dust, also of damp, also of unwashed shirts. Your room speaks silently to me of male preoccupations and transience and impermanence. You are often away, and when you come back you do not feel settled or comfortable.

I know this room as I know you. I have inhabited it mentally from the day I first knew of you. It is real to me because it is how I visualised it, how I have imagined it when I have known you are here. I know the rest of the apartment in the same way, my interest in you extending to every detail of you.

Susan is sitting wide-eyed in the chair by the window, watching what you are trying to do. She has placed her canvas bag on the floor beside the chair and its strap snakes lightly over one of her feet. On the carpet in front of her is the opened envelope in which I gave her my story. A dark pool of wetness lies in the weave of the carpet beside the overturned beer can. You are a few feet away from Susan, frozen in your truculent search, exactly as you were when I decided to call a halt.

What do you hope to achieve as you search so aggressively for me? If you found me what would you do? Do you seek some kind of violent conclusion to our dealings? Surely I cannot matter to you any more, as for weeks I have left you alone? Without any prompting from me you had decided to break off your affair with Susan. That suited me, and you too, as a matter of fact. Therefore, as soon as you have finished with her I shall be finished with you. So why should I matter to you any more?

But Susan has shown you what I have written about you, and that seems to have mattered!

You clasp my story in your hand, Grey, knowing that it invalidates you. What you remember of the hospital in Devon becomes false now that you realise I wrote everything for you and about you. And because the hospital is the basis of everything that followed, everything else is invalidated too.

You thought you could trust those memories because they had conviction, but I can tell you they have not.

Do you believe me? How good is your memory? Can you believe anything you remember or do you trust only what you are told?

We are all fictions: you are one, Susan is another, I am also one to a lesser extent. I have used you to speak for me. I have made you, Grey. You disbelieve in me, but not nearly so much as I disbelieve in you.

Why resist the idea? We all make fictions. Not one of us is what we seem. When we meet other people we try to project an image of ourselves that will please or influence them in some way. When we fall in love we blind ourselves to what we do not wish to see. We wear certain clothes, drive particular cars, live in certain areas, all to project an image of ourselves. We sift through our memories not to understand the past, but to suit our present understanding of ourselves.

The urge to rewrite ourselves as real-seeming fictions is present in us all. In the glamour of our wishes we hope that our real selves will not be visible.

This is all I have done.

You are not you, but how I have made you seem to be. Susan is not Sue. I am not Niall, but Niall is a version of me. Once again I have no name. I am only I.

So here is the end, and it is probably not what you wanted. Life is not neat. It has no happy ending. Nothing is explained.

What remains for you of Susan?

Nothing remains for you of her. She will leave with me.

I could relinquish you here, stuck forever in this unsatisfactory moment, a fiction abandoned without an ending.

But that would not be right, however tempting. Your own real life continues and you can go back to that. Everything will probably be much tidier, your body will heal, matters will improve. I doubt you will ever know why. You will forget, induce a negative hallucination. You are no stranger to doing that, because for you forgetting is a way of failing to see.

The summer was hot again that year, and at the end of June there came the prospect of a full-time job for Richard Grey. His friend at the BBC put him in touch with the head of film drama. After an interview he was told that a freelance contract would be his from the first week in September.

Given the long summer to fill, Grey was stricken with his customary restlessness. He did a freelance camera job in Malta, but it was soon over and afterwards he was at more of a loose end than before. Financial compensation for his injuries at last came through from the Home Office: it was less than he had expected, but more than enough to cover his immediate needs. He was no longer in pain, and his body was working normally, but he bought a new car, one with automatic transmission. The old one had begun giving him trouble, starting with the annoyance of a flat battery. When Alexandra returned from Exeter to complete her research notes he waited around for a week or two, then suggested a holiday.

They took the new car across to France, driving slowly from place to place, following whim and a certain curiosity of memory. They visited Paris, Lyon and Grenoble, then drove south to the Riviera. The crowds of the high season had not yet built up. Grey found Alexandra's company delightful, even though she was several years younger than him. They were falling in love, their romance counterpointed by the exotic landscape through which they were passing. They never spoke of the past, or of how they had met, or of anything that was not their immediate world of the holiday and each other. They spent a long time on the south coast, sunbathing, swimming, touring around to see the sights. They visited Saint-Tropez only briefly, but here Grey came across a little shop that sold reproduction postcards. There was one he particularly liked: a photograph of the harbour when it had still been used only for fishing. He bought a copy of it to send to Sue. *Wish you were here*, he wrote, in a deliberately elaborate hand-writing, and he signed it with an X.